LOVE'S LEARNING CURVE

LINDSEY PENNINGTON

12-153-44 PUBLISHING

Chapter 1

Closing another box, Skylar Nash longed to put everything she had just packed back in the exact same place she had found it. To go back in time to when the dresses, skirts, and shirts now packed were so neatly organized in the closet All color-coordinated from red to purple and every color of the rainbow in between.

A wave of sadness hit her hard, causing her to sit heavily on the bed. The entire room around her was full of color and life, making her heart feel hollow. This room was so much her mom that her bring gone seemed unimaginable even now.

A short month ago, Skylar had been enjoying a much-anticipated trip to her longtime girlfriend Iris's parents' house in Colorado when she got the call—the one that nobody ever wanted to get. A voice from her past told her that Karla Nash had been in a car accident, and that it was bad. She needed to come home right away.

In that single moment, her world fell apart, and so far, she hadn't found a way to put it back together yet. Her mom had been her best friend. Even when she had been an angsty teenager, she still loved to spend time with her mom. Her mom had made being her daughter easy.

Not many days went by that they hadn't called each other. Even though they lived miles away, they were still close. Karla knew everything that went on in Skylar's life, and she knew her mom's life. She was the first person Skylar ever thought to call.

Skylar knew the struggles her mom was having with Kayden, who was fourteen and more like an alien than a child of hers, after raising two daughters. He had been the youngest, and there hadn't been an issue with his behavior until he turned twelve. That was when everything changed.

Meanwhile, her mom never judged as she listened as her insecurities arose and had her worried that Iris just wasn't the one. Skylar had been dating Iris for over two years, and though she loved her, she wasn't madly in love with her. Shouldn't she be madly in love? She had seen true love once with her mom and stepdad and wanted that for herself, that instant knowledge that this was her person.

On her mom's nightstand, Skylar's phone buzzed, bringing her back to the present, the one where she was in Warrington, and her mom was gone again. Slowly, she got to her feet. There wasn't anyone she needed to talk to— Kayden, Keeley, and Sierra were in school, and Iris was working.

Which just meant the phone call was for her mom, a former friend who had gotten the news of her passing weeks later. Or maybe a bank or credit card company who needed one more piece of information before they believed Karla was gone. Either way, it was better to answer now, not forcing Skylar to get a hold of whoever later.

Before she could say anything, Iris was already talking, happiness bubbling out of her. "Hey babe, how are you today?"

Feeling completely disconnected from her girlfriend's joy, she answered, "Fine."

It was a lie. She wasn't fine. Not today. Every day she hoped today was the day she didn't feel alone in the world, but it hadn't happened. But maybe tomorrow.

"Good, good." Her voice was just as bubbly, in contrast to Skylar's. Which meant she hadn't noticed that Skylar wasn't actually fine, because she never said she was fine before her mom died. Fine was exactly what she was now. But she didn't noticed that today either as she just went on talking, "So I was talking to Kindra this morning. She's moving her son into an apartment and is looking for a bedroom set for him. And that got me thinking we should sell ours and buy a new one."

Iris barely took a breath as she said it. The bedroom set Skylar had was brand-new not five years before. It wasn't theirs; it was Skylar's. But it wasn't Iris's style, and she had been hinting since moving in together last winter that they should get a new one. Something more, or as Skylar saw it, more expensive.

Not wanting to think about this, she gave in. "Yeah, sure, I guess."

Right now, she couldn't even remember what her own bed looked like. It was nothing like the black brass of her mom's bed. It had been Karla's since long before her mom's house was purchased.

"I just knew you'd say yes. Did you want me to wait until you get back to go get the new one?" Iris asked, as if Skylar was coming home anytime soon.

At this point, she had no idea how long she would be away. Right now, she was the legal guardian of two kids who were enrolled in the only school they had ever been to. The only other person who could help was Sierra, was only nineteen and in college hours away. There was so much she had to settle before she could think about going back home. And right now there wasn't space in her head to think about a new bedroom set. Not when she had to decide what to do with everything her mom had ever owned.

Shaking her head, even if Iris couldn't see, she said, "No, it'll be awhile before I can go back."

"Can you take that kind of time off of work? Have you talked to your boss?" Iris asked, even if they had talked about this before Iris went back to Minneapolis after the week of the funeral.

In fact, they had talked about a lot during that time,or maybe they hadn't. It was a blur of people, sadness, and tears. Iris had only been able to stay for a few days before she had to get back to her job. Skylar herself had been on summer break from her teaching job at the time. Only now was she missing work since the school year had recently started.

Except now she was actually jobless. How could she pretend she was going to teach in Minneapolis with everything that needed to be done here? Pretend her life was going to go back to how it had been before in a few days? To be in two places at once?

"I called and turned in my notice this morning," she admitted. Though she loved her job, going back wasn't possible, and maybe not for this entire year or so. Right now, it was better to leave the kids where they were.

"You quit?" Iris gasped loudly.

It was why Skylar hadn't run it by her before she made the call. Iris's job was the most important thing in her life. Jobs, after all, were status. And Skylar now had neither.

Rubbing the back of her neck, she admitted, "Yeah, I have to stick around here for longer than they would give me off. And it would be easier to find a replacement for me this early on in the school year. The longer I put it off, the harder it will be for them."

"So you quit when exactly? They were giving you time off to grieve. Why would you just up and quit? Things could've been settled by the time you needed to go back." Iris wasn't letting this go. Even if there was no way around it.

"I thought I told you. And it was only another few weeks, nowhere near enough time. Mom wasn't planning on dying, so she had nothing planned. I have to think about Keeley, Kayden, and Sierra. Put their needs before mine right now." Skylar had a flashback to this conversation and wondered if it had been a dream. Since her mom had died, those had become far more vivid. Or maybe it was because she was sleeping far more than before.

"I don't like that you didn't tell me. I know you have a lot to do there, babe. But in a few months, I feel you will regret this brash decision."

"It took away the stress of having to go back to work by a certain date. I just needed a little less stress right now." Not even just stress. Days were going excruciatingly slow and then were gone before she did anything productive.

"Do you want me to come one weekend? I can take off a Friday, and we can spend some time together. I have some stress reducers that I know that you enjoy," she said suggestively.

Skylar left her mom's room and wondered when Iris suggesting sex hadn't turned her on, but right now, she felt nothing. It felt like a lifetime since they were together instead of two weeks. But maybe it had been more than that since the distance between them had been there before her mom died.

Knowing she needed to be more present in their rela-

5

tionship, she agreed, "Yeah, I would like that. I want to see you. I miss you."

"How about in two weeks?" Iris said, the sound of flipping of her planner pages clear over the phone, "Three, no four weeks. I'll keep that weekend open for you. Maybe you can come down one weekend before that. Your brother and sister are old enough to stay home alone for a few days."

"No," she said a little too quickly. "Kayden can't be left alone. He's acting out, and I can't just leave him."

The fact that he had taken the car for a joy ride the day before when she was napping had told her he wasn't to be trusted. At all. Thankfully, he had only made it a block before a neighbor who happened to be an off-duty cop had stopped him. Who knew where he was going?

"You haven't told me about that. Maybe Sierra can watch them?" Iris pouted.

"She lives on campus. She can't have her little sister and brother spending the weekends." Skylar knew she wouldn't ask her to come home just so Skylar could go to the city to have sex. "Sorry, I'm just not …"

"Hey, I have to go—big meeting. I'll call you tonight, and we can plan more." Iris hung up before Skylar could respond.

Skylar wanted to smile at her girlfriend's busy schedule, but couldn't. Once upon a time, it was sexy-hot how that woman wore power suits and was a manager, but now it was like she was going too fast for Skylar to keep up with. And that was even before Karla died.

Before she could put her phone down, it rang again in her hand, something Iris usually did just to say goodbye because she forgot. Or maybe it was her who had done that, back when they had first started dating.

"Bye, love you," she said before Iris could. Maybe it

would make her smile, since she was upset about Skylar quitting her job.

"Is this Skylar Nash?" the voice on the other end asked tentatively, unsure.

Instantly she blushed and wanted to hang up, except they had said her full name. "Oh god, sorry, thought it was someone else. Yeah, it's Skylar. What can I help you with?"

"This is Leila Hensley at the high school," the voice said, but she didn't have to. Skylar had listened to that voice an hour a day in English class for years. Even after all these years, she would've recognized it anywhere.

"Miss Hensley, how are you doing?" She had seen her at the funeral, but couldn't remember if they had spoken. It had only been a few weeks, but she couldn't remember anything about that day.

Her mom and Miss Hensley had been friends for years, even if Skylar hadn't seen what they had in common and still didn't. But after working in education for a few years herself, she knew you found friends where you could.

Her mom wasn't what you thought of when you thought of a math teacher. She was a hippy through and through. But Miss Hensley was the most straight-laced English teacher Skylar ever had. Never once had she seen her not in earth tones and usually in black with blouses and slacks. Casual Friday wasn't a thing for her.

"I'm managing," Miss Hensley said, with a hint of sadness in her voice. "I was calling because of Kayden. There's been an incident."

"Shit," she said without thought. The last thing she needed today was her brother acting out at school, but she realized what she had just said and to whom and blushed at what she said. "Shit, I'm sorry for swearing."

"Don't worry, Miss Nash, you're an adult now. I

7

assume this isn't the first time you have sworn. Could you find time to come down to the school for a talk?"

Miss Hensley was the only teacher in the school who routinely called students by their last names. It made you feel special when you were in the ninth grade, being called something as important as Miss Nash. Now it was so routine to be called that, Skylar rarely noticed. That was until her former teacher said it, but now, instead of making her feel like an adult, it made her feel sixteen again.

"Yeah, I just need to put pants on, and I'll be down there." Skylar cringed. Had she just said that? Did Miss Hensley think she was naked? "Why did I just say that?"

There was more than a smile in the woman's voice when she said, "We appreciate everyone wearing pants, Miss Nash. Take whatever time you need to dress appropriately. See you when you get here."

Closing her eyes at the humiliation, she said, "Yeah, see you in a bit."

Chapter 2

Leila Hensley sat in her desk chair and looked at the phone she had just hung up. The last thing she wanted to do was call Skylar Nash. Dealing with her brother's issues wasn't what the younger woman needed to do today. Everyone in the school was missing Karla Nash as the school year started, but not like her kids were. It had only been a month.

Losing his mom had hit Kayden hard, but he had been getting into trouble before that had happened. For two years now, he had been disrupting class and being an all-around jerk. Karla had been at her wit's end with him, and Leila knew Skylar wasn't ready to be the kind of parent he needed.

"She isn't coming." The redheaded teen smirked smugly from his chair, slouched down as if he hadn't just done what he did.

"She's coming," Leila assured him. Not that he cared. He never did when his mom was called. But usually, her trip was just down the hall from her classroom.

Sometimes Leila wondered if it was because his only

living parent worked at the school that he had rebelled. That he was too comfortable in the building and with the staff. It didn't help that the school had grades pre-k through high school in the same building.

Then sometimes, she wondered if it was that he was missing the father figure he never got by losing his father so young. Leila had never met the man, who had already died by the time she moved to town. But there were quite a few other students in school in the same situation for some reason or another, and they weren't acting up.

Kayden's issues had been on her mind long before his mom was killed. Karla had confided in her and asked her opinion about what to do with him. Not that Leila knew she hadn't raised kids. She had always been happy enough to send them home to their parents at the end of the day.

Leila had a hard time with fourteen-year-old Kayden Nash. The first time she met him, he had just started kindergarten so many years before. He was an adorable little boy who smiled and waved at her every day as he walked past her door on the way to his mom's. His sister Keeley was two years older than him and almost always with him.

Unlike his sisters, he had red curls and freckles, and he reminded her of someone she used to know in college. But that hadn't been why she liked him. He had just been a likable kid for many years. All of Karla's kids had been. But now, years later, the red hair had been shorn so short you couldn't even tell the color, and that innocent little boy was completely gone.

His oldest two sisters didn't inherit either of those features, but took after their mom with light brown hair and flawless skin. But once you got past their looks, the sisters weren't alike at all. Keeley and Sierra were far more studious than her older sister, who Leila still couldn't believe she had grown up to be a teacher herself. That one she didn't see coming.

From his chair, Kayden yawned and stretched before telling her, "Why don't you just get it over with and suspend me? Sky doesn't have to be here for that. I can walk home."

Leila wondered how dumb he thought she was, because that suggestion nearly made her laugh at its ridiculousness. His cockiness was bothering her today. It was only the third day of school, and she was already annoyed with students. It wasn't even just Kayden she had lost patience with. Had she been in education too long?

Controlling her eye roll, she said, "Your punishment will be up to Mr. Gerard, not me. But I'm sure he won't send you home to enjoy a few days off. Not when you already have work you haven't turned in, and that is just for my class."

"Why turn in anything? You will give me whatever grade you want to give, anyway. Why even try?" he asked, trying to get a rise out of her.

"Because when you try, your grades improve. I would like to see you try this year, Kayden. Last year is over; let's start anew. You are smarter than it looks on paper," Leila said just as the principal walked into the room.

Tony Gerard had been at the school for a few months, and his philosophy about punishment was far different than hers. Not that she would ever complain, though she desperately wanted to.

It wasn't even because the school board had hired him instead of her for the job. Even if she had been working like a dog for two years to get her administration license just to work at this school. The former principal Rick Hardy had even given her the heads up that he was retiring earlier than anyone else, so she could prepare. But it hadn't been enough.

She didn't knew why they had passed her up, but she had her suspicions. The school board wasn't as progressive as they liked to pretend to be. No matter what her qualifications, at the end of the day, she was gay and not from the area. One was bad enough, but both, it seemed, couldn't be overlooked.

"Kayden, what is going on today?" Gerald ignored her completely and focused on the student.

Not that she wouldn't do the same thing, but his assistant hadn't given him the entire story because she didn't know it. Leila hadn't felt the need to tell her everything since she would just have to repeat herself to Gerald, anyway. And Bonnie was a known gossip who couldn't keep anything to herself. Though Karla was gone, Leila knew she wouldn't want everyone to know what her son had done.

"Miss Hensley has a stick up her ass and no sense of humor." Kayden smirked at her. He knew she was pissed, knowing just what buttons to push. All of them.

"If the situation calls for humor, I can laugh. This did not," she informed him, ignoring how Gerard didn't do anything about the boy's swearing.

Biting her lip, she controlled the smile that threatened at the memory of his sister's instant apology for doing just that a few minutes before, which caught Leila off guard with how cute it had sounded coming from her. It was something she never would have done at her brother's age. None of Kayden's sisters would have.

Turning from Kayden, Gerard frowned at her. "Miss Hensley, can I talk to Kayden for a moment?"

All she could bring herself to do was nod because Gerard was going to be this kid's friend, not the authority figure he needed. The school year was only a few days in, and she was starting to see the pattern already. She hoped it was only because he was new, and he would grow a backbone soon.

"Kayden, you know we don't allow smoking on the school ground. It's a law we have to follow." Before she could make it to the door, Gerard was talking, making it sound as if he would allow it if he could. Hell, be probably would if a student asked. It seemed he was far more into being liked than doing his job.

Smirking, Kayden straightened. "I bet it's also against the law for her to come into the guys' bathroom."

"Leila, did that happen?" Stopping at her at the door's threshold, because she didn't like her name being used in front of the students. She had told the man on his first day. And third. And again yesterday.

Turning back, she said, "He was smoking. Someone had to go in there and stop it. Was I supposed to wait for a male teacher to come along? Because I assure you I'm as capable as anyone else in the building."

"Girls are not allowed. What if she saw my junk?" Kayden grabbed himself as he said it, as if his oversize jeans couldn't cover it properly.

"Be happy it was me, Mr. Nash. I don't care about your so-called junk." That wasn't even just because she was gay, but because he was a kid. Her students were her students. It never mattered what sex they were. They were students.

"Leila, you should be aware that you are not allowed in the men's washroom." Standing up, Gerard had a concerned look on his face. Yes, for her, not for the smoking student.

"Boys," she spat out the word, because the staff had their own washrooms, so the student ones were mostly for boys, "and if rules are being broken in there, I'm going in."

"Leila, we'll talk about this later." Dismissing her with an exasperated look, he turned to the student again before sitting down on the chair next to him. "This time, I'm not going to call your parents."

Leila turned on him. This was an automatic call to the parents and a harsh punishment. After all, it was the first week of school. Briskly, she told him, "I already called his sister."

"That wasn't necessary, Leila." He said her name again. She didn't like how informal he liked to be. She had spent over a decade being Miss Hensley and wasn't ready to let that go yet. Not for this guy.

"Yes, it is, Mr. Gerard." She emphasized his name, taking a few steps into the room. "This is a violation of school rules and not the first one this year. He has already been warned twice, and we have only been here a few days."

"But this is the first time he was smoking," Gerard pointed out, defending the student.

Controlling her anger, she asked, "Is he allowed to break every rule once before he gets in actual trouble? Is everyone allowed to do that? He's practically an adult."

"We are just getting used to the new school year, aren't we, Kayden?" He reached over and tapped the boy's knee.

"Yeah, new school year, Leila. Just learning the rules," Kayden said boldly, realizing he had an ally in the new principle.

"It's Miss Hensley to you, Mr. Nash," she reminded him. Even if she had been his mom's friend, neither of his sisters had ever been allowed to call her by her first name.

"Kayden, why don't you run to class while I talk to

Leila." Gerard nodded at Kayden. It seemed he wasn't even going to talk to him about what happened.

"Sure. Thanks, Tony. You're the best principle I've ever had." Kayden jumped to his feet and headed out the door, whistling.

Leila would also be happy if she had just gotten off the hook for a major infraction, because no matter what the nitwit in the principal's office thought, smoking was suspendible. First and every time.

Kayden slammed the door without even asking if Gerard wanted it shut. Once the room had stopped ringing, Gerard turned to her. "Do we have an issue, Leila?"

Nodding, she turned to him. "Yes, we do. First, you do not call me Leila in front of a student, ever. I prefer to be called Miss Hensley, and I have requested you do so. Second, Kayden needs to be punished, or he will keep pushing boundaries until he finds one. He needs to find it here in school and not in the real world, where there are actual consequences for breaking rules."

"Cut him some slack. His mother passed away this summer." Gerard sat down on his desk and relaxed.

"Really? I didn't know, Mr. Gerard," she said sarcastically. "Thank you for reminding me that one of my best friends died in a car accident twenty-nine days ago. I guess I should let her son get away with murder, even if he knows better, because of it."

"It's smoking, not murder. He might have been smoking all summer, for all we know. With his parents' consent," Gerard argued with a dismissive wave.

"Parental approval doesn't mean he can smoke in school. And knowing his mother means I know he wasn't allowed to smoke at home. And I know that because I talked to his mother all the time." She wanted to be done with this conversation because she was afraid she was going to murder him.

Getting up from the edge of his desk, he moved to his chair. Leaning back, he said, "You don't know who and who does not smoke in this school."

"Do you want me to make a list of the students who actually smoke? Because I can. I spend enough time with them to know each and every one of them. Smell them."

After twelve years at the school, she knew more than she cared to about almost everyone. The students might have thought they were being sneaky, but she knew. Talk made it back to the staff, and the staff talked to each other.

Gerard fidgeted as he sat in the chair, "So, I don't know the students I met three days ago as well as you do. Is that what you are saying?"

He didn't get it, and she was afraid he might never. "I'm just saying that maybe you should listen to the teachers who know the kids before you take the kid's word for everything."

"I'm giving them the benefit of the doubt. Every student starts at square one with me. They don't have last year's issues hanging over them like you. It's all fresh. You obviously wouldn't let him get away with a stern warning, so what would you have done with Kayden?"

"In-school suspension for two days, maybe three," she said easily. After all, she knew how smoking had been handled in the past.

"Why not just suspend him and send him home?" he asked curiously.

"Because his sister can't handle him," she answered honestly.

"I think only I can make that call, Miss Hensley," the woman herself said from the doorway.

Leila hadn't noticed that it was even being opened because she was so mad at the man in front of her.

Turning, she saw Skylar, so much like the student she had once been in the doorway, in ripped jeans and a snug T-shirt that had a rainbow heart on it. The only thing that showed she had aged was the strain on her face and the tattoo running up her right arm. Leila caught the hurt in her eyes before it vanished, replaced with anger.

She had said the wrong thing.

Chapter 3

Karla Nash had been a teacher Skylar's entire life, but she wasn't the reason Skylar had chosen to be a teacher. That had been because of Miss Hensley. Though she'd disliked her through most of her high school career, because meeting her rigid standards hadn't been as simple as school had always come to Skylar.

That meant Skylar had only decided to become a teacher when she was in the middle of her freshman year of college. It was then that she had realized how prepared she was compared to her fellow students for college classes. Only then did she understand that it had been Miss Hensley who had prepared her for her future. And she wanted to do that too.

But today she saw what the woman really thought of her. That she wasn't up to the task of raising her brother and sister. She was right, of course, but what choice did she have? She was all they had.

"And you are?" asked a young man with a hipster beard and a cheeky smile, who didn't seem to notice the tension in the room.

After watching the exchange for a few moments, she could tell that Miss Hensley wasn't impressed with the man. Not that Skylar pretended to know Miss Hensley very well, but they had spent many, many hours together over the years. Skylar just wondered if the man was ever going to realize it. Or if he even wanted to.

"Skylar Nash." Stepping into the room, she provided her name, and when the man still looked completely confused, she added, "Kayden Nash is my brother."

"Oh, Kayden's sister. I'm Tony." A smile spread over his face as he jumped from the desk and took her hand in an overly friendly shake. "Sorry about your mom's passing."

Taking the hand, she shook it, but when she let go, he still held on. "Thank you," she mumbled automatically. It was what everyone said to her the first time they ran into her. Whether in the grocery store or her front yard, and it seemed even here in the principal's office. Finally able to shake the hand off, Skylar got to business. "Miss Hensley called me about Kayden getting into more trouble?"

Turning away from Tony, Skylar looked at her former teacher and wondered if and when the woman would ever age or change. She looked the exact same as she had ten years before, when Skylar was in her class. A gray blouse tucked into slim black slacks, all above white tennis shoes, which hadn't changed either. No matter how dressed up she got, she always wore tennis shoes during class. So much so that if she wore dress shoes, it looked odd.

The only thing that had actually changed was her hair. No longer was it in a pixie cut. Now it was almost to her shoulders, but it was still the dark black it had been years before.

Gerard indicated for Skylar to sit down. "Yes, it seems Leila went over my head and called you when we can handle it here. A simple mistake," he said, casting Miss Hensley a look of dismissal. "She was just getting back to class."

Taking a seat in one of four chairs in the room, Skylar caught Miss Hensley rolling her eyes, something she had never seen before. Not even when she and Karla had gotten together to chat in their off time. Miss Hensley had never rolled her eyes.

A look at Principal Tony Gerard, she saw he hadn't noticed, because he was focused on Skylar. He had been hired before her mom had passed, but not soon enough that her mom knew much about him. And they hadn't met in person. But based on how he had dismissed a teacher so callously, Skylar knew her mom wouldn't approve because Skylar herself didn't approve of that move.

Turning to leave, Miss Hensley stopped in front of her and touched her upper arm gently, the touch warm against her bare skin, and she wondered what her teacher thought about her tattoo. Why it mattered, she didn't know, but she wondered just the same. Miss Hensley was the most straight-laced woman Skylar had ever met, which meant probable disapproval.

Her touch was more comforting than anyone's had been for a month, but her words brought back reality. "Yes, sorry for how that came out. It wasn't what I meant."

Bristling at the words, she shrugged to get the hand off her. "Yeah, I'm sure you meant something else when you said I couldn't handle Kayden."

Miss Hensley's brown eyes showed a moment of pain before she pulled her hand away. "I'll see you around."

"Sure, Miss Hensley," she said noncommittally, like she was a student again. But then again, she was maybe acting childish. She had been right, after all. Skylar had no idea how to control her brother. This was, in fact, the first time she had ever been called to the principal's office herself. Her only trips into this office had been with her mom to see Mr. Hardy, who hadn't been as friendly as Tony was, and she hadn't even been in trouble.

"Shut the door on your way out, please, Leila," Tony said as he watched her leave.

Skylar watched, knowing his eyes were on the teacher, but not on her back. The man was watching her ass. She would bet money on it.

Behind her, the door closed softly, and she was alone with Tony Gerard, a man who hadn't felt it was even worth the call to her when Kayden acted up. Getting up from his chair, he grabbed a stress ball from the top of his desk and squeezed it as he sat down on the front of the desk, far too close to her for her to feel comfortable.

Shifting uncomfortably in her chair, she asked, "What did Kayden do?"

Tony set the ball down and waited to speak for a moment too long. Which meant it was going to be bad. Even if this man wasn't going to call her, Miss Hensley had. And that woman followed rules. Or she was slipping, and Miss Hensley wasn't the teacher she used to be. Which would be even worse than anything Kayden had done.

"We've been having some issues with him since school began—small issues that we are working through with him. Losing his mother has affected his judgement, but we expect him to right himself soon enough," he said with a dismissive smile.

The words didn't assure her at all, because Kayden had been acting up for over a year now. After all this time, there was no "soon enough" anymore. There was just a problem.

"Issues? It's been three days. What has he been doing?" she asked, wishing this wasn't the first time she was hearing about it. She thought he was behaving in school this year despite his behaviors at home.

"Just normal behavior issues." He brushed them off as if they were no concern of hers. That she didn't need to even know what they were.

This wasn't the first time she was treated like she had no clue as to what was going on. That she couldn't possibly understand. But it was the first time she had been on the parents' side of things, and it was even worse. How could she know what an actual issue was or not if this man was hiding it from her?

"Mr. Gerard, there are no normal behavior issues. If Miss Hensley called me, there was something serious." Anger rising fast, she folded her arms.

Setting the stress ball on his desk, Gerard said with a shy grin, "Miss Hensley shouldn't have called you. There was no need. She should have called me first, but instead she went over my head. It won't happen again, I can assure you."

"Do you know what he did?" she asked with concern, wondering if the man was clueless.

"Smoking in the boys' room," he said and nearly giggled. "Like the song. You might not be old enough to know it, I guess, but there was a song—"

Not needing to know what he was rambling about, she demanded, "So, is he in-school suspension or out?"

Being in school settings her entire life, she knew that was an automatic infraction. It was one that rarely happened anymore because nobody could smoke in the building, but when it did, there were consequences. In the school she taught at, it was suspension.

Tony's smile fell when she didn't find it as humorous as he did. It seemed he hadn't expected her to know the rules.

"Neither actually. We are giving him a little leniency right now."

"Because his mother died?" She glared at him. He needed anything but leniency right now.

"Yes, he's working through the pain," he said, his eyes drifting down her chest. She just hoped he was looking at her shirt, because it stated plainly she wasn't interested in being ogled by him. That she wouldn't be flattered or interested.

Crossing her arms to divert his eyes, she stood up. Now he had to look up at her. "No, he's blowing smoke up your ass, Gerard. It took him two days to realize he can get away with shit, so he is plain and simple. If his mother were here right now instead of me, she would tell you the same thing. He was acting out last year and the year before. Now suddenly he's getting a pass on the same behavior? No, you will punish him, one way or another. This time and every time."

Gerard was squeezing his ball harder and harder as he stood up. "I have already made my decision. I assured him that this was his last warning."

Right then, she wished she hadn't just burned the bridge between her and Miss Hensley because she wanted to know if that was the truth. Skylar's BS radar said he was only telling her what she wanted to hear. But there was no way she could ask the woman now.

"If you won't enforce your own rules here, how can I enforce them at home? Because we have rules there that he's been disregarding those also, probably because he isn't held accountable to them here." Sitting down, she hated that this was an issue. She couldn't control him in school, and now she was finding out he was being coddled there.

Gerard walked around his desk and leaned against it, looking down at her. "We try to steady our students with a gentle hand here at Warrington High School, not bend them to our wills."

"He doesn't need a gentle hand. He needs boundaries."

"We give our students boundaries."

"No, it seems there were boundaries before, and they're breaking this year. What else has he done?" she demanded, needing to know.

"Nothing major," the man stated, not looking at her face, but lower.

"Then what minor things has he done?" she asked, then added so she wouldn't have to ask later, "And what punishments has he received?"

Reluctantly, he went back around his desk and opened his laptop. Then spent too long tapping the keys to find a program that was most likely already open. But she waited more or less patiently.

"He has been tardy a number of times."

"What number?" Standing, she leaned over the desk, trying to see his computer screen, but he managed to shift it before she could see anything.

Grabbing the stress ball again, he worked it with one hand, as he typed with the other, before saying, "Fifteen."

Gasping, she couldn't believe it. "It's been three days, Gerard. How is he home at the same time as his sister every one of those days? Shouldn't he have received detention after a certain number? Long before it was fifteen!"

"It's three, but …" Gerard started, but then stopped. He had no explanation.

Pushing off the desk, she started pacing and finished for him, "His mom died, not that he's taking advantage of the system."

"Since you are not an educator yourself, Skylar, I wouldn't expect you to understand. As educators, we have to walk a fine line—" he started, as if she were a high school student herself and understood nothing about the world around her.

"Excuse me?" she demanded.

"Teaching children day in and day out takes skills and abilities not every person has."

"I know about teaching children, Gerard. I have been doing it for four years now. Day in and day out, as you say, and never have I heard of a student getting away with so much in so little time."

Gerard's face paled, and he cleared his throat as if that would change the last few minutes of this conversation before saying, "I didn't know you were a teacher."

"From one teacher to another, I expect you to stop treating my brother with kid gloves. He needs to learn to control himself. If this school can't teach him that, I'll find another that will. And I'll be sure to tell the school board why I'm pulling him from WHS. A school I graduated from."

"There is no need for that." He squeezed the ball again.

She glared at him. "There seems to be. If I could spend my days here watching him, I would. Because you don't seem to care."

"We care. I can assure you we care."

"Then prove it by treating him normally. He doesn't need kid gloves. Not anymore." Getting up, she headed for the door, done with this discussion, needing air to breathe and to cool down.

"What do you teach?" he asked, stopping her.

"Math."

"Like your mom?"

"Yes, just like my mom," she said proudly.

Math had always been easy for her, and she loved

helping others with it even before she started teaching. But now with her mom gone, she was extra proud she had followed in her footsteps.

"Where are you teaching?" He finally put his stress ball down.

"Nowhere right now. I had to quit my job to be here." She wasn't going to tell him that she already missed teaching. That the beginning of the year was her favorite time.

"If you're looking for a job, we happen to need a substitute math teacher. Then you can keep an eye on your brother all day long." He smiled, as if she were desperate for a job. She wasn't.

"Don't tempt me," she said. "Someone has to control his behavior because you're failing."

That wiped the smile from his mouth but put one on hers as she slammed the door closed behind her.

Chapter 4

Whistling quietly to herself, Leila unlocked her classroom door, ready for another week. It had taken most of the weekend to get to this point. After her disastrous Thursday, and an equally bad Friday, her mood had improved greatly when she got home from work on Friday to find her jars had arrived early. As an avid canner, she was dead in the water when she'd run out of jars at the height of the season. She had more ripe tomatoes than she knew what to do with. Now they were, for the most part, in jars ready for later use.

In hopes of a better week, she had brought in a box of salsa jars to leave in the staff break room today for the other teachers to enjoy. After all, she couldn't enjoy fourteen jars of it herself. In fact, she barely liked the stuff, but she enjoyed making it.

Canning always reminded her of her grandma Hensley, who spent all summer and fall putting up jars of fruits and vegetables for the winter. As the only child of busy parents, she spent more time with her grandma than her own parents when she was growing up. Though her dad had passed when she was too young to remember, her mom, Donna, had owned not one but three car dealerships, which kept them busy, leaving no time for her. Which meant she grew up lonely.

When she'd been sixteen, her grandma died suddenly, and she was left alone. Her mom was barely home, so she was alone most of the time. By the time she graduated from high school, her mother had happily sent her to any college she chose to get a business degree so she, too, could work at one of the dealerships. Which she did with that exact goal in mind. And for that, she was proud of her.

Or was until she was in her senior year. When she'd told her mom she'd changed majors two years before to journalism. Her mom had been upset. That had gotten worse when she admitted that she also was brokenhearted because of a break up. A breakup not with a man, but a woman. That was when the proverbial shit hit the fan.

Within weeks, she was cut off and her tuition payments stopped. Access to her trust fund was gone and her credit cards were frozen. She was on her own without means to support herself. The only money she had access to was the little money her grandma had set aside for her.

Using that, she finished college at a more reasonably priced school and changed her degree to something she could use. A journalism degree had turned easily into teaching English without adding too many extra classes. Even to her young self, she knew journalism wasn't an option when she had no net if she failed.

That had been years ago, and she hadn't seen or heard from her mom since. Nor had she looked for her, even if she would be easy to find because of the Hensley dealerships. She could find her at any moment. But the sting of rejection still hurt, so she stayed far away.

Turning on the lights in her classroom, she dropped

her backpack on the desk just as swearing in the hallway sent her hurrying back toward the door. It was early for students and really early for students who hated school. Those, after all, were the ones who swore.

"Language," she said loudly to the familiar voice.

Kayden Nash was directing his anger at his sister. Not Keeley, who was supposed to be at the school, but Skylar, who wasn't.

"Tell her to leave, and I'll stop," he stated, slamming his hand into a nearby locker.

"I told you I was working here, Kayden. I don't know why you didn't believe me," Skylar stated calmly, more calmly than Leila herself would have as she worked to unlock the math room door.

"I don't need a babysitter at school!" he yelled so everyone in the school could hear.

"Yes, you do," Keeley told him from behind her sister while holding a brown leather bag. Not that she needed protection. Kayden had been overprotective of her since as far back as Leila had known them. Even if Keeley was older, she wasn't as outgoing as her brother.

"The school needs a math teacher, and I happen to teach math. I'm not here for you. I'm here for everyone." She waved a hand around, but there were no other students in the hallway.

"Don't think I'm going to acknowledge you," he spat out and headed down the hallway, away from them.

"I wouldn't expect anything less." Skylar said under her breath and watched him go as she took the leather bag from her sister, looping it over her own shoulder as she continued to work on unlocking the stubborn door.

The teenager gave her a smile and left in the opposite direction as her brother. Their relationship had suffered since Kayden had started acting out. Keeley hated conflict.

Turning back to Skylar, who was finally getting the key to work, Leila couldn't help but notice that today the ripped jeans had been replaced by slimming tan slacks and a navy button-up that was covering the arm tattoo completely. The only thing that was the same as last week were the chunky scuffed brown shoes on her feet. They looked like they would make for sore feet by the end of the day.

Leila knew Skylar was a math teacher like her mom, something her friend had been proud of. Leila knew she had a job, but that job had to be far from here. A job she should be at today, not here at WHS.

"Welcome?" she said tentatively, not wanting to say the wrong thing again.

Skylar jumped as if she hadn't known anyone was there before she turned and looked at her, her brown locks in a bit of disarray this morning. But Kayden did that to almost anyone these days.

"Oh, hey, Miss Hensley," she said, and Leila hoped she had forgiven her for the Kayden comment the week before if they were going to work together.

Stepping forward, she grabbed the door Skylar had finally managed to open. "How long are you here for?"

"Here in the school or in town?" she asked, shifting the large leather bag on her shoulder. "I guess it doesn't matter. I have no idea for either one."

"Well, if you need anything, I'm across the hallway." Pointing at it, Leila realized how stupid she was being. Skylar knew exactly where she was. Had for a long time.

Skylar shook her head in annoyance. "I know the school, Miss Hensley."

"It's not the school that you'll have questions about." Over the years, Leila enjoyed mentoring new teachers to the school.

Skylar assured her. "I also know how to handle students. This isn't my first teaching job, Miss Hensley."

"Have a nice day," she called to the younger woman, because she didn't want to say the wrong thing again.

"Yeah, you too," Skylar called after her, dismissing her completely.

It seemed that was all she did in front of that woman. Even at the funeral, she hadn't said the right thing, but then again, she had been a little in shock herself that day. Karla had been so full of life and so much a part of this school and town. How could either go on without her? Then seeing her kids lost and alone had nearly broken her.

Skylar and Sierra were trying to act so old and mature, even if they still needed their mom more than ever and had lost her. Sierra had only graduated two years ago and had been one of Leila's best students, bright and eager to learn. So different than her older sister, who struggled and needed to be coerced into doing her work.

Keeley had been devastated. Karla had always said she was the most sensitive of the kids, and that day it showed. Sixteen hadn't been a good time to lose her mom, but no age ever was.

As his sisters cried, Kayden pretend that losing his mom wasn't affecting him. That he was too mature to care about emotions. The tactic that annoyed his sisters, who needed him to be the kid he used to be. Kind and considerate.

At the funeral, Skylar had been accompanied by her girlfriend, a tall, leggy blonde in a black power suit who was on her phone more than by Skylar's side. Leila wasn't surprised she came. Karla had mentioned the girlfriend since the relationship had begun. Though she had said nothing negative about it, she hadn't said too many positive things either. Not like a few of Skylar's other relationships. There had been a few women Karla had been eager to see her daughter fall in love with. But she hadn't.

Walking back into her classroom, Leila hated the frostiness between the two rooms. There had only been one other time that she hadn't gotten along with the math teacher, and that had to do with Skylar as well. Back when she was still a student, she had talked to Leila about an issue in her life instead of her mom. That conversation had pissed Karla off for months before they agreed to not talk about it again. Leila was sure Skylar never knew it had even happened, but Leila wouldn't forget it.

"Miss Hensley, can I look at your library?" Keeley Nash asked from the doorway, her books for her first class in her arms already, even if it wasn't for another half an hour.

"Sure, Miss Nash, take all the time you need."

Leila knew she used the excuse of looking at the collection of books she had in her classroom to avoid the crowded hallways in the morning. It had started the first day of school, her first without her mom. Everyone worried about Kayden's outburst, but Leila was more worried about Keeley. Being the introverted type, she was prone to outbursts, but there was more going on inside the girl than anyone could see.

"Thanks," she said and went to the corner and busied herself as she scanned the titles she had to have already memorized.

"How was your weekend?"

"Good, I guess. Kayden and Sky fought most of it. Sierra didn't come home." The girl summed up the weekend that seemed more stressful than relaxing. But maybe she was more used to the fighting than Leila would be.

Even if the girl didn't, Leila continued to talk. "I spent

the weekend canning tomatoes and making salsa. It relaxes me after a long week. Do you do anything that relaxes you?"

"Read." She pulled out a book and looked at the cover for a moment before asking, "How do you can tomatoes, and why?"

"You take tomatoes, water, jars, and add heat. It's a lot of fun, but a lot of work also. This weekend I canned salsa." She wished she had a better explanation, but not wanting to bore the girl, she instead said, "You should tell your sister to grab a jar from the break room, and you can try it."

"Like at a restaurant? With chips? You can make that?" She added the book to her pile.

"Yes, to all questions," Leila said, knowing that the kid wouldn't read the book she picked since she should have read it two years before for this class. But she wouldn't say anything. Keeley would return it in the morning.

"That's kind of cool." She turned from the shelves as the first student for her first class came into the room, the senior whose parents farmed the land around her little hobby farm had been early for the second day in a row. She had hoped it was because he was excited for class each morning, but she was starting to think it had to do with Keeley, who glanced shyly his way on her way out of the room.

It was only after she was out of the room that Justin turned to her. "Morning, Miss Hensley."

"Morning, Mr. Sather. How was your weekend?" Her eyes caught the math teacher sitting at her desk across the hallway. Had she been listening when Leila was talking to Keeley? Could she even hear that far away?

Or, more importantly, why did Leila care what she thought of her?

Chapter 5

"It's only temporary. They needed a teacher, and I'm here," Skylar said into the phone as she told her girlfriend about her new job. Sitting on the front step, she told herself it was because she wanted fresh air after spending the entire day cooped up in a classroom. Not because she didn't want to fight with Iris in front of the kids. Not that they cared much about her personal life, but she cared.

As she watched the house next door, the owner drove into the garage and closed it. All without looking her way. So much for small-town gossip.

"Won't that slow down your packing and organizing the house? I think that will make coming back take longer," Iris complained, but what she didn't know was that little of that had been happening. She was too far in her head to do anything as productive as getting the house organized. Every time she tried, memories would force her to stop.

"Are you still planning on coming in a few weeks?" She changed the subject, not wanting to hear how all her decisions weren't enough for Iris.

Iris's voice got softer, happier. "Yeah, so far. I'm so busy right now but hope I can break away for our weekend. What do you have planned for us to do?"

Skylar's blood ran cold. Had she said she was planning something? What was there to do in Warrington? Because there wasn't anything. But instead of making something up, she got creative. "I'm working on it."

"I'm so excited to see you," she cooed, and Skylar could hear her shifting in her bed. Or the couch? Iris hadn't said where she was, but it was early in the evening, so maybe on the couch. "Have you looked at the texts I sent you with the bedroom sets?"

There had been a quick glance, but she had been in the middle of class with the freshmen and hadn't had time to actually look. Then, after school, she had spent all her time getting the kids home, Kayden to do his homework, and then supper preparation. There'd been no time. And no interest. What Iris wanted, she would get. Skylar's opinion didn't matter.

"Yeah," she lied, so Iris wouldn't have hurt feelings. "I liked them all."

It didn't work, because Iris sounded sad. "All of them? Wasn't there a favorite?"

"Yeah, I kind of like the third one." She guessed at a number. There had been more than three, right?

"The Kensington collection? I knew you would like that one. It's my least favorite," Iris said, a definite note of annoyance in her voice. As if just by choosing that one Skylar had disappointed her.

"Which did you like?" she asked as Keeley came out of the house, her tablet in her hand and a look of confusion on her brow.

"The Heather," Iris said, not knowing Skylar had stopped paying attention. "I like the simple lines, and it's a platform bed. I think I want us to have a platform bed. And it's that pale color I like. Muted."

"Do you know how to can tomatoes?" Keeley loudly whispered as Iris went on about the color of the bed she liked and, more importantly, which she did not.

Covering the mouthpiece on her phone, Skylar whispered back, "No."

If she hadn't been on the phone, she would have asked what the girl was asking. As far as she knew, Keeley didn't even like tomatoes except on pizza and in ketchup. Where exactly had her interest come from?

"It was the in the first email I sent you. Did you look at that one?" Iris asked.

"Yeah," she said and realized she was still covering the mouthpiece, moved her hand, and repeated the lie, "Yes."

"I want to try it," Keeley went on, turning the screen toward Skylar, who took it and looked at the video already running. It was of two middle-aged women working in a kitchen with a bunch of stuff she couldn't even identify. Keeley pointed to it and added, "It's relaxing."

"I saw it in person this weekend. I know we agreed not to go separately, but I was bored on Sunday and just went. Don't be mad," Iris continued on, though they had never agreed not to go shopping alone. In fact, Skylar would be happiest if she just bought the bed without her.

Skylar watched the video that looked nothing like relaxing. "This looks hard," she said and realized she had said it into the phone.

"Sky, are you even paying attention to me? Don't you care about our bedroom anymore?" Iris's voice went up an octave, her pissed voice.

"Yes, Iris, it's just that Keeley had this thing. I'm listening to you." Back peddling, she pushed the tablet at her sister and pointed to the house. She needed to concentrate on her relationship right now. Not her sister's sudden interest in canning.

In front of her, Keeley's face dropped, and she closed the window the video was on as she went back into the house. Skylar knew she had messed up. Keeley wasn't an attention seeker, never had been. Usually, Kayden took all the attention.

On the other end of the line, Iris was lecturing her. "I don't think you are listening, Sky. You are my girlfriend and aren't really acting the part right now. Do you even care about us anymore?"

"Of course I care about you, and I care about our bedroom. But today was a busy day," she reminded her. She was raising two teenagers.

"Too busy for me?" Iris demanded.

"I did not say that," she insisted, because she wasn't. She loved Iris. "I just feel like I'm doing so much around here, but nothing is getting done. That everything is on me, and I don't have time for it."

Behind her, the door opened and slammed shut. But instead of Keeley coming back, it was Kayden who came out of the house. Barely looking at her, he called once past her, "I'm going out."

"It seems like you are," Iris complained on the phone.

"No, you aren't," she said to her brother as she lowered the phone, because he was grounded, and he knew it. The school might have let him off the hook for his actions, but she didn't.

"Bug off, Sky, you're not my mom." Kayden kept moving, heading for downtown just six blocks away.

"Get back here," she called after him, getting up and following.

"Skylar, are you there?" Iris yelled into the phone in her hand.

"If you keep going, you will be grounded for the rest of the month. And if you're lucky, I won't add the next month onto it." She slipped her phone into her pocket. She had to concentrate on her brother right now.

Kayden stopped and stomped back to her. "I don't know who you think you are, but you have no control over me. So leave me alone."

"Never. Now get back in the house and go to your room." She stood as tall as she could, not backing down, but he was now taller than her. Something she now hated immensely.

With a huff, he stomped back toward the house, cursing the entire time.

She had won this time.

When the front door slammed closed behind him, she remembered she was on the phone with Iris. Pulling it out, she saw that one of them had ended the call. And that Iris hadn't called back. Nor did her girlfriend call back the rest of the night.

As she was getting ready for bed, she knew she had messed up far more today than she had done right. Tomorrow she would do better. She had to.

Chapter 6

"How was your first week?" Leila tentatively asked Skylar midafternoon Friday. So far since starting, Skylar had successfully ignored Leila, even if they monitored students in the hallway across from each other. Not that it mattered, it just hurt a little.

"About how I expected it." She didn't even look up as she straightened another desk, not expanding.

Leila wouldn't even be in this room right now if Keeley hadn't seemed off for most of the week. Every morning she chatted with the girl for a few minutes, but as the week progressed, she stopped talking about anything home related and just ignored the questions. Then today she hadn't even shown up. Leila hoped that having her sister around the school wasn't making it worse for Keeley.

For Kayden, though, it seemed having his sister in the building was having the opposite effect. By Tuesday, he had stopped breaking most rules. He had even been on time for her class all week. Even his snarky attitude had improved a little.

Leila hoped it was all a sign that Skylar was getting

more of a handle on raising the boy. Keeley had mentioned that all they did was fight, but her stories of their battles of will were humorous. From Skylar slowly taking all Kayden's video games and forcing him to do chores to get them back. To Kayden moving around the living room furniture so his sisters couldn't even get in the room for almost an entire day. Without crawling over furniture, she and Keeley were forced to go outside to get from the kitchen to their bedrooms.

Now, after a week of silence, she knew Skylar wouldn't forgive her without a little work on Leila's part. And she felt Keeley needed to get away from the house and her siblings. A little time to herself where there was no fighting.

Which was the only reason she was in the math classroom for Keeley. Not because she didn't feel right about the fact that Skylar didn't like her. Because that didn't matter one bit.

Tentatively stepping into the room, Leila pushed her to talk more. "I hope that means good. The kids seem to like you better than Mrs. Borren. That's who was here the first few days."

"Mrs. Boring still subs? She must be ninety." Skylar cracked a smile, and the tension broke just a little between them.

It was on the tip of her tongue to correct her, because she was constantly correcting students, but the nickname was far more popular than the woman. But she was a reliable sub, so she was always called.

"Just turned eighty-two, last I heard," Leila told her, because the woman always told her her age, every damn time she was in the building. She also reminded them she shouldn't have to put up with kids at her age, but she never said no to subbing.

Skylar's voice went soft. "I had forgotten about her. I

hadn't been told who the sub was. Every year, she swore at least once that she was never coming back. Yet she always did."

Relaxing into the conversation, Leila took over, straightening the desks. "If you stay long enough, you will have her personal number memorized."

Going to the front of the room, Skylar started erasing the board, assuring her, "I don't plan to stay that long. I left this town and never planned to come back."

Leila watching Skylar remove the equations from the board, noticing her boxy numbers were very different from her mom's curly ones. It made Leila miss the woman's familiarity. The school had definitely changed with her gone.

Leila pulled her attention from the board. "I wish you didn't have to be here."

"Yeah, me too," Skylar agreed, not turning around. Though she could have said it sarcastically, it was said with a wistfulness that said she was thinking of her mom, too.

With her back to her, Leila said truthfully, "I'm sorry about what you overheard in the office last week."

"Not that you said it?" Turning, Skylar's blue eyes pinned her down for an answer.

Nodding, she agreed, "That too. I just lost my temper with Gerard. Sometimes I don't understand his disciplinary tactics."

"I could tell. I don't think I've heard you lose your temper before." Tossing the whiteboard eraser onto her desk, she leaned into the sturdy metal.

"It takes a bit, but it happens." She knew she could count on one hand how many times it happened in the school. But she didn't want to talk about herself. She was here to mend fences any way she could. "Anyway, I didn't mean that you couldn't handle Kayden. I was mostly implying that you shouldn't have to have him home with you when he could just as easily be in school. You are perfectly capable of handling him. What I meant was that you just shouldn't have to for a few hours of the day. You are supposed to be getting your mom's estate organized."

Her shoulders slumping, Skylar nodded. "Thank you for the confidence, but I don't really feel it."

Bouncing on the balls of her feet, Leila didn't want to leave. She wanted to talk to Skylar more. "Are you planning on moving them to Minneapolis with you?"

Instantly, Skylar looked defeated, like the world was on her shoulders. "No. Yes. I don't see them living with Iris and me in our two-bedroom condo, but I also don't see me moving here. I don't know what to do, actually."

Leila's mind went back to the tall blonde from the funeral. She didn't look like the type who wanted to move to a small town. Who wanted a slower pace that involved two teenagers? But she didn't know the woman beyond her name, so maybe she was supporting Skylar from a distance. Hopefully, she was supporting Skylar.

Getting the last chair in a row, she cautiously asked, "And Iris? Moving here, I mean. Would she move here with you?"

Skylar looked at the ceiling for a moment before answering, "Probably not. She has an amazing job she loves there. And truth be told, there's nothing for her here."

"So you're caught between a rock and a hard place," Leila surmised, not envying Skylar and her decisions.

"Pretty wedged in, actually. I don't know what to do."

"I wish I had an answer for you, but this is beyond my skill level." Glancing at the clock, she saw the bell was going to ring, bringing their prep hour to a close, and she hadn't even brought up the real reason she was there. "So, Keeley was asking about canning this week."

Skylar seemed to shake herself before asking curiously, "She asked me, too, except we never actually got to talking about it. Where did that come from?"

Leila raised her hand and smiled. "Me, I mentioned it earlier in the week. I like to can."

Everyone around here knew about her hobby, she wasn't shy about sharing with others. After all, she was a single woman. How much food did she need? So, she gave it away when she felt like it.

"Makes sense."

Nervous suddenly, she blurted, "And I was wondering if you would let Keeley come over to my house and learn how? I think she needs a little time away from her brother. If you don't feel comfortable doing that, I completely understand. It's completely up to you."

Hoping it didn't sound like she didn't think she was doing a good job with the kids. Because that wasn't the case, she was just giving her some room to breathe. Or would she just be making it worse? Maybe she shouldn't have even asked.

"No, I'm okay with it if you are. Was she interested when you asked?"

"I didn't talk to her about it in case you didn't want her to. I don't actually know if she wants to help me or not. Maybe her interest is just talk." Leila wasn't sure anymore. It had been over a day since Keeley had last asked about the process. Maybe that phase had already passed.

Skylar shook her head. "Oh, well, I'll talk to her and see if she's interested. We could all use a little distraction right now. Can I get your number, and I'll get in touch with you about her answer?"

Walking to her desk, Leila wrote her number. Then her

name, just in case she forgot whose number it was, which was stupid because she probably didn't get new phone numbers every day. But there it was. Looking perfectly stupid, she could have just emailed or something.

Tossing the pen down, Leila took a few steps toward the door before saying, "Perfect. I can come and get her, or you can drive her out, whichever you're most comfortable with. I live a few miles from town."

Skylar's eyebrow rose in surprise. "You don't live in Conley anymore?"

Stopping, Leila looked at her. How did she known where she had lived? Had all the students known, or just Skylar? She didn't remember the girl coming over with her mom when she was in school. Not that she and Karla met at each other's houses much. They worked together five days a week. There was no need. "Not for many years."

Skylar ran her fingers through her hair, not meeting her eyes. "I can bring her out if she wants to go. Just send me the address and directions."

"I will," Leila said, suddenly excited for the weekend. To have company canning and maybe keep improving her friendship with Karla's daughter. She hated how it bothered her that they didn't get along.

As the bell rang, Skylar asked, "Saturday or Sunday?"

"Either one works. I plan to can both days. Just bring her out early in the day. I would hate for her to miss picking her own tomatoes," Leila said, needing to get to her room before the students did.

"That wouldn't be any good," Skylar called after her as she cleared the door. Leila was almost sure she had been teasing her. Almost.

Chapter 7

A few miles turned out to be eight miles and down two gravel roads. Miss Hensley officially lived in the middle of nowhere, Skylar decided as she drove Keeley toward the address that had been sent to her. Once again, she checked the map on her phone to make sure she hadn't made a wrong turn.

Back when Skylar had been in high school, Miss Hensley had lived almost a half hour away in a town twice the size of Warrington, in a little red house with white shutters. It had always looked cozy and well-kept for the part of town it was in, which wasn't exactly well-kept. But that was the exact kind of house she always saw the woman in, tidy and organized.

Skylar didn't know how she found out where her teacher lived or the exact house it was from that distance. But she had known. Just like she had known Leila Hensley lived with another woman. Even before Skylar realized she herself was gay, she knew that particular teacher was. Her girlfriend was a health teacher from Conley, who also coached the high school basketball and track teams. Of course, all the adults said they were just roommates.

As she got older and her interest in any same sex-relationship peaked, she'd actually gone to a basketball game specifically to see her teacher's girlfriend. And also to see another gay person in person, or at least from across a gym. Noreen Neerson was her name, and she was short, stocky, and liked to yell. It seemed with these two, it was a case of opposites attract. She wasn't the girlfriend Skylar had always envisioned for her teacher.

But she and Leila had been together for years by that time. They had moved to town together, even. They had a dog, or did back then, a big black Labrador named Frank. But that had been years ago, and maybe they had another dog. Or more if they lived in the middle of nowhere.

Secretly, she was happy the couple was still together. Warrington might not be the bastion of acceptance of everything, but as far as Skylar knew, Leila never hid who she was. Everyone in school knew she was gay, even in town. As far as Skylar knew, nobody had anything against it.

Miss Hensley's openness about her sexuality had been the reason Skylar turned to her about being gay. Back then, she had been sure her mom wouldn't understand. But she knew if anyone would, it was Miss Hensley. After all, she must have gone through it herself once, though she hadn't shared that information with Skylar.

"You're sure you want to do this?" Skylar asked, because Keeley had been silent this morning, or more silent. All week she had been silent.

"Yeah, it looks fun," she said to the window and not to Skylar.

Keeping toward the distant farm, Skylar set down the ground rules. Usually, they were for Kayden and not

Keeley, but Keeley was finally doing something. "Are you willing to work and not complain? Miss Hensley doesn't want a complaining teenager around her on her day off."

"I won't complain," Keeley assured her, then turned to her and said, "Didn't you want me to go?"

"Yes, I want you to."

"I could have driven myself."

"I wanted to drive you, at least for the first time. And I wasn't ready to be without my car all day." Skylar turned into a driveway after double-checking the number on the mailbox.

The yard was as neat and tidy as the woman's yard in town, only this one was larger, and there were two massive gardens to the left of the driveway. On the right was a sprawling white square house with a wrap-around porch. Beside it was an attached garage that would only hold one car. There were no cars visible, so the garage must fit whatever Miss Hensley drove, and maybe her girlfriend went to town or some place with her vehicle.

As she parked by the garage, a tri-colored basset hound lopped happily toward them. Before she and Keeley could get out of the car, Miss Hensley stepped out of the front door. In the hundreds or thousands of times Skylar had seen her over the years, she had never worn shorts, not once. Not even skirts. Never bare legs. But today she was in cut-off jean shorts that were worn and faded and short—not obscenely short, but there was a lot of tanned leg showing. Then there was the black tank top covered with an open red and black flannel, but the outfit was something straight out of her teenage dreams. Miss Hensley barely dressed.

She once had crushed on Miss Hensley? That was years ago, and she had nearly forgotten it completely, even if it had been pretty heavy for a few years. And she knew she wasn't the only one. She might have been the only female, but she secretly reveled in the fact that she was the only one who had a chance.

Back then, the teacher was still in her twenties, not that she wasn't still gorgeous, but she was now in her thirties and might not entice those dreams in her students anymore. But they hadn't seen her in the shorts, which was probably for the best. And bare feet, Skylar tried not to stare. Bare feet.

"Don't worry about Russell. She's more of a lover than a fighter. Give her a few scratches, and she will love you for life," Miss Hensley called as she came down the steps as if she wasn't in her bare feet.

Keeley was the first out of the car to meet Russell. Slowly, Skylar got out, feeling like a kid in her sleep pants and university sweatshirt. Sadly, she was even in her glasses still, which she regretted completely. She didn't know Miss Hensley was going to be gorgeous on the weekends. Now she felt like a slob. She tried to divert the woman's attention from her and her outfit. "What a gorgeous house."

Leila looked behind her. "Thank you. Mostly I bought the place for the yard. The house was just a bonus. A little big for my needs, but I still love it."

"How long have you been here?" she asked, ignoring how much she liked this at home with Miss Hensley.

"Seven years. I had always wanted to be in the country. I saw this in the paper and jumped on it." Russell went back to her and nudged her leg, making the woman reach down and scratch the dog's ear.

"You lucked out." Looking around the yard, Skylar realized she had bought the farm the year after Skylar had graduated. Which was why she hadn't known. But that didn't explain why her mom hadn't mentioned it in the years since.

"I know." She turned her attention to Keeley. "Morning, Keeley. Are you ready for an adventure?"

"Yeah." She was still on the ground petting the dog, who was going between the two people who were willing to pet him. "I like your dog."

Leila stuffed her hands in the back pockets of her jean shorts. "That's good; she'll be under your feet all day. Well, except when she's with her puppies."

"She has puppies?" Keeley asked in surprise.

"Russell is a girl?" Skylar said at the same time, eying the dog.

Miss Hensley laughed lightly at their reaction. "Yes, we'll go look at them first, or I'll never get any work out of you." She turned to Skylar, who wasn't going to leave quickly but could resist puppies. "She's a girl. I was planning on getting a male but fell for her. On the way home, I decided she didn't know Russell wasn't a girl's name, so I kept it."

Skylar loved the sound of her laugh. It wasn't something that came out in school. Sure, she would smile and chuckle, but never really laugh. It seemed maybe Miss Hensley was different at home than at school, like everyone else. It was like seeing behind the curtain, and Skylar liked it a little too much.

"I don't need to see the puppies," Skylar argued, feeling like she was intruding, not wanting to spend more time with this version of her former teacher.

"There are nine of them, and they're the perfect age." Miss Hensley grabbed a sliver of Skylar's sweatshirt and pulled her toward the house for a moment before letting go, but it was enough to push her to follow.

Russell seemed to sense they were going to see her babies and headed toward the door as fast as she could, which wasn't fast at all. Mostly because she had to make sure they were following every few steps. Before stopping at the closed door to wait for them, the dog looked back to still make sure they were coming. So proud that they were following her.

"Just go in. They're right there in the mudroom," Miss Hensley called to Keeley, who was leading the way.

"Is, uhm, is Noreen home today?" She stumbled over the question. She had been looking for signs of the woman, but there hadn't been any. But what would she have been able to pick out that was the other woman? She didn't even know what was Leila's.

"Noreen?" she asked in confusion.

"Your girlfriend, right? Noreen." She said the name again, wondering if what she remembered had been rumors or truth. It had been so long that she couldn't even remember where she had heard it the first time. And now she doubted herself.

Miss Hensley shook her head at the name before saying, "She was, but that was years ago. A lot of years ago. I'm not seeing anyone now."

Skylar knew she was blushing, knew she had stepped in it, and now it was her turn to apologize. "Sorry, that was a rude question, Miss Hensley."

Leila nearly touched her arm, then pulled back but smiled. "We aren't in school, and you are no longer a student. You can call me Leila. And it's okay. We broke up a long time ago. And I'm not on that Facebook thing, so you couldn't know my status."

"Leila, then. You're not missing anything," Skylar said as she looked at Russell, who seemed proud to have everyone looking at her puppies. Blushing, she realized exactly how that sounded, so corrected herself, "I mean, with Facebook, not being single."

"I know. But I miss not being single sometimes."

Picking up one of the squirming puppies, Leila handed it to Skylar, who instantly fell in love. Puppy smell and puppy kisses made her laugh, and she wished she could spend the day right here.

Bringing the puppy to her face, she kissed the nose just moments before the tiny claws latched onto her glasses. Then, just as fast, he was chowing on the rim as they slid down her nose. Since she was holding the puppy with two hands, she was at a loss to save her only pair of glasses from falling to the floor.

That was, until Leila reached up and slid them off completely, her fingers grazing Skylar's ears and forehead as she did. Meeting her brown eyes, the older woman . smiled at her. Or at her predicament.

Chapter 8

A smiling Skylar in black-rimmed glasses holding a puppy was simply adorable. The woman in her comfy clothes with the wiggly little puppy was almost too much for Leila to resist.

Of all the outfits she had thought Skylar would wear to bring Keeley to the farm, pajamas weren't on the list. But Leila was very surprised and happy to see them. Not that she should be. After all, the woman was over ten years younger than her and a former student with a girlfriend.

Leila wasn't supposed to notice that Skylar was cute. She always wondered why Skylar had never been picked for the trivial beauty pageants that took place during homecoming and prom every year. Karla hadn't been upset that Skylar was never chosen, even if she was excited when Sierra was.

"I'll just go clean these." She held up the glasses and went into the kitchen, away from Skylar Nash.

Slowly, she cleaned the glasses and looked over all the items she had laid out this morning to prepare for Keeley coming over. Now that the girl was here, Leila was a little nervous. She had never canned with anyone but her grandma. Not even in the years she lived with Noreen. In fact, she didn't start until she bought the farm, and the farm came after her relationship with Noreen was over.

It was a surprise that Skylar knew she had dated Noreen, but not that they had broken up. Karla knew it had happened and had been a shoulder to lean on in the first confusing months. But her daughter was oblivious, and she had been a senior when it happened.

Noreen had broken her confidence for a while. Or more like a lifetime, because she still wasn't confident in dating and relationships. To be told that you were more of a habit than a lover had hurt her.

They had only been dating for a few months before they graduated, both with teaching degrees. Since they were dating, they applied for jobs in the same area. Each had gotten a job, but in different schools—rival schools, in fact. Moving in together hadn't even been discussed. It was a given. By the time they were getting into their jobs and routines, they had settled for each other as well. It wasn't a love match, and in the end, love never came. Habit came, and they stayed because it was just that: a habit.

If there had been any more lesbians around, one of them would probably have realized a lot sooner that there was more to life than what they had. Instead, they just stayed until Noreen had found someone else—a parent who had recently come out had caught her eye. Leila wasn't heartbroken or devastated, except that she had lived for years with a habit. Wasted years.

Letting Noreen go was easy. Even the sudden loneliness wasn't hard to get used to. It was during those early weeks when she was learning to do everything alone that she had run across the ad for the farm and took a leap she wouldn't have before.

She had always wanted to live in the country. Noreen hadn't, so they lived in town. But with Noreen gone, there wasn't anything keeping her in town. And since she and Noreen had been renting, moving had been a breeze.

Not that she and Noreen didn't still get along. After all, she had gone to the couple's wedding a few years ago. It had been beautiful, and she was happy that Noreen had found someone who truly loved her. Something Leila couldn't do.

Leila had loved and lost once and knew she would never find that again. Even today, she was living with the knowledge that sometimes you only get one great love, and she had let hers slip through her fingers without the fight it deserved. It had been years, and she still regretted what she had done.

"Wow, this is a lot of stuff," Skylar said, the puppy still in her hands as she looked around the room, making Leila jump and bring her back to the present.

"I think I have everything we will need." She handed her the glasses, but since her arms were full, she put them back on her, blue eyes watching her closely. It was oddly familiar.

Skylar let it happen, as if this was a thing they did. Skylar didn't say anything about it as she asked, huskier than Leila remembered her voice being, "Keeley wants to know if the puppies have names."

"Just two. I wait for them to grow into their personalities before I name them," she admitted, but it was more like she wouldn't name them because she didn't want to get attached. She was already attached to two.

"Which ones?" Skylar asked as she went back into the mudroom.

Following her, Leila realized she enjoyed having

company. It was something that so rarely happened that people being there was odd. A nice odd today.

"Hilary." She picked up the one that was fighting with another puppy and barking as she did it. Then picked up one that was sleeping in the corner all by itself. "And this one is Nancy."

"First Ladies?" Keeley asked, catching the meanings first.

"Nope, Nancy just came to me one day, but Hilary was a friend of mine from college. This guy acts just like she did back then." Setting them both back down, Hilary headed to the pile of puppies, and Nancy just turned in a circle before laying down to continue her nap.

Keeley picked Hilary up before she made it to the pile. "Will your friend be upset you named a dog after her?"

"She will never know. I haven't spoken to her since I left college," she admitted, and Hilary wouldn't want to see her again. They hadn't exactly parted on good terms.

"Oh, an ex?" Skylar asked, all excited for some gossip.

"Not every woman is my ex, Skylar." She stopped talking, realizing she had called her by her first name in front of her sister.

With her attention on the puppy, Keeley didn't seem to even notice. "That's what Mom always thought about Sky's friends, that they were dating or something."

"I hope you don't know what the 'or something' is." Skylar bumped her sister's shoulder with her own.

"It's sex, Sky. I know what sex is. Geez, I'm sixteen, not a baby."

Leila tried not to laugh at the sisters. "Now that we have established that, are you ready to head to the garden, Keeley?"

The girl set the puppy down and turned to Leila. "Yeah, I'm ready."

Turning to Skylar, she grabbed and slipped on her garden shoes. "Miss Nash, you can stay and play with the puppies as long as you want. Just make sure they're in the pen when you leave."

"I will, and you can call me Skylar when we're not in school," Skylar said her words back to her, only they sounded far more flirty than when Leila had said them, or at least she hoped they did.

"I will, Skylar." She used the name, liking it far too much.

As she ushered Keeley out of the room, she caught herself taking one last look at Skylar's ass as she leaned over the fence to pick up another eager puppy. Turning away from the site, she cursed herself for even looking. It wasn't even like her to act like that. But since seeing Skylar again at the funeral, she couldn't stop her eyes from noticing everything about her. How she was now an adult, and a nice-looking one.

Out the door, she let it close gently and turned to the girl. "Grab those pails, and we will head to the garden."

"What are we making today?" Keeley asked, as she did what she was told.

"Spaghetti sauce or salsa, your choice." It didn't matter to Leila; she had enough of both to last years.

"Can we make salsa? It was good." The girl followed close as they walked to the garden furthest from those.

"You tried it?" Leila asked in surprise. She hadn't thought that Skylar had gotten a jar. The Science teacher usually took most of it.

"I barely got any. Kayden ate almost all of it in one sitting. He's a pig."

"Boys are like that," Leila said, though she knew all teenagers were like that.

"I don't think they're all that bad. Some have to be

nice, or girls wouldn't date them," Keeley surmised, the pails swinging by her side as they walked. "Or boys, I guess. Boys can date other boys. Just like girls can."

"That's right, Keeley, they can." Smiling, she liked this kid.

In the garden, she showed the girl exactly what they were looking for in a good tomato. She saw Skylar walk out her front door and get into her car. Calling Russell to her, she waved at the woman leaving the yard in her little SUV. It was bright green, exactly what Karla would have picked out for her kids. But she wondered if it was the type of car Skylar would pick out for herself. If she had that flare for color her mom had.

But she decided it didn't matter. Skylar's preferences were none of her concern.

Chapter 9

"You've got to be kidding me. I'm not going out to Miss Hensley's house. Not today, not ever. I hate her. I don't need to see where she lives," Kayden whined as he stared at the TV, an action movie playing.

"Yes, you will, because I'm going to get your sister, and I'm not leaving you home alone." This morning had been different. He wasn't up and wouldn't be before she got back. Now he was awake and had been on the couch all day. He needed a change of scenery and one she controlled.

"I won't leave the couch, I promise." He grabbed it like the couch itself was going to leave him.

"You breaking promises is why you are coming with me. You're still grounded from that smoking incident." She just pointed at the door and waited. It didn't take long before he groaned and slowly got up, making his way to the door.

Today had been no picnic, just Kayden testing her, and she had failed some of those tests, but so had he. Which was why she wasn't leaving him home. When she had headed to the grocery store, aka a drive and a talk with Iris, she had come home to smoke billowing from the oven from a sleeping teenager and a forgotten pizza.

The only thing that didn't make her blow her top was that she had successfully apologized to Iris and had promised she was heading down there on Friday. It would involve bribing Sierra to come home for the weekend and paying any price her younger sister asked, but she needed to spend time with her girlfriend. Phone calls were not enough anymore.

Based on how her body had reacted to Miss Hensley's —no, Leila's legs—she needed to see Iris and get laid. Not that she was going to lead with that when she talked to Sierra, but she would bring it up if she had to. Though Sierra wasn't the person who could control their brother, she could handle babysitting for a day or two. Skylar would clean up any damage and be happy doing it.

"Come on, the sooner we get there, the sooner we get home." She checked her hair one last time in the hall mirror before heading out the door.

After this morning's embarrassment of an outfit, she had made a point of looking like a put-together adult this afternoon. No need for Leila to think of her as a kid anymore. Or so she argued with herself when she put on the jeans she had bought a few weeks before coming here and a blue striped shirt that Iris always liked her in.

"You know me and miss perfection don't get along. She refuses to give me anything above a C, and I'm doing A-quality work," he argued as he slipped into her passenger seat.

Skylar was skeptical. "Are you sure it's A-quality work? I haven't seen you put over ten minutes into all the home-work you have. Or are you focusing all your attention on English for some reason?"

"It doesn't matter how much time I put in, she will give me a C, maybe D," he grumbled as she backed out of the driveway.

"You mean when you turn in assignments? And turn them in on time?" she asked, because he wasn't turning them in to her for math.

"I've seen her throw my homework away," he argued, as if she would even believe him.

"Are you trying to convince me or you? I had her as a teacher as well."

He seemed to think better at keeping on that line of argument. "She's just the worst."

"She probably thinks the same about you." Skylar wondered what Leila really thought about her brother.

Leila. It had only been a few hours, and she was already wondering how she was going to call her Miss Hensley during school hours. She was now Leila in her eyes. Though she had always known her first name, being able to call her that was completely different.

Driving the miles back to the little farm, Skylar was glad for the silence. Iris had been happy to talk to her, but she was still a little miffed about being hung up on her during her argument with Kayden. Which had been an accident, because she had thought Iris had done the hanging up because Skylar wasn't talking to her anymore. Instead, she had just hung up on Iris, then didn't call her back.

But then again, Iris knew she was fighting with her brother, so maybe she could have called instead of getting upset and holding a grudge. Now three calls later, she was still bringing it up. Skylar just hoped the woman would forgive her completely once they could spend time together alone.

"This is so lame," Kayden mumbled as they pulled into

the yard, though she could see him looking around with interest.

The two were no longer in the garden, but Keeley was leaning against the railing, talking to someone on the other side of her. When they got close enough, Skylar realized it was a boy from school, a Cody or Cory Sather, and she wondered where he had come from.

Getting out of the car, Kayden acted like the young man was there to spend time with him and not already talking to his sister. Shaking her head, she let him go. There was no stopping him, anyway. A teenage boy's self-importance knew no bounds.

That was before Russell came running toward him with a deep, menacing bark, happy to see someone new. But that wasn't how her brother took the greeting. Kayden's reaction was to scream like a little girl and turn tail, running back to the car faster than Skylar had ever seen him go.

Instead of getting back into the car, he slid onto her hood and pulled his feet up before Russell made it down the last step from the porch. Now she was just loping toward the teenager in the car with her tongue hanging out.

"That's Russell. She's harmless," Skylar assured him as she squatted down to pet the little dog.

"She's not harmless!" he yelled from the hood, not moving. "I think she bites."

"She's too lazy to bite, Mr. Nash. But if you're worried, I'll put her in the house," Leila said as she opened the door to the house and stepped out. Now in just a T-shirt, the flannel was gone, and her hair had been pulled back from her face with a clip.

"I'm not scared," he argued, but didn't move from the top of the car.

Catching her eye, Skylar knew Leila was trying not to laugh at the brave teenager on the car as Skylar grabbed the dog's collar to take him to the house. "Come on, Russell, let's go inside."

Bitting back the need to tease her brother more about his sudden fear because she needed to stop doing that. She wasn't just his sister anymore. She had to act like an adult —one he was supposed to respect.

Russell went willingly and headed for the door so quickly, Skylar could barely keep a hold of her. Whether it was because of the puppies or because she liked it inside, she didn't know. When they got close, Leila stepped aside and held the door until they were through it.

Leila slipped inside after Skylar and let the door close behind her. Her eyes focused on how well the worn, stained T-shirt hugged Leila's curves. Suddenly they were alone in the room that had seemed big this morning but was suddenly small.

"Thank you, Skylar, for bringing her out. I didn't realize Kayden was scared of dogs." She looked out the window at the teen on the hood, still worried about a dog getting him.

"He isn't anymore," she insisted. Sure, when he was a toddler he feared dogs, but he had outgrown that years before. Or she had been sure he had.

"It seems like he is." Through the window, Leila looked out the door at the teenager getting off the hood of the car.

Keeping her attention on the dogs and not Leila's body or wanting to watch her brother scratch the green paint of her beloved little SUV, Skylar turned her attention to the other teenager there, "Has Cory been over all day?"

"It's Cody, and he came about an hour ago. I hope you don't mind. Seems he was driving by and saw us this morning and stopped when he could this afternoon. His family owns the land surrounding the farm. In fact, his great-grandparents lived in my house before I bought it."

"No, it's fine, just Keeley doesn't talk about boys, so …" She didn't know what to say. It wasn't like she talked to her sister about her love life. The girl was sixteen; she shouldn't have one.

"He has been smitten with her since last year," Leila said quietly, as if saying it too loudly would spook the budding romance.

"He told you that?" Skylar asked in surprise.

With a head shake, Leila corrected, "He didn't have to. I see what's going on in school. I think he finally got the courage to talk to her."

"Did my mom know?" Skylar grinned, loving that her sister had an admirer.

"I don't know. I didn't tell her. Sometimes these things just blow over without anything happening. Would you like something to drink?" She kicked off her sandals before going into the kitchen.

"Sure, whatever you have," she responded just as Keeley slipped into the house, being careful to keep Russell inside.

Keeley shifted nervously from one foot to the other for a moment before asking, "Miss Hensley, can we take the puppies outside for a little bit?"

"Not if your brother's afraid of dogs," Leila said as she pulled out a container of lemonade.

"He's not afraid of puppies," Keeley stated incredulously.

"How about just a few, and you three can play with them, but bring them in if your brother is uncomfortable?" Leila agreed quickly, as she came back to the mudroom to help Keeley get two puppies into her arms.

Smiling, Skylar realized that one of the two was puppy Hilary. Sky knew there was a story there, one she sort of wanted to get out of the older woman. Sort of a lot.

"And we're leaving soon, so enjoy the puppies while you can," Skylar added. No need to spend all evening here. After all, Leila had put up with Keeley all day.

Keeley's face fell instantly at her words. "But Sky, I thought we could try the sauce I made. We made salsa and spaghetti sauce."

Leila handed her a glass of cold lemonade, but directed her words to Keeley. "If your sister has something already planned, I'll just send a few jars home with you. You can eat it sometime during the week."

"Can we please stay?" the teenager whined.

Trying to signal to her sister to not push her luck with her eyes, she failed. So she had to say out loud, "You've been in Miss Hensley's hair all day, Keeley."

"I truly enjoyed our day. And I told her we could try the sauce tonight if you were okay with it," Leila confessed as she took a seat at the kitchen table.

"If you're sure you want us, but only if I can do most of the work so you can rest. You've been working all day." Everything that had been laid out this morning was gone. So they had used it all, cleaned it, and put it away. Exhausting.

The least she could do was pay Leila back with a meal, even if it was made in her own kitchen. That and she suddenly didn't want to leave so quickly. Leila's house had a relaxed, homey feeling that the house she had been raised in no longer had.

Chapter 10

Sitting down for the first time all day, Leila let herself relax. Yes, it had been fun teaching Keeley how to can, but it had been a long day of teaching instead of going at her own pace. Usually what she did today was a two-day process, with a rest between each step. But she didn't want the girl to have to come over another day, and what would they talk about during the resting periods? She didn't think Keeley was up for deep conversations with her English teacher.

Not that Keeley hadn't talked. She had actually talked a lot. It seemed she was happy to finally have a conversation with someone when her brother wasn't there to take over. So Leila had made sure that they didn't talk about him. Mostly, Keeley talked about school and classes and her dreams for the future. But sometimes, she asked questions about Leila. Personal questions. Like, where did she grow up, and what were her parents like? Both those questions she dodged, instead talking about Russell and the puppies and her plans for the puppies, which was selling them. But that had upset the girl a little, so she deviated to the other dogs she'd had and why she never had cats. Which had been a simple answer. She wasn't a cat person.

After telling Skylar where the pots were, she looked out the window to see the three teenagers sitting in the grass, playing with the two puppies. Even Kayden seemed relaxed with puppies. Though he was sitting furthest away and not holding one.

"So what's in this secret sauce?" Skylar asked as she filled the pot with water for the noodles.

"You'll have to help one day and find out. It's the only way to learn my secrets," she teased.

Asking them to stay had been an impulse, one that she should have ignored. Because now she was alone with Skylar in the house. Skylar, who was in threadbare jeans and a white T-shirt that showed off the tattoo on display today. It seemed this was her usual attire, and Leila could appreciate how well she pulled it off.

"I don't think I want to spend a day doing something that would cost a few bucks to buy." She turned off the water and walked the pot to the stove carefully.

"It's a lot better than what you buy." Leila, in fact, didn't know. It had been years since she had bought anything tomato-based beyond ketchup.

"And you do this every year? Spend days canning? Do you eat it all during the year?" Skylar looked at the jars sitting in a tidy row on the counter. Two dozen of them.

"Not always. But I make it through some of it. Some I give away." Blushing at the admission, she knew she had an addiction and no outlet for all the jars.

"Some? Yet you keep doing it." Skylar raised an eyebrow in question.

"I like it," she argued. "Did you want to see it?"

Skylar was reaching to turn the stove on but pulled

away and, in a teasing tone, asked, "It? You mean your stash of jarred food?"

"Yes, that." She headed toward the basement door without getting confirmation from Skylar that she wanted to see it. But she needn't have worried because the other woman followed quickly. "It's down here. When I bought the place, there was already a room built in the basement for the jars, which is what got me started."

She led her down the steps into the cement block basement. That wasn't just a little spooky. Looking around, she wondered what Skylar was thinking of the place. Her mom's house was almost a hundred years newer than this one, and she herself lived in a condo. Those were newer also. This was completely different than those.

Skylar didn't say a word about it, though. "Did you see this room and buy the place on the spot?"

"No, of course not," she argued and admitted a secret she hadn't told anyone. "I saw the attic bedroom and bought the place on the spot."

"Really?" Skylar asked in surprise.

"No, but it was the deciding factor. It took a little back and forth to actually secure the sale." She opened the door, flipping on the lights she had added herself to make the room less like a scary prison for unwanted guests.

Letting Skylar in first, she wondered what the younger woman actually thought. This was a little nuts. She had to stop. But it filled her time, and she enjoyed it. So what if it was bordering on obsession? That she secretly dreamed of the day when all the shelves would be filled and, even more secretly, wished she had someone to share it with.

Skylar was, in fact, the first person to see this room. Not even Karla had seen it. It was far too embarrassing to show just anyone. Which left her wondering what she was doing right now with the younger woman.

"Wow, Leila, this is … just wow." Skylar stepped into the room, her eyes darted to every corner. "How long did this take you?"

"I have been canning for six years, but that first year wasn't much. It took a little practice to get good at it." In fact, there was nothing in the room from that first year, and little from the second. Which made the stash even worse. What was the place going to look like in five years?

"What are these?" She pulled a jar from a shelf and held it up to the light.

Leaning against the doorjamb, she answered easily. "Cherries in a simple syrup."

Skylar put the jar away and pulled out another a few shelves down. And held it up to her, barely looking at it.

"Applesauce. I make it every year and usually go through a lot of it. By myself," she admitted. It was her favorite.

Setting the jar back, she pulled out another, but this time didn't ask anything about it. "Who taught you to do all this? Or did you learn it on your own?"

"My grandma taught me when I was a kid. Back then, canning was a chore, but now I just enjoy it." Which was true, but she had to invest in a few books on it after not even thinking about the process for a dozen years. She hadn't remembered much of what her grandma had taught her.

Skylar went back and pulled out the same jar of applesauce and held onto it as she moved around. "Do you ever sell the stuff?"

"No, nobody would want it," she assured her.

"I bet they would. I mean, not everyone, but I think you could make money from it."

"I don't need money."

"But you can't eat all this either. Maybe you want to

take in a few teenage boys. They'll have this room cleaned out in a day or two."

Laughing at the image, she shook her head. "Too many teenagers during my daytime. No need for any at night, too."

"I know what you mean." She looked around at jar after jar but still held the apple sauce two-handed, like it was the puppy from earlier, like it would get away from her. "You have given some to my mom. I recognize the handwriting on the labels. She used to give me jelly all the time. Every time I saw her. I have so much in my cupboard at home. Why do only some of them have labels?"

Leila watched her walk around the room, touching a jar here and there. "I only label them when I'm giving them away. The rest I know what they are based on where they are in the room."

"This one has a label: rhubarb sauce. Gross, I can't stand that stuff. My mom, on the other hand, loved it." Skylark pointed out the oval label.

"I know." She looked at her bare toes. "Those were for her, before …"

"Oh," she said and backed away from it, then started to look at other jars. "This is fascinating. Why don't you date?"

"Excuse me?" Her head snapped up at the question.

Skylar turned a jar of pears but didn't pick it up. "You're a catch. How are you still single?"

Caught off guard, she stammered, "That's, ah, that's a long story, one I prefer not getting into."

Skylar just nodded. "You're still in love with your ex?"

"Yes, you could say that." Not the one she was thinking about, because she was completely over Noreen. Had been for a long time.

"What's it like?" She pulled a small jar of raspberry

jelly off the shelf and paid no attention to Leila as she asked.

"What are you talking about?" Leila asked in confusion. This conversation wasn't making sense.

"Love. To be so in love with someone that everyone else pales in comparison. That you would rather be alone than be with someone who wasn't her?" Turning finally, she was holding two jars now and had a confused look on her face.

Leila didn't know what to tell her, so she went with the first thing that came to mind. "Like your world is complete."

Looking at the floor, Skylar was silent for a while before admitting, "That makes no sense."

Smiling, Leila told her, "It will when you meet the one. Isn't your current girlfriend the one?"

"Yeah, I think so." Skylar never looked up from the jars in her hands.

Leila wasn't ready to talk about Skylar's relationship with her girlfriend. It just reminded her that Skylar had a girlfriend. Even if she wasn't interested in Leila and never would be.

"When you feel it, you will know. And you will never forget it," Leila said wistfully at the memories of so long ago. Something she never liked to think about. "We had better get back upstairs."

Skylar looked around the room one more time and nodded, coming toward the door. Leila turned and left first, letting her follow. Knowing she would think about Skylar in her happy place for a long time to come. Probably long after the younger woman went back to her real life.

Chapter 11

Skylar felt the pain in Leila's words more than she heard them. She regretted bringing up the topic, but she couldn't believe the women in this town and surrounding area had overlooked this woman. That nobody had noticed how quirkily cute she was.

Looking around the room once more, she again wondered how many hours she had spent filling this room, all for just her enjoyment. Not just the work of canning, but getting the ingredients and supplies. How many hours was she in her garden to get enough product to fill all these jars?

Leila had turned to head up the stairs when Skylar touched her arm. Stopping her instantly, she turned and looked at her with those expressive brown eyes. Not moving her hand, she asked, "Can I try these?"

"If you want," Leila said quietly.

"I do. Thank you for sharing your secret stash with me." She leaned in and whispered, "I'll not tell a soul."

As close as she stood to her, she could feel Leila's breathing hitch when she whispered, making her look at the lips Leila was biting so delicately. Leaning closer, she felt herself tilting her head as if she was going to kiss her.

Snapping out of the trance, she took a step back, pretending that what had almost happened hadn't. Because she in no way had nearly kissed her former teacher in the basement of her house. Because she had a girlfriend and Leila was a friend, nothing more. And in actuality, barely a friend.

"I, um, the pasta needs to be added to the water," Leila stated in near-panic and rushed up the stairs.

Watching her go, Skylar hoped it was because she was concerned about the water and pasta and not worried about the fact that Skylar almost kissed her. Because she had to know that hadn't actually happened.

At a slower pace, she grabbed a jar of strawberry jelly to add to her other two jars before shutting the light off and closing the door to Leila's secret room. As she went up the stairs, she told herself to act normal, because they were friends. And friends didn't have awkward near-kisses.

"I grabbed a jelly too, strawberry. It's my favorite, and I thought I would try it." She forced herself to sound like they were having a normal conversation about food.

Leila only glanced at her as she dug in the freezer. "I got that one from a book, but go ahead and take whatever you want. I only have frozen meatballs. Do you think the kids will mind?"

"They'll be fine. Whatever you have." She was a little surprised the woman didn't have a stash of handmade meatballs in her freezer. "Do you still get to can with your grandma?"

Standing up, Leila didn't look her way. "No, she's passed. It was a long time ago, so don't feel sorry for me."

Setting her jars on the table, she didn't say the usual sorries about her passing. Maybe Leila was as tired of that as Skylar was, so instead, she asked, "What was her name?"

"Virginia, Gin."

"Hensley?" she asked, knowing Leila wasn't relaxing like she should.

Turning on the oven, she answered, "Yeah, she was my dad's mom."

"Are your parents still alive?" Skylar took the bag of meatballs from her and indicated that she should sit down. This, after all, was her meal to make.

Letting go of the bag, Leila admitted quietly, "My dad is. I don't know about my mom."

"You don't see her anymore?" That surprised her.

Sitting down, Leila said, "She didn't want a gay daughter, so no, I don't see her anymore. Not since I was twenty-one."

Skylar regretted asking right away. Her mom had been so accepting, and she hadn't met many gay people whose families had disowned them. It never even dawned on her. "Shit, I'm sorry, Leila. That sucks."

"Yeah, I'm used to it now." Leila shifted uncomfortably, then asked, "So, how are things going with Kayden? He seems to be keeping out of trouble."

There was no way Skylar was going to prod, so she went with the change of topics. "I don't know if being at the school is helping or if he's just saving it up for something big."

"Helping. Kayden has never shied away from making trouble," the woman said, and Skylar was happy she agreed.

"I don't know how my mom did it," Skylar admitted, letting her head fall forward, hating how her voice still quivered when she spoke about the woman. "And I can't ask her. All I want to do is talk to her. Once more."

"I know, Skylar. Me too." Leila's arms wrapped around her. "She always had the best advice."

"I need it right now," Skylar said, letting herself enjoy the warmth of Leila's arms wrapped around her. It made her feel content and, at the same time, it made her heart jump in her chest. She was going to lean her head onto the woman's shoulder when the door slammed open. The sound had them both jumping apart and looking guiltily at Keeley, who didn't even look their way as she grabbed a few more puppies.

Trying to get her heart under control, Skylar dared not look at Leila. What was it about being alone with this woman today that made her forget Iris so completely?

As Keeley left, she held up another two puppies to show them she was taking the puppies outside before heading out. Skylar just hoped the kids were keeping track of them. What would she do if they lost puppies?

Leila took another step backward as she said, "Why don't you go sit in the living room? I bet you don't get a moment to yourself anymore. I can handle doing this."

"You spent your entire day with Keeley. I can't ask you to make us a meal on top of that," she argued, but only half-heartedly. She wanted to go sit down. Or at least in another room to get her head back on straight.

"Good thing you are not asking. I'm insisting. There is a bookshelf you can look at. I think you'll find something good. Take whatever you think you would like. I know where to find you."

Taking Skylar's long silence as an argument, Leila walked over to the stove and gently pushed Skylar toward the living room. "Not another word. Go sit, relax while the kids are still interested in puppies. Take the time when it's offered."

Leila turned her back to Skylar, as if that would make

the discussion stop. And it seemed to work as Skylar walked into the homey living room with its light gray couches with what looked like homemade blankets in reds, draped over them. On one wall was a built-in bookshelf that held well over a hundred books. From paperbacks to hard covers, they filled the shelves from floor to ceiling.

Since Leila had told her to look, she did. But not only at the books, but the knickknacks on the mantel and the pictures on the walls of far hillier country than what surrounded Warrington. The only picture in a frame was of an older woman in bib overalls and flannel with her arm around a younger version of Leila.

Picking up the picture, she stared at the girl, who had turned into Leila Hensley. Her dark hair was long in the photo, and her cheeks had a definite sunburn to them. Leila's outfit screamed the peak of fashion twenty years ago. Grinning, she liked that the two were smiling so big as they each held up a giant tomato. This was obviously the much-loved grandma.

Setting the picture down in case Leila came looking for her and found her snooping, she turned to the bookshelf. There was a wide variety of books, from the classics to books on gardening and, of course, canning. But what interested her the most was the section of romance novels tucked away at the very bottom of the shelves. Some straight, but more were not, and Skylar recognized the authors as ones she had read before.

Pulling one from the shelf, she went to the couch and sat down, getting comfortable for a few minutes. She should be helping Leila, but she enjoyed having a moment to herself. And she was afraid if she actually went into the kitchen, something else would happen. Something beyond an embrace or a near-kiss.

Not that she was attracted to Leila. The only thing

between them was friendship and an old crush that had died years ago. Except today was the first time they had spent more than ten minutes alone together, and they had almost kissed. Not to mention the hug that was far too perfect to be called innocent.

Or was Skylar worrying about it too much? Leila probably didn't feel either of those things. Because not only was Skylar a lot younger than her, but she was also in a relationship. She wasn't supposed to almost kiss anyone. Right?

She knew she needed next weekend more than she had thought. She was throwing herself at anyone. Well, not anyone, just one anyone. But that was bad enough. She needed together time with Iris, and it was starting to affect her relationship with everyone.

Chapter 12

The last period bell rang had come none too soon for Leila. The seniors were restless as the excitement of the first weeks of school waned. Now it was just another year of school, and the temperatures were dropping to prove it.

Last weekend with Keeley had been the perfect temperature for working in the garden. Today it was twenty degrees colder, with no end of the chilly weather in sight. Summer was letting go, and fall was setting in, and it was going to be a long time before it came back. This weekend she was going to have to start getting her property ready for winter. There were so many projects she had put off, and now they would need to get done, or they would have to wait another year.

Keeley had stopped by Monday morning to say thank you again for the weekend, but Leila hadn't seen her since. Leila hoped she had found friends to spend her time with and wasn't hanging out in her sister's classroom instead of hers, but she hadn't dared check. In class, she still sat alone and didn't talk to anyone.

Leila had seen Skylar a few times across the hall but

hadn't gone out of her way to speak to her. The younger woman hadn't seemed interested in conversation with her either. Though she had thought they had gotten close during the weekend at her place. Maybe she was wrong. The family hadn't stayed long after the meal had finished, just long enough for the kids to do the dishes. By that time, Cody had already gone home, and the two remaining kids didn't see the need to linger.

Skylar had taken three jars and a book home with her, promising to return it when she was done, but so far she either hadn't finished or had forgotten to return it. Either was fine; she could replace it. It didn't matter. She didn't have a shortage of books.

But Leila couldn't stop herself from thinking that Skylar was just plain ignoring her again. This time because of what had almost happened in the basement—or the hug she shouldn't have given the young woman. Or both. Or none of it. She was probably overthinking everything that had happened.

Leila wouldn't blame her. The almost-kiss was probably all in Leila's imagination, anyway. And she hadn't meant anything by the hug except to comfort the woman. After all, Skylar was still upset about her mom's death. That didn't mean Leila forgot she was dating Iris. Iris of the power suits and phone stuck to her ear when Skylar needed her presence the most.

Not that it was any of Leila's business, it was Skylar's.

"Miss Hensley, I was wondering if I could come out again this weekend? Maybe make more salsa? Kayden has already eaten the two jars that I brought home," Keeley said, her backpack slung over her shoulder as she lingered in the doorway.

Leila knew she should say no, needed to say no, but Keeley seemed so hesitant, as if she knew she would be told no. So she knew she had to say yes and try to get her other chores done some other time.

"If your sister says it's alright and can give you a ride out, Miss Nash," she said, then instantly regretted it. Picking up the girl would be the perfect excuse to not spend too much time with Skylar. Except now, she couldn't take it back.

Keeley smiled. "She already said I could if you said it was alright. And I have to ask Sierra to bring me out."

"Not Skylar?" she asked, her heart sinking using the woman's name. All the sisters were Miss Nash to her, and there was no way to identify between the different ones.

Keeley didn't seem to notice her disappointment. "No, she's going to see her girlfriend this weekend. Leaving right after school."

"Oh." Leila didn't like that. She felt hurt, but she had no claim on Skylar. Iris did.

"So if I get a ride, I can come, right?" She double checked as Skylar came out of her classroom and locked it.

Leila was already dressed in her heavy jacket, the brown leather messenger bag slung over her shoulder. She didn't look like a student anymore to Leila. She was now an adult. An adult going to visit her girlfriend for the weekend.

Shaking thoughts of what was probably going to happen between the couple from her mind, she reminded the girl, "Yeah, dress warm. It's not going to be hot this weekend."

Skylar smiled, waved at her, and called to her sister, "Come on, Keeley. We have to get you and Kayden home so that I can head out."

"See you tomorrow," Keeley said before turning and walking away with her sister.

Hours later, Leila was home and had taken a few items

off her to-do list. And now was snuggled down with a blanket and wine, ready to start the book she had been waiting for fall to read. Her favorite thing to do was light a fire and read for the entire evening. So, with a glass of wine, she snuggled under a blanket and opened the steamy romance. Except it only took a few pages before she had to admit she couldn't finish it. All she could picture in her mind's eye was Skylar and Iris kissing and touching instead of the main characters.

She knew she shouldn't be having the feelings she was having—Skylar was her friend, nothing more. She should be nothing but happy for her to get to spend a romantic weekend with the woman she loves. Happy she'd found the love she deserved. Even if the younger woman was questioning those feelings herself.

At her feet, the puppies were tussling around as Russell watched them with half-closed eyes. Mostly she was trying to nap, but the puppies were keeping her awake. Tossing off the blanket, she slipped onto the floor herself and snuggled with the warm little bodies, hoping they were enough of a distraction.

They were getting older, and she should be thinking about selling them. Basset hounds were a desirable breed, and it wouldn't take long for them to find homes. But she knew that Russell loved her babies, and she hated to take them away from her. But there was no way she could keep ten dogs in her house. Not that she even wanted to. At the size they were, they were manageable, but in a few weeks, they would be uncontrollable.

Snuggling Hilary into the crook of her arm, Leila put off that task until they were bigger. For now, she was going to enjoy them. There was time for goodbyes later. Much later.

Sitting on the floor, she felt the loneliness of her home.

Even with the puppies and Russell, she was missing actual humans after the Nashes had been there the weekend before. For a short while, her house suddenly felt like a home with a family and noise. The silence tonight was almost too much for her.

Was it time to think about starting to date again? To dip her toe into that again? She wasn't sure there were a lot of options around town, but there were more than when she and Noreen had broken up. Or maybe she had just been paying more attention since then.

There were at least two women around town who had shown an interest in her in the last year. Both were close to her age. But was she interested in them? She hadn't been a few months ago. What had changed? Well, she knew what had changed, but she wouldn't admit that Skylar was making her feel desperate, old, and lonely.

Chapter 13

"Did you want to get together with your friends tonight?" Iris asked from the couch. Only an hour before, she had snuggled in with Skylar to watch TV. She was overly dressed for lounging with her girlfriend, but Skylar wasn't complaining that Iris wanted to look nice.

It hadn't been to watch Parks & Rec with Skylar either. She had instantly demanded she turn the TV down and find something else to watch because it was giving her a headache. Which wasn't true. Drinking most of the night away had given the woman a headache. Once the TV was at a near whisper, she had fallen asleep for the next three hours.

"No, I came down this weekend to spend time with you. They don't even know I'm here." Skylar came back from a fridge raid with cold pizza and a high-end beer, not the kind she usually drank, but the kind that was now in her fridge. An entire case of it.

"Shoot, I have another work thing tonight, and I know you'll be bored if you go."

The information was news to Skylar. Not once all week

had Iris hinted that they wouldn't spend their weekend together.

It was now Saturday afternoon, and they were just getting to spend time together, or time together, where Iris wasn't wasted or sleeping. Because instead of waiting at the apartment for Skylar to arrive the night before, she had gone out with her friends. Where they had gone and for how long, Skylar didn't know, but when Iris came home at close to four in the morning, she was wasted—so wasted she passed out, still dressed beside her in their bed.

That meant that instead of spending the evening with her girlfriend, Skylar had spent it alone, ordering pizza and reading the book she had borrowed from Leila. It was an author she had read before, but not this book. All week she hadn't found time to read it and almost didn't pack it. Now she was glad she had because she was almost done with it. Which meant she had nothing to do if Iris left her alone for another night.

"How long will you be out?" She set her beer down on the coffee table just a little too hard, causing Iris to flinch, but she didn't care. She was mad. Why had she even come if Iris wasn't going to make time for her?

"Only a few hours. I thought you would be happy to get to spend time with your friends. Don't you miss them? I thought you guys were close." Iris turned it around like the lawyer she was would.

"I guess I could call Steph and see what they're doing," she said about her college friend who still lived in town with her girlfriend.

Iris grinned and tapped Skylar's leg as if she were proud of her for having a friend. "See, you have something to do."

"But I wanted to spend time with you. That's why I came for the weekend." Leaning into the couch, she knew she was complaining, but Iris had to know she wasn't happy.

"We are together now," Iris pointed out.

"You're hungover."

Stiffening, Iris scowled at her. "So? How many weekends have I spent with you hungover? More than I can count. I do it once, and suddenly you're acting like a child about it. What else are you able to do that I'm not?"

"Nothing. I just thought you'd be here when I got back. It's been weeks. I thought you would miss me. That you would cancel your plans knowing I was coming home today," she grumbled, knowing that was what she would do.

Snuggling up to her, Iris threw her arms around her. "Of course I miss you, Skylar. I miss you every day. It's you who doesn't miss being here with me."

"I miss you, and I miss being here with you." Wrapping her arms around her girlfriend, she kissed her hair.

"But you don't make plans to come back. You even took a job there. I don't think you are ever coming back." There was a whine in her voice that grated on Skylar's nerves.

Pushing her annoyance and anger away, she had the woman she loved in her arms. She should be enjoying it. Instead, she was thinking about how much she wished she were back in Warrington. Not bickering with Iris.

Pulling her closer, Skylar said, "I'm coming back. I just don't know what to do with the kids. But I'm trying not to disrupt their lives any more than they already have been. I don't want to bring them to the city and watch their behavior issues get worse."

It wasn't the first time she had talked to Iris about her concerns, but it was the first time they had done it face-to-face. The other times had been over the phone, and those

calls had all been interrupted by Iris's work or more important things. Like dirty talk.

"What about your sister? She's an adult and can take
care of the other two."

"Sierra's in college," Skylar said, as always. It was like
Iris didn't care that Sierra's education was important.

"And you were here with me and a great job. But you
put that all on hold. She can do the same thing."

"Not the same," Skylar argued. Sierra needed to get
her education. Skylar already had hers. Jobs could be had
anywhere. Case in point, she was already employed, even
if not full-time.

"It is the same. You just don't push her. You need to
stand up to her and tell her that she needs to grow up and
take on some responsibility." Iris pushed herself from
Skylar's arms and stood up, adjusting her silk shirt and
checking for wrinkles.

Iris going out tonight was the reason she was all
dressed up right now. It had seemed odd when she had
spent so much time getting dressed, though Skylar had
hoped she had planned a date for them. Instead, she
wanted to go out again ... without Skylar.

"She's only nineteen. She isn't ready to take on two
teenagers, especially one who is rebelling." Skylar
couldn't understand why Iris thought Sierra was the
answer.

Iris rolled her eyes. "And you are? Because every time
you call, you complain about him. Well, guess what, Skylar,
I can't help you from across the state. I'm so tired of the
calls for help when I can do nothing."

"I don't need anyone's help, Iris. I need someone to
listen to me. Because I have nobody to talk to in my life.
Except you," she admitted. Since they had started dating,
she had let her friends go one by one in order to be there

for Iris until she didn't have real friends at all anymore. She hadn't even talked to Steph in months.

"Well, I have problems in my life too, but I don't bring you into them. I work on them myself." She snatched the empty beer bottle from the coffee table and headed to the kitchen.

"Fine, I won't bring it up again." Skylar got up from the couch and headed for the door. She was tired of being yelled at.

Iris turned from the counter in the open kitchen and demanded, "Where are you going?"

Pulling her jacket and grabbing her gym bag, she needed to get out of there to think. "Out with my friends, since you don't have time for me. I need to get away from here right now."

"Fine, go cool off. See you later tonight." Iris didn't even sound upset that she was leaving. But then again, she had asked her to.

"Maybe," she said as she slammed the door, debating if Steph or Jordan would have a couch she could crash on because she didn't want to come back here.

An hour later, she parked in front of the gym her friends now owned. When she had roomed with Steph Reynolds during her freshman year of college, she never would have guessed that years later, they would still be friends. Usually college roommates ended up hating each other after a time. Except nobody could hate Steph, and she had easily accepted Skylar into her large friend group.

Steph's best friend at the time, and still to this day, was Jordan Owens. Over the years, they had spent a lot of time together since all three of them were some sort of queer and they became close. Even if they had never shown a romantic interest in each other. That might be the true reason why they were close still. She had never had a romantic thought about either one of them.

Heading toward the gym the two had opened a few months before, Skylar was happy to see that the parking lot was semi full. It was, after all, Saturday afternoon. There had to be better things to do than work out. At least Skylar always found something else to do.

It took only five minutes to learn that Stephanie was out of town for the weekend and that Jordan was teaching back-to-back classes. But that the receptionist would give her a message if needed. Declining the offer, Skylar headed back out into the cold.

Without a thought as to what she was going to do now, she got back into her car and headed back toward her apartment. It had been hers first. Iris had moved in with her after her own lease was up, and they had been dating for a few months. If anyone should leave, it was Iris.

As she drove, she wondered if Keeley had gone out to Leila's again. Now she wished more than ever that she was in Warrington instead of here this weekend. She would much rather be teasing Leila about her addiction than here fighting with Iris in person.

When she had grabbed it, she had planned to eat the apple sauce a little at a time all week, but instead, she ate it all in two sittings. It was exactly what she had needed after Kayden had been caught cheating on an assignment in health, only to get a slap on the wrist instead of the punishment he deserved. Which meant she was forced to ground him at home and added, not letting him go see the puppies that weekend when someone was going to pick up Keeley.

She didn't know if Sierra would bring him with her anyway, which was probably fine. He had been hinting at the fact he wanted a puppy all week. Even her reminder that puppies grew into dogs hadn't dissuaded him. He didn't just want any puppy; he wanted one of Leila's puppies.

Once Russell stopped barking, he got over his fear of her quickly. But who wouldn't with the overly friendly dog? She had the perfect personality. By the time they left, he had acted all gushy as he said goodbye to the dog.

Which reminded Skylar she had wanted to do something special for Leila, for being so nice to Keeley and to Kayden, even if she didn't have to. She had thought about finding a store that specialized in canning, but when she saw a bookstore on the way back to her apartment, she knew what to get her.

Inside the cozy little bookstore, she headed straight for the romance section. In her perusal of Leila's home library, she had noticed a few books from Skylar's favorite authors were missing from her collection. So she picked out a few books for Leila and a few for herself, in case Iris had to leave for work and couldn't get out of it. Only once getting into the car did she realize she had spent over an hour in the store.

By the time she made it back into the apartment, it was empty. Which didn't bother her as much after their fight. They both needed cooling off, but she had hoped that the fight would spur her to cancel her plans. Just this once.

It was after eight when Jordan called and forced her to go out. Something she wasn't all that excited to actually do by then, but after telling Jordan about the fight and Iris's leaving her alone for the evening, Jordan had insisted.

The night turned long, and she ended up crashing on Jordan's couch instead of driving home. Which was a good thing, since she'd had too much to drink to get herself across town. She had been sober enough to text Iris where she was and not to worry—something the other woman hadn't done the night before.

By morning, she was sober as she made a quick stop at the condo to grab her things. That had turned into a long talk with Iris, who had been waiting for her. She apologized and promised to be around more the next time Skylar came home, no matter what was happening at work. Skylar had promised to try to come again the next weekend, hoping Sierra would be able to watch the younger two again so soon.

And by the time Skylar left, she felt their relationship was on more solid ground than it had since her mom had died. And that she had overreacted to Iris. Iris even admitted she was too focused on her job with Skylar out of town. But what else did she have to focus on?

They had even kissed goodbye with far more passion than any other time that entire weekend. But that wasn't saying much. Because it was only their second kiss of the weekend.

Chapter 14

Running late wasn't something that Leila was used to. She never ran late. After years of having to be at work at the same certain time, she never had issues. Until she didn't sleep well all weekend because Skylar was spending it with her girlfriend.

When Keeley hadn't shown up by eleven on Saturday, Leila had put her canning things away, opting to spend the day working on her winter projects. It hadn't bothered her that Keeley didn't show up; it had bothered her that nobody bothered to tell her she wasn't coming. Because if it was a matter of a ride, she would have gone to get her no matter what she had said.

On Sunday, she had gone to Conley to go shopping. There were just things you needed to buy that weren't available in town. What was usually a pleasant way to spend a day had turned into a boring, lonely trip that ended early when she decided it wasn't worth her time.

Now it was Monday morning, and she was half expecting Skylar to not even be there. That her weekend had been so great she had decided to extend it. If Leila had ever had a girlfriend who lived far away, she would have done it in a heartbeat.

Rushing down the hallway, she unbuttoned her jacket one-handed as she went. It had been a chilly morning, and she knew it wasn't getting warmer. She always hated this time of the year. It always reminded her of college when the days got shorter and the temperatures dropped as she waited for a call from her girlfriend, who had dropped out of school because of a family emergency. A call that never came.

Down the hall, two football players were tossing a ball around, something they knew better than to do. Before she could call out to stop them, the ball flew her way and slammed into her shoulder. Not hard, but with enough force to cause the hand holding her café latte to slam into her chest, spilling coffee all over her white button-down. It had been so hot she couldn't drink it until the day had actually started.

Her cotton bra and thin shirt was no match for the steaming hot liquid. The burning sensation made her drop the cup and her keys completely as she pulled the fabric from her body in surprise, but that didn't stop the pain at all. The damage was already done.

"Are you okay, Miss Hensley?" Tyson asked with worry and concern lacing his voice.

"I wasn't aiming for you. Tyson missed the ball. I would never throw a ball at you." Avery picked up the now empty cup from the ground. The remaining was coffee already soaking into the stained carpet.

"Out of the way, boys." Skylar easily pushed the boys, who were almost a foot taller than her, away, gently taking Leila's bag from her shoulder. "Are you okay, Leila? Is that coffee?"

"Yeah, I um, I … Hot coffee." She sucked in air through her teeth.

"You two go to the office and get Miss Perkins," Skylar said the name of the school nurse who no longer worked in the school. Not for a few years, but Skylar wouldn't know that.

"Lark," she corrected without thinking and didn't see if the kids actually went or not as Skylar led her into the math classroom.

"Keeley, shut the door." Skylar took control as the noise level in the hallway started to rise. Skylar turned her attention to Leila. "How bad is it, Leila?"

"I don't know, I …" She looked down at the obvious stain covering her shirt, but couldn't see what it looked like underneath and didn't really want to.

Skylar followed her eyes and saw the stain. Her first reaction was to pull the shirt from where Leila had it tucked in, her fingers grazing bare skin as she did it.

"Keeley, go to my car and get my gym bag. I know I have an extra shirt." Skylar never left her side as Keeley rushed from the room. Turning back to Leila, she said, "Let's get as many layers as we can off."

Gently, she helped her remove her jacket. An item which, if she hadn't unzipped on the way in, it would have deflected any liquid that came her way. Instead, she had stupidly opened it.

Skylar put the jacket on a desk, went to the front of the room, and pulled out a handful of tissues from the box. Bringing them back, she handed them to Leila. "Here, dry off a little. I know it won't make the pain go away, but it's something."

"Thanks." Taking them, she patted at the shirt front, but a few tissues weren't going to clean up the mess, mostly because the liquid was already soaked into the fabric of her shirt and had cooled to chilly already. "I figured you would be gone today."

Skylar was watching her cleaning the fabric, but looked up in confusion. "Why?"

Tapping gently at the stain, she blushed, unable to believe she had said that. Why had she said it? Now she had to explain what she had meant. "To spend more time with your girlfriend."

"No, I didn't even think of it. Maybe next time." Skylar took the tissues from her and started to unbutton the shirt as she dabbed at the newly exposed red skin.

Watching her, Leila couldn't even imagine stopping her, even if every touch of the tissue stung just a little bit. The pain was worth it to have Skylar so close, to be almost touching her skin. When she encountered the formerly white bra, Leila hissed at a particularly tender spot. "Did you at least have fun?"

"Yeah, it was okay." The light touch of Skylar's fingers as she unbuttoned the shirt to just under Leila's breasts before she stopped made her skin heat up even more.

Trying to distract herself, she grabbed at conversation topics. "Keeley didn't come out Saturday."

Skylar nodded as she kept dabbing, even if there was no liquid for the tissues to soak up. "Yeah, Sierra seemed to be too busy with her friends to be able to bring her out. I talked to her, and next time, she'll make the drive."

"Next time?" she asked, wondering if there would be a next time.

"If there's a next time," Skylar said as the door opened, and Mrs. Lark rushed into the room carrying a first aid kit, followed by the principal and two other teachers. Suddenly, the room was getting full of people, and Leila realized she had her shirt half unbuttoned. Not to mention that Skylar was touching her with only a thin layer of tissues between them.

Pushing the hand away, she pulled the shirt closed. The wet fabric was cold and felt nice for a moment before it wasn't as cold anymore. Feeling exposed, she hated everyone in the room. Skylar seemed to know what she was feeling and forced everyone but Mrs. Lark out of the room, even managed getting Gerard out.

Even in her shocked state, she noticed how his eyes barely let her breasts the entire time he had been in the room. Leila knew that it wasn't the burn or the coffee stain he was fixated on. His eyes couldn't look away from breasts no matter who they were on.

"I have an ointment that will take the sting away, but if you think you need to see a doctor, I would go now. Gerard will be trying to talk you out of it, but if you wait, insurance coverage might be an issue," Mrs. Lark whispered to her as she handed her the tube of ointment, not even asking if she should apply it.

"I don't know. It's not as bad as it was. It was only coffee," Leila insisted, sure the pain would pass quickly.

"Which can be scalding hot. We both know that. Let me look." Mrs. Lark frowned at her. So much for the woman not seeing her virtually topless.

Opening the top half of her shirt again, she let the woman look. Her looking at Leila's naked skin was clinical. Nothing like when Skylar had done the same thing. Even their touches were completely different. In fact, she barely noticed when Mrs. Lark touched the skin, whereas Skylar's touch had left tingles that she had been sure were a part of the burn.

"I would say only first-degree, but that doesn't mean it won't hurt for a few days. The ointment will help some. Did you want me to put it on?"

"No, I can do it. Thank you, though," she said to the woman whose face showed obvious relief she wouldn't have to apply a cream all over Leila's chest.

"Sure, Leila. I'll keep everyone out so you can do that. No need for an audience." The woman walked toward the door.

"Thank you," Leila called after her, holding the ointment in one hand while holding her shirt closed again with the other.

"Sure, we have the two boys in the office. They're very upset about what happened," the woman said before opening the door.

"It was an accident," she assured her.

"Glad to hear. The team really needs those two." The woman's husband was the football coach and had an interest in who would be sidelined for a game or two for burning a teacher.

Before Leila could say anything, she slipped out just as Keeley came in with a grey duffle bag. But the girl didn't stay, just dropped the bag just inside the door and shut it. But it was open long enough to hear Mrs. Lark and Gerard discussing her injury. Or more to the point, Gerard downplaying how bad it was based on his not seeing it.

Skylar went and grabbed the bag and pulled out a T-shirt that she smelled and set aside. "They smell clean, but I can't say whether they are or not. It's been a long time since I went to a gym."

"But you had the bag in your car?"

"I almost went this weekend but decided against it. It was the only reason the bag was in the car. You're in luck." She pulled out sweatpants and a sweatshirt.

"Just the sweatshirt," Leila said, knowing she couldn't teach in what she was wearing and didn't want to go home because she was afraid she wouldn't come back.

"The pants?" Skylar picked up a pair of gray joggers and held them in the air.

"No, I'm in no way wearing those in front of these kids. My pants will be dry soon enough." She wasn't looking forward to an entire day in wet pants and wet panties, one item Skylar hadn't offered her a replacement for. Which was probably for the best. No way would she wear her panties, but knowing what they looked like wasn't a good idea either.

Walking the shirt over, Skylar teased her. "You'll smell like coffee all day."

"Good thing I like coffee, but I might pass on it in the morning for a while." She took the shirt and pointed at the door. No way was she stripping down in front of Skylar Nash. Because she had already decided that she wasn't wearing the wet bra.

"I do too, but I don't bathe in it." Skylar smiled as she went to the door and slipped out.

Leila stood there for a moment, laughing. It was exactly what she needed.

Chapter 15

When Leila had decided to stay at work and tough it out, Skylar was pissed. She should have gone to a doctor instead. What was she trying to prove by sticking around?

Every time Skylar walked even close to the door, she checked to see if she could see Leila. If she was doing okay.

Every hour she had caught at least one glimpse of her, now in Skylar's own old gray college sweatshirt. Now, five hours later, Skylar hoped Leila's pants had dried out.

Now it was the last hour of the day, and she was debating going to Leila's house after school to make sure she took care of herself because it seemed she didn't know how. Because if she knew how to, she would be home right now. Of course, that would have been after she went to see a doctor this morning.

This hour her class was taking a test, the first of the year. And the twenty-two heads were all focused on that. Not her trying to sneak another look across the hallway. So far, this hour, she hadn't seen Leila at all.

"Sky," a voice stage-whispered from the door, a voice she knew instantly as Kayden.

"Aren't you supposed to be in class?" Scowling, she went to the doorway. Most of the class was now looking her way instead of at their tests, so she pushed him into the hallway.

"I need to talk to you." He shifted nervously from one foot to the other.

Leaving the classroom, she glanced into Leila's room, but still didn't see her. Which was normal, since she couldn't see a lot of the room from her position. She folded her arms as she turned to her brother, who was supposed to be in that classroom.

"What is it, Kayden?"

"I heard a rumor about Miss Hensley," he said, looking up and down the hallway.

"What? Aren't you supposed to be in her class?" She nearly went over to look in the classroom again, but decided to wait until after this conversation.

"That she took something, like a drug." He rubbed the back of his neck nervously, looking back into the classroom he had just left.

Rolling her eyes at his dramatics, she told him, "It was probably something for the pain from her burn. I wish she'd gone home and rested this morning."

"No, not like something normal, something more on the illegal side," he said the last, but as quietly as possible.

"Miss Hensley would never do that." She almost laughed at the mere suggestion. Leila was the most straight-laced teacher at this school. No way would she break a rule, much less a law.

"She maybe didn't know what she was taking," he said critically as he looked down the hallway again.

Her blood ran cold. "What was it?"

Kayden leaned closer to her. "Okay, the rumor is that what she took isn't bad, but it will make her feel good. Really good. But it's not mine, and it's not my fault she took it. She wasn't supposed to take it. She never takes pills at school. Everyone knows that."

"What the hell have you done?" Now she was truly worried about the woman and mad at her little brother.

Stepping back, Kayden put up his hands. "I said it wasn't me. Some other guys had been storing something in her desk. And I guess with the coffee thing this morning, she took it. I told them not to leave it in her desk for too long, but she never takes pills."

"What was it?" she demanded.

"Nothing that won't wear off in a few hours." He wasn't saying, and she knew he wasn't going to tell her. Not without a little coaxing.

Grabbing him by the ear and squeezing, she said, "Tell me now, or I'm walking you down to the principal's office. I don't give a rat's ass what he does with you, but at home, you will not see the outdoors until summer. And that Xbox? You can kiss it goodbye forever."

"I think, no, I don't know for sure," he said, trying to slap her hand away from his head.

Letting him go, she was pissed at him. She was in the middle of a test, and now there was a crisis across the hall-way. "I have to get her out of here before someone realizes what is going on, and her job is affected. When did she take it?"

Shrugging, he straightened the jacket he insisted on always wearing. "Last hour, I heard, but it's kicking in."

"Shit."

"Yeah, she'll be pissed if she does something stupid," Kayden agreed, as if he wasn't partially to blame for this happening. He knew there were drugs hidden in her desk and never told Skylar.

"Miss Nash, is there an issue here?" Mr. Gerard walked up to them, and though he sounded concerned, his face showed more excitement than anything.

Pushing her brother back toward Leila's classroom, she told the man, "Yes, Miss Hensley is in a lot of pain from the coffee this morning. I'm going to take her home."

"You have a class, Miss Nash," he reminded her, as if she needed reminding.

"Which is why it was nice that you came by. You will need to watch both of our classes for the rest of the day."

Looking into her classroom, his smile faltered. "I don't think so, Skylar. You are required to stay here until the end of the day."

"It's either you watch the classes now, or we wait for the end of the day, and I take her directly to the emergency room. Then we'll have to report the incident to the school board and explain why she was still in school hours after the incident." She knew there was no way she would ever take her to the ER now because the school board would be far more concerned with why she was on drugs while working than any burns she had sustained. But she wasn't telling Gerard that. The less he knew, the better.

"Oh, well, if you have to go, go." He waved her off.

Walking back into the classroom, there was a lot of scuffling as kids returned to their chairs, and she knew the tests were garbage now. But she didn't care. Her only concern was getting Leila out of the building quickly. "I'm leaving for the day, and Mr. Gerard will finish administering the test. If you have any questions, just ask him."

All eyes swung to him, who had followed her into the classroom. "I didn't realize you were giving a test. You should probably stay to finish that."

Grabbing her car keys and jacket, she assured him, "Don't worry, Mr. Gerard, this was actually a practice test. The actual test will be tomorrow."

The last bit caused moans and grumbles from the students, who had thought that they were going to get away with cheating on the test. But it was going to be worse for her since she would have to create an all new test within a day and take care of Leila. A Leila she had no idea what was going to be like.

Kayden was still pacing in the hallway when she came out. Walking up to him, she told him, "After school, you and Keeley walk home."

"But it's like a mile," he argued.

"Walk. Don't let me hear you got a ride. She can, but not you. I want you to think about what happened here and what your role in it was."

"Fine," he grumbled.

"When Miss Hensley is back to normal, I'll come back to town. But that means you guys will be on your own tonight. If you do anything beyond your homework and TV, I'll ground you until you don't remember what the outside world looks like." She walked into the classroom her friend was in.

Leila was sitting at her desk, her attention on a pencil, paying no attention to the students looking at her. Insead, she was focused on spinning it in her hand with a look of fascination on her face.

From the back of the classroom, she told the kids to get their stuff and go over to the math room. Nobody questioned the request, just grabbed their stuff and walked over. They all seemed to know something was wrong with their teacher and were relieved when another teacher showed up to take over.

Getting Leila out of the building was easy because she

seemed up for anything she suggested. Anything. Overly accommodating didn't even come close to explaining her attitude. She didn't even question leaving before the last bell. But maybe that was because she didn't realize it was still during the school day.

Twenty minutes later, she unlocked the door to Leila's farm house and held the door open for her, forgetting until too late about Russell and the puppies. Good thing Russell didn't even care who was coming into the house. All she cared about was getting a few scratches in before she went outside to do her business. Her little brood of nine whined from inside a kiddie pool that seemed to contain them, but Skylar could tell it wouldn't be long before they were getting out.

"Puppies. Don't you love my puppies?" Squatting down to pet them, Leila let them lick her, so happy they were there.

"I do," Skylar agreed.

"I want to keep them all. How can I give them away when I love them so much?" She picked up three at once and kissed each of their noses.

Skylar took them away from her one at a time, setting them back in the kiddy pool before getting her to her feet and directing her to the kitchen. "How about we leave them for a minute and change clothes?"

Leila frowned and looked down at the shirt she was wearing. "Oh, yeah, I'm in your sweatshirt, Skylar. Skylar. I love that name. It's so pretty. Skylar, Skylar, Skylar. You are pretty, Skylar."

"Thank you, Leila. You are pretty, too," she admitted, hoping the woman didn't remember any of this later.

Leila smiled and then covered it shyly as she said, "Not like you."

"How about we take a nap?" Skylar suggested.

"Okay, but I'm not really tired," the ever-accommodating Leila replied.

Ushering the woman toward the stairs, she said, "Let's try, anyway."

It was the first time Skylar had been upstairs in Leila's house, and like the downstairs, it was comfortable and homey. There were four bedrooms, but only one had furniture in it. That one had to be Leila's room.

Before she could stop the woman, she had slipped out of her pants. Leaving them on the floor, she pulled the sweatshirt down to cover her perfect butt, but not before Skylar got an eyeful of the barely there red thong and more of the golden legs she couldn't get enough of. At least Leila didn't notice her staring as she crawled into bed under the covers. "I thought *we* were napping. I don't want to nap alone. Can you nap with me?"

"No, I think you should sleep alone. I have things to do," Skylar lied. She was just going to read or spend the next few hours trying to figure out why her former teacher had on sexier panties than she did.

"Please, just until I fall asleep?" With innocent eyes, she tapped the bed.

"Okay." Reluctantly, Skylar slipped off the jacket she was still wearing and laid down on top of the comforter.

Leila lay quiet for a moment before turning toward her and whispering loudly, "I can't sleep. Can we just talk?"

"Sure, what about?"

"Tell me about your weekend. Did you go out to eat? Dancing? A party?" She sounded so excited by the idea of going out on a date. Was it the drugs or the real Leila missing that part of life?

Turning toward her, she answered honestly, "No, it wasn't the best weekend."

"Oh, I thought it was going to be amazing. Did you at

least get to have sex? I'm sure you did. It's been years since I've had good sex. I mean, fantastic sex," Leila moaned as she said it, then licked her smiling lips, which caused Skylar's heart to race a little.

There was no way Skylar was going to answer that, even if Leila wouldn't remember it. Not just because it was personal, but because then she would have to admit it had been a while since she'd had really good sex as well. Sure, sex with Iris was good, but never fantastic.

"Can I ask you a question?" Skylar knew she shouldn't take advantage of her state, but she wanted to know so badly.

"Anything." The woman's brown eyes were wide in anticipation.

"You and Noreen, how'd you know you were in love with her?" she asked tentatively.

Leila was quick to answer. "I didn't."

"You never knew you were in love with her?" Skylar asked in confusion.

Shaking her head, she clarified, "I was never in love with her. I wanted to be, but it never happened. I settled. We settled. Then it wasn't enough anymore."

"Then who's the woman who made your world complete?" she asked in confusion.

"Lauren Almquist. I loved her with everything I had. For a time, our lives were perfect." There was a dreaminess to her eyes as she spoke, something that hadn't been there when she talked about Noreen.

"What happened between you? How did it end?" She took the woman's hand.

"I thought I could do better than her." Leila looked at their joined hands as she spoke.

"You broke up with her," Skylar surmised.

"Worse. I cheated on her." Leila blinked a few times

and yawned, but still stared at their hands. "I was so stupid back then."

"We all make mistakes in our lives," Skylar said, wondering when she had known this woman. Because she met Noreen in college.

"I wish I could just apologize," Leila said as her eyes closed.

Watching the woman sleep, Skylar stayed in bed with her. She just couldn't see her cheating on anyone or anything, and maybe it was the drugs that were talking and not the real Leila. Except she sounded so sincere about it. With so much regret.

Chapter 16

The pounding in Leila's head was worse than the pain in her chest from being burned. Sitting up, she was surprised she was in her bed and even more surprised it was night. The last thing she remembered was lecturing on The Scarlet Letter. Then nothing. But somehow, she had gotten home and into bed. Though she was still wearing Skylar's sweatshirt, she wasn't wearing her pants anymore.

Crawling out of bed, she headed straight to the bathroom, holding her throbbing head the entire time. She was still exhausted, but there were a few things she needed to do before she actually went back to sleep. Her only hope was that the headache would be gone by the time she woke up the next time.

Once her bladder was empty, and her teeth were brushed, her head had started to feel better. But her stomach had started to remind her she had skipped lunch and, based on the darkness outside, supper. So, with just the sweatshirt on, she headed down for something to eat. After that, she would call the school and leave a message about taking a day or two off. Until she figured out what had happened today, she wasn't going anywhere close to that building. She had never lost time before, and it was freaking her out just a little bit.

At the bottom of the stairs, she realized a light was on in the living room. She turned that way, only to jump out of her skin when someone asked, "How are you feeling?"

"Holy fuck, Skylar, you scared me to death." Her hand landed on her racing heart. "What are you doing here?"

"Making sure you're okay." Closing the book in her hands, she set it on the end table.

"I have a headache, but other than that, I'm okay." Reaching up, Leila touched the subsiding aching.

"The burn?" Skylar asked.

"Not as bad as the headache." The skin pulled on her chest, but the pain she felt that afternoon had subsided considerably. "Did you bring me home?"

"Yeah,"

"Why?"

Skylar was silent for a bit too long before saying, "I'll explain in a bit. Are you hungry?"

"Famished. But don't worry about me. You can go home." It was late, and Leila knew she was going back to sleep soon. She could easily make something herself, but knew she wouldn't if left up to her.

"Not a chance. I'll just go make you something. You sit down and rest your head." Skylar got up. Instead of the jeans and blazer she had been wearing earlier in the day, she was in gray sweatpants and a red T-shirt that had what was obviously the mascot from the school she used to teach at, a different pair than she had pulled from her gym bag earlier in the day. "I hope you don't mind I started a fire?"

"No, that's fine." Looking at the flames for a moment, she wished she had spent the evening with Skylar here in front of the fire instead of sleeping. "Was there enough wood?"

"I had Kayden bring in enough wood to fill your firebox. Then I made him clean up the mess he made in the house." Skylar headed for the kitchen. "Is soup okay?"

"Yeah," she said absently. Anything would do. Then added, "He didn't have to do any of it, actually."

In the room, Leila knew she had been planning the meal since there was a can of soup on the counter. Skylar went right to it, opened it, and started heating it up in the pot that was waiting. The scene in front of her was just so homey and domestic. How long had it been since someone else had made her a meal?

When the soup was heating, Skylar finally turned back to her. "Yeah, he did. After you fell asleep, I went back and got the kids. Keeley played with the puppies and Russell while Kayden raked the leaves in part of your yard. The sun set before he could do the entire thing, but he will be coming out again this week to finish."

"Skylar, he didn't have to." Sitting down, she remembered when the cold chair hit her legs that she wasn't wearing any pants. Pulling the sweatshirt down her legs, she tried to cover the fact, but was sure Skylar had noticed.

"He wanted to. Actually, he suggested it. Then he played with the puppies for a while so they would sleep better before I took them home."

"Why would he want to rake leaves?" she asked in confusion.

Kayden hadn't struck her as an overly helpful kid. Not anymore. The Kayden of five years ago would have raked her leaves without a thought, but that kid was long gone. There was no way he would suddenly change back.

"He feels guilty." Skylar turned around to shut off the stove, busying herself by filling the bowl. "He heard a rumor about you taking something that wasn't what you thought it was."

"I took aspirin," Leila argued, the ones that'd been in her desk for years. She almost never got headaches, and not usually at work.

"What kind?" Skylar brought over the bowl and a small plate of crackers.

It was exactly what her mom would have done. Karla was a nurturer through and through. Most of the time, Skylar didn't remind Leila of her, but right now, there were so many similarities. She held her tongue, not needing to remind Skylar of her loss today.

Instead, she just answered the question. "Over the counter. I've had them in my desk forever and hoped they would work. It seems they did. Too well."

Skylar sat down and rested her hands on the table. "No, you took something else. Kayden wouldn't say exactly what, but it was illegal. Someone was storing the drugs in your medication bottle. I talked to him tonight, and he admitted the owner felt it was safer than lockers since the cops sometimes searched lockers. And everyone knew that you never took the pills in your desk."

"What? How does everyone know that?" She had stopped eating after one bite, unable to stomach food after what she heard.

Yes, she knew there were probably illegal drugs in the school, but she had never guessed they were in her desk. How long had they been there? Who put them there? What was it?

Skylar ran a hand through her hair. "In his defense, he came to me when he heard what was going on. I was able to get you out of the school without anyone catching on. I have been with you the entire time. Mostly, you slept."

"Mostly, only?" Leila tried to remember what had happened. Had anything happened?

Skylar grinned and patted her hand. "You were chatty until you passed out. It was like you were drunk. A happy drunk."

Relief washed through her. She could have done anything. Back when she drank to excess, she had been a happy and horny drunk. A clumsy lover, but horny as all get-out. At least maybe she had outgrown that. Or at least Skylar maybe hadn't noticed it.

Changing the topic from herself, she asked, "Whose drugs were they if not Kayden's?"

Cringing, she realized that she made it sound like Kayden had drugs. Or that he would definitely know who it was.

Skylar tapped the table with her fingers a few times before admitting, "I'm not saying it wasn't Kayden. I'm just saying *he* said it wasn't him."

"Gerard doesn't know?" Grabbing a cracker, Leila leaned back in her chair and nibbled it, the soup no longer appealing to her.

Skylar shook her head. "I didn't tell him. I figured you would be put under a microscope for no reason. It wasn't your fault, but you had drugs in your system. I also didn't take you to the ER for that reason, though he thinks that's where I took you."

"Wise decision." Munching, Leila hated she didn't trust the principal at all. In the weeks since school started, she had noticed that he took the students' word as gold and assumed the teachers were lying about everything. Over a dozen teachers had been talked to about their "attitudes" already.

"As for Kayden, I have already grounded him until the end of time. But I also told him that he owes you, and if you need him to do anything, he will be doing it. Raking leaves, cleaning those gardens, moving dirt piles and bricks for no reason, build an addition, whatever you need."

Grinning at the list, she said, "I don't think he has the skill level to build an addition."

"Just make sure the list is long and tedious."

"Can I think on it?" Leila asked as she finally started eating the soup.

"Of course, I wouldn't want to rush you."

"Thank you. And thank you for bringing me home. It seems you spent the entire day saving me."

"All in a day's work for a math teacher." Skylar rubbed her knuckles on her t-shirt as if polishing them.

"I didn't do or say anything embarrassing, did I? Before I passed out, that is." Leila pushed the empty bowl away from her, needing to reassure herself she didn't.

"Nothing to be concerned about," Skylar assured her, but there was a blush across her cheeks that had Leila worried. But before she could ask anything more, the woman got up and went to the living room but returned quickly, saying, "When I was in Minneapolis, I got you a gift for being so nice to Keeley. I worry about her sometimes."

Watching her sit back down, Leila insisted, "You don't have to get me a gift. I truly enjoy spending time with her."

Setting a plastic bag with an obvious bookstore logo on it, Skylar pushed it toward her. "I know, but I was in a bookstore and found a few books to add to your collection."

Opening it, Leila looked inside and smiled, pulling the books out one at a time, looking at the front and back of each one. Holding up one in particular, she said, "I don't have any from this author."

Skylar took each book as Leila set them down and put

them in a neat stack. "I know. I remember not seeing her name, but I thought you would enjoy her work."

"I'll love them, I'm sure. Thank you, Skylar," Leila said and then stifled a yawn.

"Are you still tired?" Skylar grabbed the bowl and took it to the dishwasher.

"Yeah," Leila admitted, though she wanted to keep talking to Skylar. To have her to herself, even just for a few minutes. Even if she wasn't hers to have.

"Go to bed. I'll let Russell out in a while and head out myself. Don't worry about work tomorrow. I already talked to Jan in the office. She was a little upset you were under the weather. It seems you never call in sick." Skylar grabbed the bag from the table and tossed it in the garbage.

"I don't. But I'm sure I'll be fine by morning." Leila got up. She wasn't going to argue with Skylar; she was exhausted.

Skylar shook her head. "Tomorrow you won't get a choice. You're off already and can do anything you want. I don't care, but do not go into the school."

"I'll restrain myself," Leila said, but she had no idea what she was going to do with a day off. Which was why she never used them.

Behind her, Skylar called, "I would expect nothing less."

Not responding to her obvious joke, Leila headed back up the stairs as she heard Skylar walking around the kitchen. She hated to admit how much she liked her being there. Liked Skylar in her life.

She pushed that thought away because Skylar wasn't in her life, not like that. And she never would be. They were just friends and would never be more than that—no matter how much she wished it would be.

Chapter 17

Pacing Leila's front porch, Skylar listened to the phone go to Iris's familiar voice mail, happily telling her to leave a message. Again. It was late in the afternoon, and she had been trying the woman since morning. Why wasn't she answering?

After all, she had told her they would talk today, even if Skylar hadn't been able to go back to Minneapolis for the weekend again. That difficult call explaining that it would be impossible had taken place on Thursday evening. It was now three days later, and they hadn't talked since.

Iris was upset, and that was understandable. But there was no way Skylar would leave the kids home alone after what had happened on Monday. With so much going on with Leila and her burn and the side effects of the drugs, Skylar had forgotten to call Sierra most of the week. By Wednesday, she had decided that she wouldn't even call her sister about it. Kayden would have to spend most of the weekend at Leila's, and Sierra wouldn't want to spend her time at the farm. Which Iris wouldn't understand. So she had lied to Iris and said that Sierra was busy and she couldn't make it home.

So now she was trying to settle the ruffled feathers her decision had made, even as she kept an eye on two teenagers who would rather be anywhere but there this weekend. Even Keeley hadn't wanted to come out and help Leila. Mostly because it was just house cleaning, something that Skylar was sure Leila hadn't gotten to because of her burns. Though she didn't complain during the week at school, Skylar had noticed.

Today, she hadn't complained at all either, and Kayden hadn't needed to help her. She was okay doing everything herself. She always had in the past, not that her arguments swayed Skylar. This was different.

They had been at the farm for hours now, and Kayden had cleaned dead plants from the garden while Keeley washed dishes and learned to make a soup that they ate for lunch. Once that was over, Kayden had to do the dishes and clean the kitchen while Keeley and Leila got to read. Skylar made sure her brother actually did what he was supposed to.

She was still keeping an eye on the two as the kids raked leaves while tried to call her girlfriend. Even though she knew that the puppies they had begged to bring outside were being watched, she still worried that one would get away from the teens and run into the woods. It had already happened once.

So far, she hadn't found out who had drugged Leila, and Kayden kept insisting it wasn't him. She wanted to believe that, but as a teacher, she wasn't so easily persuaded. Her brother had done a lot of nasty things in the past, and this could have been another one of those things.

Not that she could do much about it since she had

failed to mention it to Gerard, and so had Leila when she had finally gotten back to work. She just went back to being her normal self.

They hadn't talked much after she got back, either. Leila had thanked her for forcing her to take the day off. She had needed it. And though Skylar had driven Kayden out each evening for an hour behind the rake, they hadn't had a moment alone. Leila insisted on helping the kids and not just supervising, so the yard was pretty clean, but every day another million leaves fell, making the group start again.

"They can go home," Leila said while walking out onto the porch, her hands wrapped around a large cup of coffee.

Skylar stopped herself from grabbing the cup away from her, scared she would spill and burn herself again. Skylar knew that the woman had on two layers since she could see a black T-shirt under the flannel she had worn the first time Skylar had brought Keeley out. Only today, it was paired with black corduroy pants.

"No, there's still an hour of daylight. If I have to change my plans, he's damn sure going to complete every second of his punishment," Skylar insisted.

"You could have put this off another week. The leaves haven't all fallen yet." Leila looked up at the trees that still had a lot of leaves, despite how many had already been cleaned up. "You have to learn to trust them a little bit."

Letting out a pent-up breath, Skylar admitted, "Not after Monday. I don't think I'll ever trust him again."

"He's growing up. He wouldn't have told you about the drugs last month," Leila assured her, sitting down on the rocker. Then she indicated Skylar to sit down also in the other rocker.

Giving in, Skylar sat down heavily and gently rocked with one foot. "I don't see it."

"I do." She leaned back and set the coffee on the wide arm. "Your mom would have been proud of how well you are taking care of the kids. Though she would be worried you're sacrificing your own life for theirs. Have you gotten a hold of Iris? That's who you're calling, isn't it?"

"Yes, but no, she doesn't answer," she replied and blew a lock of hair from in front of her eye. "I told her on Thursday and haven't heard anything from her since then. I'm worried that this might be the last straw. I haven't been present for her since Mom died and, in reality, I don't see it happening again for a long time."

Leila quirked an eyebrow in question. "You don't want to go back?"

"Of course I do, but Keeley and Kayden need the stability being here brings. Without that, I don't know how they will react." Hearing the puppies' tiny barks, she let herself believe that they weren't running off on the kids because Leila didn't react. But the last thing she needed was a lost puppy on top of everything else.

Taking a sip of coffee, Leila let the silence hold for a moment before saying, "Maybe the same, maybe better. It might be what you see as stability to them is a constant reminder of Karla. They can't get away from the memories. She's at home and at school. Everywhere they go is her ghost."

Skylar's anger rose at her words. "You're saying that I'm wrecking their lives by keeping them here? That I should have just left and took them with me?"

"No, I'm saying you're doing your best, and *that* is what's best for them. I just wonder if you are staying here because *you* need to be here, not them. Your gut response is to curl up with the ghost of the past, and that's what makes you feel better. But maybe the rest of your siblings don't feel like that."

Getting up from the chair, she started to pace. "Which is wrong. I'm where I need to be, Leila. We need to all be here right now."

"What about Iris during this? Is it possible you're screwing up your relationship with your girlfriend by not taking her needs into account? You need to focus more of your attention on her."

"That's none of your business. Stay out of my relationship with my girlfriend; focus your attention on yours. Oh, except you don't have one." Skylar instantly regretted the words. Leila had been nothing but open and friendly to her. And she just threw her single status in her face.

"You're right, I don't." Leila she got up. Her demeanor had changed quickly.

"You're so quick to solve everyone's problems except your own. Here's a little insight on your love life, Leila. Get over your ex and move on," she sneered, wanting Leila to see what a low blow her questioning her relationship was.

"I'm over Noreen." Her voice was quiet.

"I was talking about Lauren." Skylar said the name with a smirk because her friend probably didn't even know she knew the name.

Her face paled instantly. "How did you hear about her?"

"It doesn't matter." She dismissed the question.

"You can show yourself out. Kayden has paid off whatever debt you think he owes me. Have a nice weekend." Tossing her remaining coffee from the cup over the railing into the yard, Leila turned, walking back into the house and letting the door slam behind her.

Standing on the porch alone, Skylar knew she had stepped over a line, a line she hadn't even seen but should have known was there. She had taken advantage of Leila in her weak state to obtain the information and had thrown it back in her face.

Before she could go after her and apologize, her phone rang in her hand. One glance said it was Iris. Answering it as she went to gather up the kids, she knew Leila was right. She needed to apologize for not being there for Iris and anything else Iris felt. Because she had let their relationship slide. She just hoped it hadn't slid into nonexistence.

Chapter 18

Leila's week had been long, but at least she had made it to work every day. Even the days she hadn't wanted to see people—which had been all of them.

After the Nashes had left on Saturday, she had let herself mope around the house, drowning in her memories. It was what Lauren's memory always did to her. Even to the point of bringing out photo albums, the ones she usually left buried in boxes in the back of her closet.

Then she had lost hours looking over her past self in happier times. Back when heartbreak wasn't on her radar, and she was still dreaming of being a journalist for a big newspaper. She had spent her days learning about how to chase a story and her nights with the love of her life. Some evenings were parties and events they attended together, and others were spent alone. But at the end of every day, they were together.

In picture after picture, she could see the two of them growing up. They had met freshman year and, by the end of it, practically lived together. Which was why, when sophomore year started, they were living together and stayed together until the moment Lauren went home during their senior year.

It had been late in the evening during a party at the house they shared with a few other girls that Lauren's twin brother had called. Only bring a few days into the school year hadn't mattered. Leila knew it was over. She knew that Lauren would run home to help Lee with his kids. He was her twin. The Almquist twins had lost their parents together in a car accident, and it had made them close.

Even though Lauren had promised to call all the time, she hadn't been out of the closet with her brother, so calling her girlfriend would be tricky in a time before everyone had a cell phone. In the end, there had only been one call.

It had been nearly twenty years since she had met Lauren. A lifetime. Yet sometimes it felt like mere days had passed since they last spoke. Their last phone call had been stiff and felt wrong, which was why she hadn't called again. Which was why she had tried to forget about the redhead the only way a college student could—by finding someone new.

It was days like these that made her long to call Karla. She had been the only woman in town who had known about Leila's heartbreak. It had been Karla who she had confided in when Noreen had left her, Karla who she had admitted she hadn't loved the woman, and now Karla's daughter who threw it back in her face.

How Skylar even knew about Lauren, she didn't know. It was something she never brought up, but maybe at some point Karla had, except that would have been out of character for the woman. The mother-daughter relationship wasn't something Leila had much experience in. Her own mom, after all, had been a businesswoman, and not a motherly one. She spent more time worrying about their car lots than she ever had about her daughter. Mostly, Leila had wondered if she even remembered she had a daughter when she was growing up. Instead, nannies had provided day-to-day for her, and when they weren't available, it was her grandma.

After she had outgrown the nannies, all she had was a grandma, but when she passed, there was nobody. Her teen years had hit her hard. Being gay hadn't been something she had been emotionally prepared for. Maybe she still wasn't.

She was spending far too many hours thinking about Skylar Nash. That woman was just a friendly coworker, but Leila thought she was cute and funny and was insanely jealous of her current girlfriend.

After the conversation on the porch, she knew she should actively avoid the woman. And for days, she had been doing just that. There was no need to tempt herself with the younger woman. After all, Skylar should only be there for a few more weeks or months. There was only so long they could put off hiring a new math teacher, then she would be gone because she needed to get back to her life, or there wouldn't be a life to get back to. Even if Skylar hadn't realized that yet, Leila had.

Principal Gerard walked into her classroom at the end of the day, Friday afternoon. "Leila, how was your day?"

"Good, Mr. Gerard," she answered, picking up a forgotten book from the floor, trying to ignore the fact that he was looking at her butt as she did it, just like she was ignoring that he was calling her by her first name. "What can I help you with?"

"I've had some parents approach me about your class requirements. It seems they're a bit unobtainable." He sat himself down on the top of a desk, something she never let her students do.

Putting the book on her desk, she tried to control her rising anger. "They're the same ones that I have had since I started here. Ninety percent of the students have no issues with it. The rest aren't trying hard enough."

"As usual, I'm concerned about those ten percent, and so are their parents. Some of these kids have busy lives, Leila."

"They're teenagers who spend hours wasted on screen time," she reminded him.

Gerard gave her a smile, like she didn't understand anything. "Many are involved in extracurricular activities."

Sitting down in her chair, she argued, "Sports isn't an excuse. If students can't get their work done around the sport, they shouldn't be in the sport."

"Penalizing a student for being active in school isn't what we want here." He got up and walked closer to her, as if that would change her mind.

"They shouldn't be treated special either." This wasn't the first time she'd had this conversation, but it was the first time it wasn't with a parent or coach.

"I'm not asking you to treat anyone special," he actually said.

"Yes, you are. That is exactly what you are asking." She shook her head and turned her attention to the homework she was correcting. "Which is why I'm not going to talk about it any further with you. I know the student whom you want to treat specially, but if he hopes to keep playing sports next quarter, he has to get his homework done more often." Then she looked up and added, "Or maybe copy his girlfriend's homework more often because they always have the same answers."

He made a small sound of annoyance. "There Is no proof of that happening."

"Yeah, the papers themselves are not proof," she told

him, holding up a paper, just not one of the students she was talking about. But she was sure it made the same point.

"He's doing great in other classes," Gerard argued.

"I don't care." And she highly doubted that. The kid had struggled for years and usually found someone to copy answers from before he found his latest girlfriend. But her grades weren't as stellar as he needed to pass all his classes. Grabbing the papers, she shoved them into her bag and slung it over her shoulder. "Now I want to head out to start my weekend. Are we done?"

"I guess." It seemed he had lost his argument.

She was sure he would be back when he figured out another one, and she turned to leave quickly, which left her time to grab her jacket before heading out of the room.

As she closed and locked the door, Skylar's voice made her jump. "What did Gerard want?"

"Me to drop my standards for a kid who can carry a ball," she told her, shrugging, not caring if the man heard. But if Skylar was asking, he was long gone.

"Oh, one of those. For some reason, I thought he wouldn't be that sort of principal." Skylar laugh at her own words. "I'm kidding, Leila. He's a total people pleaser and wants nothing but to be popular."

Door locked, she turned to the woman standing in the middle of the hallway, her own messenger bag over her shoulder. "Are you saying he isn't already popular?"

"He's never been popular," the younger woman said with surety. "So, I just wanted to say sorry about last weekend. I sort of took my anger at myself out on you."

"Don't mention it," Leila said, because she didn't want to talk about it again.

With a hand on her arm, Skylar stopped her as they

walked toward the door. "No, I'm going to. I never ever should have said what I said. I'm truly sorry."

"I understand where you are coming from. You're right. I don't have kids, so I don't know how to raise them." Ignoring the touch, Leila gave her a thin smile, not meaning it. She just wanted to go home and be alone.

Dropping her hand, Skylar adjusted the strap of her bag. "Neither do I, but it wasn't even that. I'm sorry I said anything about your past relationships. That wasn't my place."

Not saying anything, Leila let the silence settle between them. What was she going to say? It was okay? Because it wasn't. It had gutted her, and for no reason. Turning toward the door, she started walking again. "Well, I need to get home. The puppies and all."

"Yeah, sure," Skylar said from behind her. "I found her."

"Who?" She stopped but didn't turn to look at the younger woman.

"Lauren Almquist. You said you didn't even know where she was. You said that when we talked about her, that is. But, anyway, I looked her up on the internet. I think I found her." Skylar came toward her, or at least her voice got closer, quieter.

Turning, she fixed a neutral expression on her face. "I'm not interested. That was twenty years ago. I've moved on."

Skylar looked surprised. "You're not even a little interested?"

"No, that part of my life is over." She shrugged.

"How can you be this stubborn? I spent hours looking for this woman, and you don't even care." Skylar folded her arms.

"I didn't ask you to, Skylar," Leila reminded her, then

added her own dig. Because she was being petty. "Shouldn't you be spending hours getting your girlfriend to forgive you instead?"

Gaping, Skylar accused, "That's low, Leila. I'm serious about the fact that I found Lauren. Don't you want to know where she is?"

"She's in Campbell," she said easily. Where else would she be, after all? It was where she was from.

Before Skylar could answer, Leila headed out of the building and into the afternoon sunshine. It seemed she and Skylar were some of the last in the building, since theirs were only two of the six cars in the parking lot. Too bad she and Skylar had parked close together that morning.

"You already know? Have you ever gone to see her? It's like three hours away."

Instead of turning around, she said over her shoulder, "No, and I don't plan to."

Suddenly, Skylar was in front of her, physically stopping her from going forward. "You're kidding me right now. All you want to do is apologize, and you won't. Instead, you do nothing."

Leila shook her head at the audacity of the woman. Where did she come off? She didn't know anything about Leila. "Nothing? Skylar, nothing? Did it ever cross your mind that I picked this school a state away from where I grew up because it was the only way I could be close to her?"

"Have you already seen her someplace? Did you talk to her? What happened?" the younger woman questioned with excitement, but she didn't move from in front of Leila.

Running a hand through her hair, she looked around the parking lot, wanting to leave, to not talk about this here or anywhere. But the only way to get that to happen was to get Skylar to leave her alone. Something that wasn't happening until she had all the answers she wanted. So she said the only thing that mattered, why she never once tried to contact her in twenty years. "She isn't out."

Skylar looked confused. "Didn't you date in college? For years?"

Rolling her eyes, Leila said, "You're from another generation, Skylar. Being gay wasn't the 'in' thing for people my age. So not being out *is* normal. You got to come out in high school, and nobody cared. My generation wasn't that lucky."

"Do you know for sure she isn't out?" Skylar asked as Leila walked around her.

Hurrying to her car, she opened the door and finally answered, "Of course not, but I'm not going to out her. I have done enough to her."

"Have you ever thought that she's waiting for you? Like you're waiting for her?" Skylar demanded as Leila slipped into the driver's seat.

Looking out the windshield, she let the question settle around her. Did she think Lauren was waiting? Yes. In her dreams, yes. But real life wasn't that easy. Twenty years was a long time. But then again, so was a week, a month, a year. Those milestones had passed just like this one would.

But all of it came down to the fact that it wasn't up to Leila to find Lauren; it was up to her. Because Leila knew that when Lauren came out, it would be for a love she couldn't live without. They were together for three years, and Lauren had never made that move. Not for her. Not then, and certainly not now.

If she was out, she was in love with someone else. If not, she was still in the closet and content there. Either way, Leila wasn't welcome in her life.

"It doesn't matter." Leila slammed her door and turned on her car.

Skylar backed away from the car with her hands in the air like she was being robbed. Apparently, the younger woman thought that life was easy was on herself. Because Leila had learned a long time ago that it wasn't. But she was happy Skylar hadn't been jaded like she was.

Chapter 19

Pulling up in front of Leila's house unannounced the next morning was sort of stupid, Skylar decided. There wasn't just a small rift between them right now. But it was her fault, so all she could do was try to fix it and find a way to be her friend again, even if she should be working harder on the rift between her and Iris. Because even if they were talking, it wasn't exactly smooth sailing after her canceled weekend.

That had been a week ago, and Iris was still bringing up the fact that Sierra was selfish during every call, which made Skylar feel guiltier and guiltier since it wasn't her sister's fault at all. Looking back, she knew she should have tried harder and not spent so much time focusing on Leila when she could have been devoting that time to her girlfriend.

The guilt kept adding on when Sierra had called to say she was coming home for the weekend and could watch the kids, so Skylar could go see her girlfriend. But she hadn't jumped at the chance because the next weekend, Iris was supposed to be coming to visit her in Warrington.

After her weekend of being left alone because Iris had to work, she decided she was being selfish, knowing that Iris wouldn't abandon her for work while in Warrington. Sure, she would probably work a little, she always did, but there would be no work event she couldn't miss or overtime she needed to get in.

Deciding it was a good time to see her sister, the one she didn't see that often, Skylar had been disappointed when Sierra canceled Friday morning. Which meant her trip would have been canceled anyway, and this way, Iris wouldn't be mad about it.

Now in Leila's driveway, she kept telling herself that leaving the kids alone for a few hours was different from them being home alone for days. She had just started to trust Kayden again, a tiny bit of trust that could easily be broken by leaving him home alone. She just hoped she felt that way tomorrow.

Getting out of her car, she felt a little afraid. Leila knew she was there because she could hear Russell barking in the house, her deep woofs permeating the entire yard easily. But Leila hadn't opened the front door, nor had there been any movement at the windows.

Suddenly she was worried that maybe she was gone, which was why she should have called ahead. But then there had been a greater chance of being told no. A little road trip was exactly what they needed to mend their frayed friendship. Or that was Skylar's hope, at least.

Walking up onto the porch, she was debating if she should knock on the door, because there was no way Leila was going to hear that over Russell's bark. But her other option was to turn around and leave. Too scared to even try.

Squaring her shoulders, she put her hand up to knock on the door that Russell's puppies were behind and just hoped Leila could hear her. Just as she was going to pound on the door, the glass front door opened, the one that went directly into her living room. A door Skylar had never walked through. She had always gone through Russell's door. Assuming that it was the front door.

Leila popped her head out. "What are you doing here, Skylar?"

Turning, she gave the woman a little smile as she moved to the other door, just glad Leila had come out. "Not Miss Nash anymore?"

"I can easily correct myself." Leila held open the door so Skylar could go into the house. Today Leila was in blue jeans and a red sweater, very cozy looking for this chilly fall day. And she looked a hundred times better than Skylar's own leggings and oversized sweatshirt. The woman relaxed in a better outfit than Skylar normally wore to work.

"Okay, okay," Skylar slipped past her into the warm house, happy she had made it this far. If Leila was still completely upset with her, she wouldn't have made it into the house. So Skylar pushed her luck. "So I decided we needed a road trip. I want to show you how sorry I am by treating you to a day out."

"Pass, I have things to do," Leila said quickly. She hadn't even thought about it.

"Like what?" Skylar pressed.

"Like, I don't have to tell you what I'm doing. My life is my life. Treat Iris to a day with her girlfriend. I'm sure she would love a day alone with you." Leila didn't leave the doorway and didn't even look over at her barking dog, who felt she was missing out on something important by being stuck behind a gate in the mudroom.

"Please, Leila, just today. If you are still pissed at me by the end of it, I'll stop trying to apologize. Forever." She crossed her heart with her finger, hoping it wouldn't come to that.

"What about leaving Keeley and Kayden alone?" Leila questioned, her arms folded, but she didn't kick her out. In fact, Skylar could tell she was going to give in.

Smirking, Skylar knew she had her. She was cracking. Skylar admitted, "It's not overnight, just during the day. I'm trying to trust them more. Which just shows you how important I think apologizing to you is. You know you are my best friend."

Okay, that was a stretch, but Skylar felt it could be true. She enjoyed spending time with and only close friends caused distress when there was a fight. If Skylar felt nothing for the woman, she wouldn't be here to mend the fences.

"You have other best friends, Skylar," Leila assured her.

Grabbing the woman's jacket from the hook on the wall, she handed it to her. "I have the entire day already planned. All you have to do is get in the car." When Leila did one of those rare eye rolls, she knew she had won.

"I'll need to change."

"I like what you're wearing, but if you have to, hurry." Skylar wrapped the jacket around her arm. "I'll let Russell out one more time, so we can head out when you're done."

Minutes later, the woman came down, now in black slacks, but still in the sweater. Why did she think she couldn't go out in jeans? Skylar didn't know, but she wasn't going to question her. Not today. Maybe another day. When they were friends again.

Russell was already back in the house, and Skylar had been playing with the puppies as she waited. She could tell why Kayden wanted one so badly. They were adorable, and those long ears and sad eyes made you want to take them home. All of them.

Setting down the puppy, Skylar straightened and smiled at her friend. "Are you ready now?"

"As ready as I'm going to be." Leila slipped on her jacket as they walked out of the house and toward Skylar's car. "Where are we going?"

"That's a surprise. One you don't need to know just yet." She slipped into the car, and Leila rolled her eyes again as she buckled her seat belt.

It was going to be a fun day. She just hoped Leila thought so at the end.

Chapter 20

"I don't remember my mom having problems finding and keeping friends. In fact, her college best friend was at the funeral. Mom made adulting look easy," Skylar admitted two hours into their trip. The drive had been pretty, but they hadn't actually stopped anywhere yet.

Leila could understand the friend's situation. After Karla died, she was in the same boat. Only then realizing that she had only one true friend. That her life had been comfortable and quiet, and she didn't need many friends to be happy. Just one. Which was why she was sure she had turned to Skylar, an easy replacement for her mom. Except, the dynamics between them were very different from those between her and Karla. For one, Leila had never once been attracted to Karla.

"That she did. I don't think there was an adult or child in this town she didn't know or didn't talk to and consider her friend," Leila told her, but Skylar would have already known that. The funeral had been huge.

In the afternoon sunshine, the younger woman was

gorgeous. Though Leila remembered her being cute in high school, it hadn't been an attraction cute, just an observation cute. Many of her students over the years were cute, after all, even some who had stuck around were still cute. And still not attractive to her. Not like Skylar Nash was now.

Which was why she shouldn't be in this car with her. She had promised herself to keep her distance. Yet the moment Skylar wanted to spend time with her, Leila was all-in.

Beside her, Skylar didn't notice how Leila was looking at her as she leaned an elbow against the door and stared in front of them. "I wish I knew how she managed to get along with everyone. It was a secret I wish I had asked her before."

Pushing down her attraction, she said, "I think it was just her personality. She was so outgoing and could talk to anyone. She rarely got riled up, and almost never got mad."

It had been from Karla that Leila had learned how to control her anger. Something that came easy now, but when she had started teaching, it had been a struggle. It took a lot to rile her up, even though Gerard managed it weekly.

"I don't remember her being mad at all. And I did some dumb stuff growing up." Skylar looked over at her. "Even when I came out, she was accepting and loving. I was so lucky."

Leila let out a little chuckle. "Don't think that one didn't rile her up a bit. She just managed to calm down and be the exact kind of mother she needed to be for you."

Skylar looked at her in surprise. "She hid it well, very well."

Leila nodded and looked at the road stretching in front of them. She still didn't know where they were going, but didn't ask either. It didn't matter anymore. She was with Skylar. Turning to her, she asked, "You know she knew already when you told her, right?"

Skylar shook her head in denial. "There was no way she could have known. I kept that to myself."

Shifting in her seat, Leila informed her, "So, the day you told me—"

Skylar interrupted her, "Thanks for that. I didn't realize for years how helpful it was to have a gay woman to talk to about what I was feeling. Many women I know never had that. It's why I never hide who I am from my students. Because one day, one of them may want someone to talk to."

Warmth instantly spread through Leila's body at that. That she had made a difference in someone's life. That by making that difference, that person was trying to make a difference. It was also the reason she never hid who she was. She wanted to be there for those who needed a role model. Even if she wasn't role model material.

"I'm glad I was there when you needed someone." Leila took her hand and squeezed it, then let go because she shouldn't be touching her, and the picture in the woman's mind was a little wrong. "But I did the one thing I never wanted to do after you came out. I ended up outing you to your mom. One day, I went to her classroom to talk to her. I thought she already knew that you had told her. It had been weeks."

"It took weeks to get the courage up," Skylar said, though she didn't sound as mad as Leila knew she should be. "How did she react when you told her?"

Leila just stared at the road ahead of them. "She was

mad, as mad as I have ever seen her. Called me a few choice names."

Slipping her sunglasses off, Skylar asked, "And here I thought she was all cool with it. I wonder if she ever was cool with it?"

"She was. Oh, Skylar, she was so proud of you and everything about you. She was never upset at you being gay. She loved you and accepted you for who you were. Always. She was mad at me." Leila pointed at herself.

"What did you do?" She tossed the glasses on the dash.

"You confided in me. She felt I had overstepped. And I did. I should have told you to talk to your mom. It wasn't my place to talk to you. She was right. You should be leery if a student ever wants to talk to you about their sexuality," Leila admitted. It was what made teaching hard. You wanted a connection with your students, but that connection was a tightrope.

Skylar grabbed her hand and held it. "No, Leila, my mom was wrong. You know that, right? She knew better than to accuse you of something. She should have been happy I was comfortable enough to go to you since you were friends. Isn't that what you want as a parent?"

"She was mad because you came to me and not her. I think she felt you weren't as close as she thought you were. That bothered her the most." Leila didn't let go of the hand, just kept holding it.

"How long was she mad at you?" she asked curiously.

"A few months. Most of that year, I guess. I can't remember anymore." It was a lie. It had been the entire school year and summer. Only that fall after Skylar had graduated had they started talking again. It was a long time during which her relationship with Noreen had fallen apart.

136

"I'm sorry she treated you like that. I didn't even realize it, and I was right there."

"You were going through something yourself. And you were a kid learning who you were."

Skylar focused on the road ahead of them as she drove. "I always told people how my coming out was so perfect, and now I'm going to have to rethink that because you took the burden of the parental disapproval during it."

Leila shifted in her seat. She would take that burden for any of her students any day, no matter which one. Nobody deserved it. "Better than you. Take it from experience; you're better off without that disapproval in your life."

"Do you think your mom knows you're okay? I wonder if she worries about you?" Skylar asked. It seemed she remembered that Leila and her parents were estranged.

Shaking off the hand, she pretended to look for something in her purse. "I don't know and don't care. It's been years. I'm over it."

"Are you?"

"Yes. I wouldn't trade a trust fund for the life I have now." She stared back, as if breaking eye contact would mean she wasn't over her mom's behavior.

Skylar turned back to the road. "What kind of trust fund were you supposed to get?"

"The kind that meant I would never have to work a day in my life. Nor my children. My mother owned a chain of car dealerships."

"New or used cars?" Skylar asked with interest.

"All new. My mom wouldn't have it any other way." Once Leila had been old enough, her mom had showed her love by giving her cars. Every year she had the newest model, whichever model she wanted. It hadn't been enough for Leila. She wanted her mom's love the affection. That was never on offer.

"You probably could've gone back, told her you were kidding and gotten back into her good graces." Skylar turned onto another tar road going no place.

"I was too busy proving to them I didn't need their money. Still am and still don't. I'm happy with my life. I don't need money to be happy. That is something I had to learn on my own because my parents weren't happy until there was a lot of money coming in." Leila insisted money wasn't what she missed about her mom. It was her mom, the mom she could have been if she wasn't so busy. Or maybe cared. "Enough about me. How's Iris?"

"We talked a lot this week. Way more than any other week since Mom passed. I feel we are getting back to being us again. I'm working to get back to what we were before," Skylar said as the car sped up.

"That's good to hear," Leila lied, hating that she was so jealous of them as a couple.

"Yeah, we actually talked about the future. Me moving back. I know I might have to be here the rest of the year, and she knows it. But it's been a few months, and it's going okay. We just have to work at spending more time together. Weekends and such. She's coming up next weekend."

"That's good." They passed a sign that actually said Almquist on it. Lauren's last name, but she had missed what else it said. Panicking, she asked, "Where are we going?"

"A brewery," Skylar admitted sheepishly.

"No, really, where are we going?" Leila demanded, because it wasn't just a brewery, that was obvious. Skylar was up to something.

"Okay, don't get mad. Lauren has a brewery." She slowed the car to turn onto a gravel road, one that had a billboard that plainly said Almquist Brewery.

"No." Leila was panicking.

Patting her arm, Skylar said calmly, "Let's just go see. Have a drink and leave."

"No." She took a deep breath. This wasn't how the day was supposed to go. She should have said no.

Skylar took her hand. "Consider it payback for outing me."

"You didn't even know about that," she argued and watched an extensive building come into view. A building that had to be the brewery. Was it Lauren's?

"I do now, and I need a drink." She turned into a farmyard with a parking lot in front of a large barn with some sort of tin building attached.

Lauren's eyes looked at the farm. That was probably where Lauren had grown up. A place Leila had wanted to go to for three years and never got the opportunity. It looked exactly like she had imagined it.

"I'm mad at you still," Leila assured her as Skylar parked the car alongside another from a different state.

Shutting off the car, Skylar leaned toward her and whispered, "I'll protect you from your scary ex."

Pushing her away, she insisted, "I don't need protection."

Leaning back in her seat, Skylar nodded. "I know, Leila, you need closure. This woman has been in your head for twenty years. It's time to move on. Seeing her will do that. Then you can open your heart to someone else. And besides, she probably isn't even here. What are the chances?"

Leila rolled her eyes at that. Skylar didn't know Lauren. She would never leave her brewery if she had one. If she enjoyed something, she gave it her all and maybe even more. It would border on obsession.

Nodding, she knew Skylar was right. She needed to get over Lauren before she could open her heart to someone, and she wanted someone. Based on how much she wanted Skylar, she knew she was ready.

Opening the door, she took a deep breath and hoped Lauren didn't recognize her. She wanted to be over Lauren without Lauren finding out. Was that too much to ask?

Chapter 21

Leila had expected the brewery to be very different from what it actually was. But then again, she knew Lauren and had based her imagination on Lauren's decorating skills. Which, when they were dating, consisted of motivational posters her parents had gotten her over the years. Posters that hadn't been hung with care and most had been crooked.

Which was why she had been sure there would be at least one poster of a cat hanging from a branch telling everyone else to hang in there. Except there were no cats and no motivation, simply shabby chic and farmhouseIr throughout the refurbished barn.

The high ceilings and shiny bar along the back wall were gorgeous. So much so that Leila had stopped moving as she looked around the room and just gawked. Then she remembered Lauren was supposed to be here some place. A woman she was sure she would notice instantly, and one who would notice her. And probably be mad.

Beside her, Skylar leaned into her and bumped her shoulder before slipping her hand into Leila's, leading her toward the bar—not letting her bolt like every fiber in her body was demanding of her. Instead, they made their way to two empty stools.

"This way," Skylar whispered as they went, wrapping her arm around her waist, because Leila wanted to run. She just hoped it didn't show. "It's going to be okay. I don't think she's even here."

"Me neither." She let out the breath she hadn't even noticed she had been holding.

Settling onto the stools, Skylar let go of her hand and started to unbutton her jacket, still looking around.

"What brings you ladies in today?" asked the young bartender in a white T-shirt as she set Almquist Beer coasters in front of each of them with one hand. The other was rested on the head of a curly haired baby who was snuggled into her with a baby wrap.

"Rumor has it you are the place to get great beer, and we are in the market for a great beer." Grabbing her hand again, Skylar took the lead in the conversation, which was for the best. Leila was still looking around, on edge, expecting Lauren to pop up anywhere.

"You came to the right place. We have amazing beer. From light to dark and everything in between. I'm Nissa, and I can get you whatever you desire. Right after I see your IDs." The woman looked directly at Skylar, obviously not questioning Leila's age.

Skylar didn't even notice that Leila didn't move to take out her ID as she pulled her own ID from her back pocket and handed it over. She must still get carded all the time. "I saw on your website you won a few awards last year. Impressive. We decided to take the long drive to see for ourselves."

As the ID went back to Skylar. Leila felt old, too old to be out doing whatever she was doing with Skylar. Which wasn't a date, because Skylar was still dating Iris, and nothing was changing that. Skylar had just said they were in a good place now.

"Welcome, Skylar. What can I get you two?" Nissa asked, a welcoming smile on her face.

They both nodded their heads, and Leila looked over at Skylar, hoping that the woman wouldn't ask about Lauren. It was far better not to see her after all. She had to know that.

"Can we each get a flight of your most popular beer?" Skylar asked, sounding like an expert.

"What's a flight?" Leila whispered to Skylar as she unbuttoned her jacket. It was getting a little warm in the barn.

Instead of Skylar answering, Nissa did, "It's six different beers in smaller glasses so that you can sample more than one kind."

"Six?! Can we share?" Leila asked, because after six beers, nobody was driving home, and she didn't want to be drunk by the end of the day.

"If you're willing to drink out of the same glass," Nissa said, a smirk on her mouth, because she thought they were a couple. She had pegged them as gay, but seemed to think they were a couple. Which was ridiculous. Skylar was far too young for her.

"Yeah, that won't be an issue," Skylar informed the woman, then turned her attention to the baby. "Cute baby. Your boss must be pretty lenient that you can have her here."

The woman grinned and rubbed the dark curls again, and the baby looked out at them with deep blue eyes as she said, "Him. I have my way of getting my own way around here."

Turning, the woman started filling tiny glasses, leaving

Leila and Skylar alone. Neither spoke as they looked around, both probably looking for the same thing, except Skylar didn't know what Lauren even looked like. But Leila did.

Nissa was back quickly with their drinks, and before Skylar could pull out her credit card, Leila handed hers to the woman, who took it with a smile and headed to the other side of the bar to the cash register. It might not be a date, but Skylar had driven. Drinks were on Leila.

"You didn't have to buy. Today was my treat to you," Skylar insisted.

Waving her off, Leila turned to the beer. "Which one looks good to you?"

"I like the light ones." Skylar looked over the drinks as Nissa came back with the credit card.

The woman's smile was gone, as was her pleasant manner as she snapped the card onto the bar in front of Leila. Her friendly demeanor was completely gone. Instead, she seemed like she regretted serving them and started wiping down the bar in front of them.

"Then I'll try the darker one first." Leila picked up the darkest one on the end.

"If you don't like the dark ones, I can ..." Skylar argued, trying to take it from her.

Holding it away from her, Leila argued, "No, I do like them. In fact, the first beer I ever had was a dark beer."

"Of course it was," Nissa stated before she tossed the towel down as she turned and walked away from them.

"What's up with her suddenly?" Skylar asked, watching her go.

"No idea," Leila admitted as she picked up the glass and smelled the familiar smell.

Before she could take the first sip, the hairs on the back of her neck stood up as something shifted in the room, something that Leila wouldn't have been able to put a finger on if she hadn't felt it many times before. Just not in a long time. Lauren.

Setting the drink carefully down on the bar top and not the flight, she turned in her chair and saw her coming out a door marked brewery. She looked the same but still older, more mature, all at the same time. Her red hair was still short and similar to the style it had been the first time she saw it. If Leila had to guess, she would say her jeans were the exact same ones she used to wear. At least the cut was. Only her heavy black jacket was something she knew Lauren wouldn't wear willingly. It was a color she always said reminded her of her parents' funeral.

Though Lauren was looking at the bar, she wasn't looking toward her. Instead, she was looking at the other end of the bar. Not that Leila looked at who or what she was looking at, because she didn't even glance that way.

Instead, she wondered if this was how their lives might have turned out, Lauren brewing beer and Leila doing god knows what, because she wasn't interested in beer at all besides drinking ccasionallyionlly. Or would they have never made it to this point? Would what they'd had evolved into some else? Something less?

Beside her, Skylar put her hand on Leila's knee. The warm hand on her chilled leg made her realize that what she felt for Lauren was something she knew she would never have again. But it was different from what she wanted now.

In their years apart, Leila had grown up and needed something Lauren wasn't and had never been. She still loved the other woman, but she wasn't in love with her. There was just a familiarity that she missed. Something she hadn't found with anyone else since.

Even from across the room, she knew the moment

Lauren felt her presence. The moment the woman looked over the crowd and recognized her. Only then did she change directions and start her way. That was when Leila captured Skylar's hand in hers. Would she start by yelling? Or just ask them to leave?

As she clung to Skylar's hand, Lauren walked toward her, a smile on her face, the single dimple showing, "Leila Hensley, is that you?"

Slipping her hand from Skylar's, Leila slid off the stool and turned to her former lover. "It is. Hello, Lauren. How've you been?"

"You look … wow. What happened to the long hair?" Lauren reached up but stopped herself just before she touched it. Only then did Leila remember all the nights in bed when Lauren had made her promise to never cut her hair. A promise she hadn't kept long because, by the time she had moved to Warrington, it was shorter. Right now, it was actually the longest it had been since the big cut.

Self-consciously, she touched it herself. "Too much work, I guess. You haven't changed a bit."

Lauren laughed and rocked on her heels. "I have changed, or so I have been told over and over again. For the better, I have been assured." Lauren looked over at the dark-haired bartender behind her bar. "Nissa, we're going to grab a table. Join us when you can."

Nissa's arms crossed over the baby on her chest, and she grunted, "Okay."

"I'll take your flight." Lauren took the beer, leading them to a table close to the bar, still smiling. "Leila doesn't even like beer."

Leila was nearly relieved. She had been so sure Lauren would kick her out. Maybe even make a scene as she did it. It was what she deserved.

Sitting down across the table from her former love, she

said, "You were more into mixed drinks, if I remember correctly. Now you run this. Always the bartender."

Lauren laughed and looked around. "This would be nothing without Nissa. She's the brains and the beauty behind the place. I'm simply the muscle."

Lauren's eyes drifted to the bar and the angry bartender. Leila recognized the look instantly. Lauren was in love with the woman. And based on the bartender's reaction, she was in love as well.

It made her happy Lauren had found the love she deserved. Seeing them, Leila knew it was a deeper love than they had shared. Based on solid ground and reality. Something she hadn't been able to find herself … and probably never would.

Chapter 22

"Nissa the bartender?" Skylar asked in surprise, looking over at the woman, who was very obviously jealous of Lauren's attention on Leila. And based on her attitude since seeing her credit card, she knew exactly who Leila was.

Which meant that she and Lauren were close enough for Lauren to tell her about her first love. She probably even knew more than Skylar about how it actually started and ended. Was Lauren still hung up on Leila like the other woman was? How big of a mistake did she make by taking Leila here?

Stopping herself, she wondered why it would be a mistake. If the former couple rekindled their relationship, that would be great, wouldn't it? Then why was Skylar hating the idea so much now that it could happen?

"Yeah, her." Smiling, Lauren waved her over before turning back to Leila. "Where did you end up? New York, Chicago, Washington? I bet New York. You always wanted to be in the city."

"You wanted to go to New York City?" Skylar turned

to Leila in confusion. The woman who bought herself a farm in the middle of a large city?

Both of them ignored her question as Lauren went on. "I have looked at the big papers for your byline but have never seen it. I always thought it would be amazing to tell everyone I used to date that woman who broke whatever story wide open."

"You wanted to be a reporter?" Skylar was beginning to wonder if she knew anything about the woman she came in here with.

Leila took pity on her and finally answered a question. "That's what I was going to school for. I always dreamed of being an investigative journalist. I only had a few semesters left when I transferred colleges."

"She'd switched her major from business," Lauren explained, like they had never been apart. "What did you get your degree in?"

"How do you know I got a degree?" Leila asked her in a teasing voice. When Lauren gave her a goofy look, she laughed and added, "Teaching."

Lauren nodded in approval. "Your personality is perfect for teaching. Let me guess, English? At a college someplace?"

"High school, actually. Some junior high." Leila explained and then picked up a little glass of beer and handed it to Lauren. "Do you want a beer?"

"No, you enjoy it." Shifting in her seat, Lauren took off her bulky jacket. "How did your mom react to that?"

"She never knew, actually. Disowned me for other things. Coming out to her went down like a lead brick. Cut me off completely." Leila was more forthcoming with information for her old friend than she had ever been with Skylar. It made her jealous of their instant connection.

"Still?" Lauren leaned back and ran a hand through her hair, messing it up completely.

"Yeah, she was never going to get over that. It's what I …"

Lauren finished, "Always said. I'm sorry she turned out like that."

"It's how it is."

"I just hoped for better." Leila smiled at Lauren and let go of her hand as if she just realized she was holding it.

"I brought another flight," Nissa stated, nearly slamming the wooden flight down on the table. How the beer didn't spill, Skylar had no idea, but she knew exactly why the woman was so mad. Lauren was hers, and Leila wasn't going to be getting in the way of that.

Lauren turned to the woman and grabbed her hand. "Sit, Nissa, meet Leila. We went to college together."

"More than that," Nissa mumbled as she sat down, adjusting the baby on her lap as she did. Once he was sufficiently comfortable, she looked up with a fake smile. "So, what brings you to the brewery, Leila?"

Leila took the hint and turned to include the woman in their conversation. "I want to apologize for everything. After you left, I went a little crazy thinking it was my chance to play the field. My chance to see who else was out there. In the end, there wasn't anyone. In the process, I hurt you. For that, I'm truly sorry. That night? I saw you."

Lauren looked surprised as Nissa shifted her chair closer to her possessively. "I didn't think you did. I was sure you didn't."

Leila shrugged. "I always saw you. That night I knew I had messed everything we might have had up."

"Yes, you did," Nissa stated, and Lauren gave her a look. "What? You just want me to make small talk with the woman who hurt you? To stand by and let it happen again? I think not."

"That's not why I came. Truly," Leila told the woman.

Skylar jumped in, needing to explain why the woman was there, that she hadn't meant anything by it. "She's right. I dragged her here. She just wants to make sure Lauren is okay."

"She's doing great. Simply amazing, in fact," Nissa said, her eyes on Leila and ignoring Skylar completely. "Tell her, Lauren."

"I don't have to; she knows." Lauren roped an arm around the other woman and bopped the baby on the nose.

Leila just nodded at the woman. "More than happy, I would say. How long have you two been together?"

"Years," Nissa answered, though she couldn't be any older than Skylar was. "How did you know?"

Leila pointed at the baby on her lap. "The baby, he's yours, together. He has Lauren's eyes. And she doesn't stop looking at you like she used to look at me. I'm happy for you both to have found that together."

"And you two? Don't think I can't see that you two are something more than friends." Nissa pointed at the two of them.

"We're working on it," Leila lied and, based on Lauren's eyebrow, she knew it. But Skylar had forced her to come here. She would let her lie as much as she needed to.

"How did you two meet?" Nissa asked, shifting the baby as she started to unwrap the baby sling.

Leila looked at her before answering, "Skylar attended the school I teach at."

"Were you fired? You should've been fired." Nissa stopped her actions.

Leila blushed. "What? No, we've only been dating for a little while. I've known her for years."

Skylar laughed at her reaction and filled the other couple in on what she had meant. "She was living with a woman when I was in school. Now I'm a teacher as well. There, for now. So, there's nothing scandalous about it. We're just coworkers."

"Nissa has been working for hours, and I'm exhausted. Let's go to the house and catch up some more."

"It's not exactly clean," Nissa told her wife from the side of her mouth.

"It's clean enough, and she lived with me. She knows how I am." Lauren took the baby from her and pulled her from the chair.

"You don't have to keep reminding me." Nissa tapped Lauren's arm in annoyance.

"Do I need to remind you that I am married to you and have no plans to changing that? No matter who walks in the door?" Lauren took the baby from her and snuggled him into her as she gave her wife a steamy glance that said more than words ever would.

Skylar had to turn away from them because the moment was too intimate. The look made her happy for reasons she didn't want to think about. Reasons about Leila and Lauren not rekindling anything.

Chapter 23

Lauren's house was exactly how Leila would have described it: warm, comfortable, and welcoming. There was no mess and not even a hint that a mess was possible. Based on the pictures on the mantle, the couple had more than the baby, but two babies and two school-age girls. But in every photo, Lauren looked ecstatic to be living the life she was living. And loving every moment of it.

"What do you guys want to drink?" Nissa asked before she could even take off her jacket.

"Anything is fine," Skylar answered from beside her, slipping off her own jacket and handing it to Lauren.

"Wine, water, milk, apple juice—we have it all." Nissa stopped and took the baby from Lauren. They were handing him off every few minutes now that he wasn't attached to Nissa.

"Wine, if possible," Leila answered, because she needed some alcohol for this day, no matter what Skylar needed.

"Sure. It seems you two weren't so into the beer. Which

is fine. It isn't my beverage of choice, either. But it's my life and my wife's."

"Your wedding photos are gorgeous. Did you get married here?" Skylar said as she looked over the photos on the mantel herself.

"Yeah, since we already had the reception venue here, we just did it all," Lauren said as Nissa left the room.

Leila looked around the house, taking it all in. "Where are your other kids today?"

"Nissa's mom lives in town and took them for the weekend. It's just that Odin was a little clingy this afternoon, so I kept him. The rest are girls, and I think they were doing nails or something." Lauren gestured to the couch.

"Did you stay in contact with anyone from school?" Leila sat down and asked. She hadn't and was almost sure Lauren hadn't either. Their group was close, but they had both left so suddenly that getting addresses and numbers wasn't possible.

"Just Hilary, and through her, I've heard where others were," Lauren admitted as Nissa came into the room with four wine glasses in one hand and Odin in the other.

"Hilary Mathews?" Leila said and laughed. "Is she still the player she was back then? I remember the party junior year where she started the night with a blonde, found a redhead to make out with for about two hours, and then went home with a different blonde."

"I can't see Hilary being that way. She doesn't even look at other women," Nissa stated, setting down the glasses of wine like an expert, which she was.

"Hilary is married with six kids now. Stopped all that when she met Cate." Nissa handed the baby to her wife and started to unbutton her jacket finally.

"I wish I had been there to see that," Leila said. It

would have been such a change from the woman she had known for three years.

"You mostly were. She met her the night before I left. That was the girl we spent the evening looking for. Don't you remember?" She went to the mantle and picked up a smaller photo. "The dark-haired girl? Yellow dress?"

They finished together, "And strappy sandals." And they both giggled a little at the memory of the night of searching for one particular woman.

"Yes, that was the first time I'd ever heard Hilary say something about a girl's shoes before. But she didn't start dating her before I left, that I remember." She took the photo from her and looked at the family in it. One was definitely Hilary, and she had her arms around a Latina woman who was very much pregnant. Around them were five little faces that all looked the same.

"No, she didn't find her until after Christmas, then bam, they moved in together and have been happy ever since. Married, kids, all the happily ever after that she said wasn't for her. Cate changed her completely." Lauren took the picture and looked at it herself, and smiled. "They stopped by last year and surprised me. I hadn't seen Hilary since moving back home, and there she was. It was a nice surprise."

"They had just found out they were pregnant again," Nissa said. "It was right after Lauren had the twins."

"You had twins?" Leila couldn't help but ask.

Lauren smiled as she sat down next to her wife and kissed her head. Leila knew her wife had simply asked her. It was all that was needed for Lauren to do anything. Something Leila had taken advantage of far more than she should have when they were together.

"Yup," was all Lauren answered. "Nissa had two, I had two. It's only fair."

Leila wasn't asking anything more about it. It was up to the couple who carried or not. It wasn't up to her. But she was so impressed with Lauren and her ability to step out of her comfort zone. Leila didn't even know if she wanted kids, much less wanted to carry one.

After a long sip of wine, she asked, "Who else have you heard from?"

"Shelby Rockingham. We haven't seen her, but we've heard about her through Cate. She a book editor now." Lauren said.

Leila shook her head at what had happened so long ago. "Remember when she and Hilary broke up? It was like world war three happening in our living room. That woman could argue."

"They managed to break every lamp we had," Lauren supplied. "Now she's a book editor and has some famous names under her."

"Wow, she was in the same classes I was in."

"I just can't see you in the city. Where would you garden?"

"I wouldn't have lasted. I don't have the cutting edge that was needed for reporting, and I need the space I have now."

"Leila has a hobby farm, an enormous garden, and she cans everything," Skylar jumped in.

"Any animals?" Nissa asked, probably getting them off the topic of college.

"Just Russell," she answered.

Skylar laid a hand on her thigh. "Her basset hound, and she has nine puppies right now."

"We should get a puppy." Nissa turned to her wife.

"No, we have two toddlers."

"Who need a dog in their lives!" Nissa begged.

"No. We don't have time for it." Lauren sounded like she was already giving in.

"But we're home all the time. We have time, and winter is coming. That's our slow time." Nissa pushed excitedly, "Do you have pictures?"

"Not good ones," Leila said. She realized she hadn't taken a lot of pictures of them. She had just spent her time enjoying them.

Skylar bumped her shoulder lightly before pulling out her own phone. "Don't let her fool you. They're adorable. My brother has been begging for one since we met them, and he's half scared of dogs. But not these. And if they're anything like their mom, they're going to be mellow."

Leila argued, not ready to let any of them go yet. "They're adorable, but I can't promise anything. I didn't know the male very well."

"It's the parenting that counts in the end," Lauren said, taking Skylar's phone but handing it right to her wife.

"So says the lesbian," Nissa said and laughed, looking at Leila's phone and letting Lauren look at the photos with her. "We'll take this one."

"That's Hilary, I would assume, named after your friend. But Leila won't tell me the story behind the name," Skylar told them after looking at which photo it was.

"No big story, just always in the middle of everything and then making noise to get everyone's attention." Leila watched them look at more photos together, a little jealous of their closeness.

Lauren laughed at the description. "That's Hilary. I always assumed it was because she had been raised in California."

"Oh, and the top of the head has more white than any of the others. Hilary was blonde," Leila added. It sounded silly now when she said it out loud. "Where did she end up? Person Hilary, that is."

"She and Cate live about three houses down from the one she was raised in, where her parents still live. Right back in the middle of her family. But it's where I would be if I had six kids."

"Where is Lee? Your brother?" she asked, because he had to be nearby. Lauren was similar to Hilary like that. She wouldn't go far from her family.

"He's in town. He was married to Nissa's mom, but that has mostly fallen apart. Just not divorced yet. We don't get along well anymore," Lauren said, her smile faltering.

"He doesn't like that Lauren is happy, but he isn't." Nissa earned a frown from her wife, which she just shrugged off.

"That sounds complicated," Skylar said, as her phone rang, and Nissa handed it quickly back to her. After one look, she said she had to take it and headed out of the room.

All Leila knew was that the caller ID had said Iris in big, bold letters.

Chapter 24

"Where are you?" Iris demanded into the phone, as if she could somehow sense that Skylar was lying about being Leila's girlfriend for the day. And that she was enjoying it, probably too much.

Skylar was glad she had made it into the kitchen and away from Lauren and Nissa before Iris's loud voice could be heard by everyone. Then she would have to explain who she was talking to.

"Leila and I are visiting an old friend of hers," she said and winced. Maybe she shouldn't have said anything about Leila.

"Your mom's friend?" Iris had somehow remembered her, though she hadn't said much about her over the last few weeks.

Agreeing, she said, "Yeah, I said something to her last weekend that I regret and am making it up to her."

"Why? She's just some older lady, isn't she? Someone your mom worked with?" Iris said, as if anyone over thirty was old. Because Leila wasn't old by any means.

"I work with her, and I consider her my friend. And when I hurt her feelings, I felt bad."

"Because you don't have a tough skin, Skylar. When you're done with your subbing job, I think you should look at something in HR. There was an opening here that sounded perfect for you, but you missed the deadline to apply. I think I sent you an email about it." At her words, Skylar remembered the weird email Iris had sent her the month before. She had dismissed it as being sent to the wrong person.

"I've always loved teaching. I plan to stay teaching, Iris," she reminded her girlfriend.

"Until we have kids," Iris stated mater-of-factly, like they had discussed it.

"What? Are we having kids?" Skylar asked in confusion.

"Not now, of course, but one day. Don't you want to have kids with me? A family?" Iris was pouting.

Controlling her annoyed tone, because she didn't want to talk about this now, she said, "Of course I do, but I didn't think you would want them. You're so career-orientated."

"Is that what you think of me? I shouldn't have kids because my job is demanding? That I would put my career before my children? That I'm that cold of a person?"

"That isn't what I'm saying at all. Not even close. It's just that we've never talked about kids, so I didn't think you wanted them." Skylar couldn't believe they were talking about this now.

"Why wouldn't you want kids with me? Is it because of your brother and sister? I have told you over and over again that you can bring them to live with us." Iris sounded out of sorts tonight. Because she had never said that. In fact, she had always insisted Sierra needed to step up and take them.

"Iris, calm down. Can we please talk about this some other time? It's sort of a bad time for me right now." She rubbed her forehead in frustration.

"You keep saying we don't talk, but when I want to talk, you're unavailable. Have you ever thought about that?" Iris accused.

"So you're blaming me for what's happening?"

"You're the one who left."

"Because my mom died, and there's nobody else to take care of my siblings. That wasn't my choice."

"It was. You always say there was no other way. How is the house cleaning going? Have you even been working on it?"

"Yes, but it's hard," she lied. She hadn't done a thing in weeks.

"Stalling won't make it go any easier, Skylar. It's like taking off a band-aid, just rip it off," Iris said, not for the first time, but it didn't help. That wasn't how Skylar handled things.

"You have no idea what you are talking about. You have never lost someone this close to you," she argued. "Anyway, I have to go. Are you still coming on Friday?"

"I already might have a meeting scheduled Saturday morning." Iris didn't commit to the weekend. As it drew closer, she had talked about it less.

"Iris, this is our weekend. Can you please try to make time for me?" she asked, knowing she didn't deserve it after this phone call.

"Work isn't something I can control; you know that. Call me when you have time to actually talk to me."

"I will," she said and realized Iris had hung up on her before she had gotten the words out. Which hurt.

Walking back into the living room, she found Lauren and Leila laughing and Nissa looking on slightly annoyed. It seemed the stories had veered back into their college days. Skylar knew she would be just as uncomfortable if she had been there also.

Leila sat up, her smile vanishing when she looked at Skylar. "We should get going." So much for hiding her annoyance at her actual girlfriend from her fake one.

"Text me information on the puppies," Nissa said with a sweet smile. "I'll work on Lauren. I'm sure she will agree, eventually. After all, she loves me." The last, she added, to remind Leila of the fact.

"I'm sure she will. And remember, they're buy one, get one free."

"We don't need two dogs."

"That would be amazing! Two of them. Like the twins," Nissa purred.

"Remember how much work the twins are? Now imagine they're dogs." Lauren handed the baby she was holding back to Nissa as if she needed a physical reminder.

"The twins are easy," Nissa argued, probably just to argue.

"The twins aren't easy," Lauren stated, and then turned back to Leila and hugged her. "It was so nice to see you again. No forgiveness needed. I couldn't hold the past against you."

"I can," Nissa stated, and Skylar knew Lauren was forgiving far easier than anyone should. But Nissa wasn't, so they may never see each other again as it was. Dog or no dog. Leila knew where Lauren was, but did Lauren know where Leila could be found? Did Leila tell them while she was on the phone with Iris?

Out in the car, they were both silent as they left the brewery, the parking lot now empty completely. It seemed it wasn't like a bar that got busier the later the night got, but closed early in the evening.

Only as Skylar turned onto the highway did Leila ask, "What was your phone call about?"

"Iris wanting to talk. She seemed off tonight, bringing up kids and the future," she admitted, needing to talk about this with someone.

"Have you ever talked about the future?"

"Yeah, in the 'I want to be with you forever' kind of talk. Not kids, quitting jobs, and who's going to carry the baby. Seriously, I'm twenty-six. I'm not ready to start a family. And neither is she." Skylar knew she wasn't. Her gut said she wasn't, after all.

"Do you know that for sure? About her, I mean."

"Of course I do. The last thing on her mind is having kids. She's too focused on her job to even think about anything else." The woman couldn't even seem to take a weekend off. "Are you happy we went to see Lauren?"

"I am. I'm relieved she's so happy." Leila seemed to be telling the truth, seemed to be truly happy.

"How did you pick up that she and Nissa were a couple? I thought Nissa was just lusting after her boss there for a while."

Looking over at her, she said, "I know when Lauren's in love, she's in love. Her entire world is Nissa and their family. It was nice to see."

"They have only been together for a few years. Do you think you should have looked for her sooner? You could have ended up with her yourself?" Skylar didn't know why she was asking. It was stupid to talk about what-ifs. Especially if Leila wished she could be Lauren's wife.

She shook her head. "No, life turned out like it should. Lauren got Nissa. That's how it was supposed to be."

"How can you not want that for yourself? How can

you just be so blasé about losing that?" The sun had set, and the car interior was now dark except for the dashboard lights.

"I guess that's my personality. And oddly, so is Lauren's. In college, we would deep dive into personality types. Learning how people tick, and learning about ourselves in the process. I knew that she loved Nissa more than she ever loved me because she carried her baby, the twins. Lauren would never do that for me."

"Did you ask?" Skylar couldn't not ask. Maybe they were more than college sweethearts. Maybe they had planned a future far beyond what Skylar and Iris had at a far younger age. Could it be possible?

"No, because we both agreed we didn't want kids back then. Which might have changed for her, but for me, I still don't want kids."

"Really?"

"Actually, I do want kids one day, just not babies. Older kids, maybe school age and above. Maybe one day when I meet the right person."

"You could still do that, even without a partner." Adoption was just as easy for a couple as it was for a single person, and Leila would be a great mom to any kid out there.

"I could, but I want to share that experience with someone. Be able to lean on someone. Make decisions with someone. It's probably not going to happen," Leila said more quietly. As she looked out the dark window, her sadness reflected back, making Skylar's heart ache. She wanted Leila to have the love she longed for. The family she longed for.

Chapter 25

It was ten after nine on Friday and Skylar was pacing. Iris had promised to get off work early and get on the road. Except she was already an hour late, and Skylar was starting to get worried. She knew if she called her, Iris would think she was checking up on her, which she sort of was. But she was worried.

Iris was punctual. Even when she didn't want to attend whatever she was going to, she was on time—except when it involved Skylar. Then she would put in longer hours instead of spending that time with her. She had promised she was going to stop doing that. Especially if they were going to make their long-distance relationship work, which they both agreed that they wanted to.

Every night that week, they had talked in the evening. Each had made promises to work on their relationship and that they would also cut each other some slack. But if one partner put forth some effort for the other, the other had to respect that. AKA not working when Skylar spent the weekend with her.

Skylar was trying to be more Zen about the relationship. Let the kinks work themselves out. They had months, if not years, of long distance in front of them, though Skylar had promised to talk to the kids about possibly moving to the city after the school year ended. So far, she hadn't brought it up. Both the kids had been in weird moods, probably because Iris was coming for the weekend. So far, the three hadn't jelled as a group. Skylar was hoping that would change this weekend with some time together.

Tonight she had planned on making a home-cooked meal for her girlfriend and her siblings, but mostly for Iris. Then she'd snuggle in with Iris to watch a movie without the kids, because they were going to their rooms and then to bed. With any luck, they would make up for the fact that the last time they saw each other, nothing happened.

But so far the dinner was cold, and time was getting late to even start a movie. But that might be because she was in small-town America now, and movies didn't start after eight. People had to sleep, after all.

"Iris isn't here yet?" Kayden asked, coming into the kitchen to snoop around the fridge. It seemed that eating over half a pizza an hour before didn't fill him up.

"Obviously not, as you can see." She waved around the empty room, annoyed.

"Aren't we in a good mood? No wonder why your friend isn't on time," he said and shut the fridge, taking a pop and a container of leftover ham with him as he left the room, smirking.

Right then, he was the most annoying person in Skylar's life, and she had to raise him. If anyone, he should pick up on how nervous she was. This was the first time Iris was coming to Warrington since the funeral. For five days, Skylar had packed as much as she dared hoping the woman would think she had been cleaning the entire time instead of putting it off and letting life get in the way.

"Skylar, a car just pulled into the drive!" Keeley yelled from the living room. It was her queue to go to her room then, but when Skylar walked into the room, she was still there, looking out the window.

"Are you going upstairs?" Skylar asked, then realized just how bad that sounded. Except she wanted to spend some alone time with the woman, and her siblings were making that impossible.

Instead of moving from the window, Keeley said, "I think it's Sierra."

Rushing to the window, she looked out herself. "What?"

"Oh, and there's someone with her." Keeley rubbed the window as if it was too dirty to see out of instead of dark out.

"I see that." She rolled her eyes and went to the door, wondering what her sister was doing there.

Opening the door, she watched a man carrying Sierra's familiar laundry basket from the truck of the car. Sierra herself was empty-handed as she came in. As if bringing home a man meant she no longer needed to carry anything.

"What are you doing here?" she asked her sister as she stepped up onto the porch.

"I live here, Sky," she stated, annoyed.

"You didn't say you were coming home or bringing a friend. Why didn't you tell me? I could have gone to Minneapolis."

"I did tell you. This weekend my roommate is having her friends from high school stay at our apart-ment. All weekend. This has been planned for months. I told you that a long time ago." She pushed past her into the house and held the door open for the man.

"And your friend?" Skylar watched him walk into the house.

Sierra rolled her eyes. "You mean my boyfriend, Dane? I thought it would be the best time to show him where I was raised."

"You didn't tell me you were coming home. I would have gone to Minneapolis," she said again just as another car pulled into the driveway. This one, Skylar recognized instantly. Iris.

Skylar went out to greet her girlfriend, happy she had finally made it. "Hey, you made it."

"I did. What a long drive. No wonder you don't want to do it every weekend," Iris stated as if that was the only reason Skylar didn't visit her every weekend.

"It's long, but it's worth it when I get to see you." She watched as Iris got her bag out of the car and then handed it to Skylar.

She was about to give her a welcome kiss her when Dane came loping out of the house to get more stuff from Sierra's car. Pulling back, she shot him a glare, hoping he would get the hint that she wanted privacy. Except he wasn't getting it based on how slowly he was trying to get everything else from the car.

Taking Iris's bag from the car, she put her arm around the woman and led her toward the house. A house that now had more people than bedrooms and, more importantly, beds.

"So, there has been a little change of plans. Sierra just got here and brought her boyfriend," she told Iris, hoping she wouldn't be too upset.

But Iris just purred, "Isn't that sweet that she brought him with?"

"It's not because now we have a full house." She

stopped Dane from going up the stairs. "You are on the couch this weekend, budd'."

"I'll just take this upstairs to Sierra," he said after dropping a bag on the floor. Skylar knew the rest of the stuff was her sister's.

"Nope, upstairs is off limits," she announced as Sierra came back down the stairs. "No boyfriends in your room."

"That's not fair. Your girlfriend's staying in your room. That's a double standard," Sierra pointed out, grabbing a backpack from Dane'

"She's not staying in my room," Skylar stated, but it was a lie. Iris had most definitely been going to stay in her room. Until now.

"I'm not?" Iris asked, not just a little annoyed.

"Where is she staying?" Keeley asked with interest.

Skylar had no idea, because the only other room in the house that wasn't already occupied was her mom's bedroom. And nobody had slept in there since her mom had died. They all knew it, and they were all avoiding the room. Until right now.

"She'll sleep in my room," Skylar quickly add'd. "I'll just sleep on the floor. Sierra, get your boyfriend blankets while I get Iris settled."

"What is the big issue, Skylar? Let them share a room so we can share a room.." Iris said loud enough for everyone to hear.

"Sierra's twenty. She's in no way sharing a room with her boyfriend." She said as quietly as possible.

"Didn't you have sex with your girlfriends in college?" Iris asked, a frown marring her forehead.

"I did, but not in this house. Mom would have killed me." She would have never even suggested it. In fact, she had never had a girlfriend share her room in this house until her mom died.

"Your mom isn't here anymore, and I came all this way to sleep in a bed with you."

"I want to spend it with you, too, but I just can't share a room with you. Not in the open. But we can sneak around after the kids are sleeping." It was a simple plan. They would just have to get up first in the morning, which they were sure to do, anyway.

"You're so sneaky. I love it," Iris whispered.

"Let's just hope it works," Skylar said, and silently added that nobody found out.

Chapter 26

Iris was at Skylar's house right now, and Leila couldn't stop thinking about it. All day she pictured in her mind what was happening. From them getting up together to them doing everything together. Including breakfast, lunch, snacks, laughs, secrets, showers, everything.

After the weekend before, she knew what it was like to be Skylar's girlfriend and was missing what she never really had. Missing something she would never have. A closeness that would never be real.

Sitting down to read one of the books Skylar had given her, she couldn't concentrate, couldn't stop seeing Skylar in her mind. Skylar in her life.

Setting the book down, she got up and headed into the kitchen. There must be something she could bake to get her mind back on track. To stop imagining Skylar in the arms of another woman. Or the woman she was in love with. Because no matter what happened between them the weekend before, Skylar was still in love with Iris.

Yes, they were going through a rough patch; they were learning to do long distance. It was an adjustment. One they would overcome because their hearts were in it. Completely.

What was she even doing mooning after a woman when there was no way that woman returned her feelings? After all, the woman was years younger than her and in a relationship. What else had to be between them before Leila finally put this little infatuation to rest?

Going into the kitchen that was completely clean, like it always was. Nothing got out of place if nobody else was there to move it. It wasn't that Leila was picky about things being a mess, but after years with Noreen, she liked everything in its place.

That woman had been messy, something she hadn't realized until they were already living together. At the time, she had assumed either Noreen would grow up and start to pick up after herself or Leila herself would get used to it, but neither of those things happened. Years into their relationship, she was irritated when she came home from work and found a mess. That didn't happen when she lived alone.

Taking a cup from the cupboard, she didn't know what to do anymore. She wanted something she could never have and couldn't get that through her head. Tea wasn't even the answer today. Well, it never was, but it usually calmed her a little.

In the mudroom, Russell barked her menacing low rumble as a car pulled into Leila's driveway. Instantly, the puppies mimicked their mama, and their high-pitched barks filled the house. Ten dogs were way too many, and it was very obvious at that moment. Though she didn't want to sell the babies, she knew it was time.

Going to the front door, she opened it to see who was there. Since Russell and the puppies lived in the mudroom, she had to start using this door more often. It only took a few lost minutes of wrangling puppies for her to hand the room completely over to them.

To her surprise, it was Keeley, Kayden, and Skylar who got out of the green SUV. The teens rushed to the mudroom and to the puppies as their sister came at a slower pace.

"Can we get some salsa? Skylar is making tacos, and the store stuff isn't nearly as good as yours," Keeley said as they came in the door.

"We'll pay you for it, but we thought we would start here," Skylar said from the porch, her hands stuffed into her jacket pockets.

"No need to pay, of course you can have some. I have far more than I need, and Keeley did help with the last batch." She held open the door to her guest.

Skylar stopped at the open door, close enough to Leila that they could touch, but didn't. "Sorry we didn't call. If you weren't here, we would have just gone back to town and bought some."

"No, it's fine." She brushed past her as she left the door, getting some space between them. "Keeley, did you want to grab some?"

But she was talking to the backs of two teenagers who were standing at the gate of the mudroom, their attention on the puppies. And the puppies knew it and needed to be loved on now.

Skylar shook her head and shrugged off her jacket. "I think they're busy."

"Yeah, I can see that. You can just go in there and play with them, but remember to give Russell some love also," she called to the kids.

"Yes, Miss Hensley," Keeley said as her brother hopped the fence, and she followed behind him.

The teens' attention on the dogs. She asked, "How many jars were you thinking?"

"I don't know. Kayden can eat one on his own. And Sierra brought her boyfriend home. I'm sure he's just as bad. So at least three, maybe four," Skylar said, holding up just as many fingers.

Leila opened the basement door and asked in surprise, "I thought it was going to be a weekend with Iris?"

"It was. Sierra just showed up with him. So now Dane, the boyfriend, is on the couch, Iris is in my room, and I'm in mom's," Skylar explained as she tossed her jacket over the back of a chair, the sweater nothing like what Leila had ever seen her wear when not in school. Did she dress up for Iris?

"Why?" She had been sure they would share a bedroom. Why wouldn't they, since they lived together in the city?

Skylar shrugged, glancing over at the teens, who weren't paying any attention to them. "I just don't feel comfortable with Sierra sharing a bed with a guy in my house. So I'm not sharing with Iris, which was supposed to be okay. We were going to sneak into each other's rooms in the middle of the night, but we both fell asleep last night. Or Iris did. I was up listening for Dane to move around all night. It was exhausting."

"Your mom's, and if I remember correctly, you have brought girls home and shared a bed with them over the years. What's different about this?" Leila hadn't been bothered by the fact when Karla had told her that, but now it did.

"My mom told you that? How embarrassing, and I never had sex in the house." Skylar blushed when she realized what she had said and to whom, then went on quickly to say, "Anyway, I'm supposed to be their mom now. I need to set a good example."

"No, you aren't. You are still their sister. Their mom is and will always be Karla. You are not taking her place in their lives, you're just expanding your roll in it," she explained, heading down the stairs.

"But they need a mom," Skylar argued right behind her.

Shaking her head, Leila told her, "They need someone who understands what they're going through, like a big sister who is going through it as well."

"So you think I should just let them share a room? Have sex?" Skylar asked in uncertainty.

Grabbing a jar of salsa, Leila argued, "I don't. But it's your choice, not what you think your mom would have done. What does Iris say?"

"That I should let them have sex so that we can have sex. But our situations are completely different. I'm an adult." She walked up and took a salsa jar herself from the same spot.

With her free hand, Leila touched her arm, stopping her. "As is she, Skylar. And you have to let her make the mistakes you have already made. She won't learn without making them."

"How do you have the answers for everything?" Her breaths quickened as she licked her lips.

Watching that tongue dart out, Leila was transfixed as she held the jar to her chest. "I don't, but I have made mistakes you have yet to make. That I hope you never make."

Skylar's own blue eyes dipped down to the jar and moved back up slowly, ever so slowly, before settling on Leila's mouth, and she leaned toward her. Unable to stop herself, Leila leaned toward Skylar.

Knowing she needed to stop this because it was a huge mistake and actually doing it were completely different things. Because there was no force on earth that was going to stop her from kissing Skylar right there and then.

Who made the final move? Leila didn't know or care. All she cared about was that she was kissing Skylar Nash. Pressing her lips against the soft pink ones made her want more, so much more.

It was Skylar whose hands snaked around Leila and pulled her closer, tight against her, with only a jar between them. But it was Leila who nibbled at Skylar's lower lip before running her tongue over the flesh, then tilted her head over so slightly so her tongue could delve into the depths of Skylar. Loving the minty taste of her.

Matching her stroke for stroke, Leila pressed Skylar's back into the shelves behind her. Pressed between the two was a delicious feeling. Suddenly, the sound of glass shattering around them brought them both back to their senses.

Jumping apart, they looked at the three jars of something red splattered across the floor at their feet. Salsa, by the looks of it, and it was now everywhere. Such a mess, but not as much as the mess the kiss had created.

Above them, footsteps hurried their way. The kids were coming to see what had happened. But Skylar and Leila were looking at each other and breathing hard, still a little caught up in the kiss. Leila longed to pull her back to her, and do it again.

"What happened?" Kayden said with concern, something he usually didn't show toward anyone there days.

"Sorry to scare you guys. I just dropped a jar on the floor. It made quite the mess." Leila shooed them from the room, glad that not much had gotten on Skylar's jeans.

"We … I'll help you clean it up," Keeley said from

behind her brother, but she was looking at them as if she knew what had happened.

"No, no, you go. You have dinner plans to get to," she insisted and was happy when the three headed for the stairs.

"But ..." was all Skylar got out before she stopped, not arguing. Her guest, after all, was her girlfriend.

"No, just go. No need to make this a bigger mess than it already is," Leila insisted and turned away from her, hoping she didn't notice the hurt. Because now she knew what tasting and touching Skylar was like, and she didn't know how she was going to forget it. If she even could or wanted to.

Chapter 27

"Where'd you get this amazing salsa?" Sierra asked as she ate another chip full of it. Though Skylar knew she wouldn't be able to eat any of it without thinking about Leila's body pressed to hers in the storage room. Her mouth on hers and wanting to never stop that feeling.

"Miss Hensley's. She makes it," Kayden said for the group.

"You should have picked up some jam while you were there. Mom used to get some amazing jam from her." Sierra went back to stirring the meat on the stove. "I should have gone with. Miss Hensley was one of my favorite teachers in high school."

"Skylar's too." Coming up behind her, Iris wrapped her arms around her waist. The movement nearly made Skylar drop the jar she was holding, as if her girlfriend would know what she had been doing with the woman they were talking about instead of grabbing the salsa. "Isn't that the name you said was the reason you became a teacher, Miss Hensley?"

"Yeah, that's her," Skylar said, not wanting to draw too much attention to herself as she spoke about the woman. In case the entire room realized she had kissed her and liked it.

"She and Skylar are now friends." Keeley dumped the salsa into a small bowl, emptying another jar.

"Then Skylar would have the skinny on her. Is she dating anyone now? My senior year, she was seeing a woman on and off for a while. Mom had high hopes, but then nothing." Sierra told the room her gossip, then asked Skylar, "Is she?"

Feeling the need to protect Leila from any and all gossip, which included her siblings, Skylar said nothing. Leila's personal life was just that personal. Though she wanted to know everything Sierra knew about this mystery woman she had dated, because she hadn't said that had happened. But did she have to? They were only friends. New friends at that.

"Wait, she's a lesbian? Why didn't I know that?" Iris asked.

Though only Skylar had probably heard the suspicion in her voice. "Didn't I tell you that?" she asked innocently, but she knew why she had kept it from Iris. But had she? She was sure that at some point, she had told Iris how she came out to her English teacher in high school. The same woman.

"You didn't," Iris insisted in a tone Skylar was well aware of. It was the same voice she always used when she thought another woman was interested in Skylar, whether it was true or not.

"They are so close that Sky gets to call her Leila," Kayden informed his sister, making the name sound far more exotic than it was.

"Hensley, is your new friend, Leila? That you spent last weekend with?" Iris demanded.

"Just Saturday. I needed to apologize for something I said earlier in the week." She didn't need all her siblings knowing about this and wished Iris would stop talking about it.

"What did you do?" Sierra asked with interest as she set out the makings for tacos.

"I don't know," Iris answered Sierra in a tone that said she should already know.

"We went for drinks, that's all," Skylar lied. It wasn't even close to it all. But there was no way she was telling everyone in her family about the brewery and Lauren. They simply didn't need to know anything about it. Nor did Iris.

"Can we talk?" Iris's tone made Skylar want to say no. These talks never turned out well for her.

"I think supper is about ready," she argued, hoping for a reprieve.

"Not yet, go talk. We have this taken care of, don't we?" Sierra asked the room, who agreed.

Iris all but pushed her up the stairs toward her bedroom because there was no way she was going to fight in her mom's bedroom. It was going to be bad because she had just been caught lying about another woman. Not that anything had happened. Well, until tonight, that was. But that wasn't coming up.

The door was barely closed when Iris turned on her. "You have been hanging out with a lesbian? What the hell, Skylar?"

"Why does it matter that she's a lesbian? We are friends, *just* friends." She folded her arms. She could be friends with anyone she wanted, after all.

"Except every time I call, you are with her. Or have just been with her." Iris matched her stance.

"Not every time," she insisted, though knew she was right. They were together more often than not since she was burned.

"You were with her all last weekend," Iris brought up that fact again, exaggerating it again.

"We went to a brewery, that's all. One single day, not all weekend."

"You were drinking beer all day? You barely like beer." Iris raised a perfect eyebrow at her.

"No, the brewery was a few hours away. There was a long drive, and we had lunch during the drive." Sure, in retelling, it sounded bad.

"It sounds like a date."

"It wasn't anything of the sort. She was one of my teachers and my mom's friend. Not someone I'd even be interested in. In fact, we went to see her college girlfriend, the woman she's still in love with." She knew she was over-selling the fact she wasn't interested in Leila. Something she wasn't as sure of anymore. Not when she could still feel her lips on her own, feel her body pressed to hers.

Shaking off the thought, she focused on her girlfriend, a woman she had loved for well over a year now and wanted to stay in love with. They had a good life once and could again. As long as she stopped thinking about a certain teacher.

Iris took a deep breath. "They're getting back together?"

"Of course not. The other woman is married. Happily," Skylar said, then realized she could have invented an entirely new relationship for Leila, one that didn't involve her for Iris.

"So she's trying to destroy two relationships at once? Nice woman." Holding up two fingers, before Iris picked up her bag from the floor. Her clothes were all over the room after one day there. It now looked just like their bedroom back home, a mess. "I think I should leave."

"Iris, no." She turned her back to her and pulled her close, ignoring how different her body was from Leila's. "It was my idea, not hers, and she's not ruining anyone's relationships. We are here together, and it seems we are doing nothing but fighting, but I don't want you to leave. Please stay."

Leaning into her, she said, "Skylar, there are too many people in this house to do anything. I thought I was coming here for alone time, and I can't get you in the same room with me for more than a few minutes before someone takes your attention. This isn't working like you said it would."

"You have it now. All on you." Kissing her lightly, she focused on her girlfriend like she should have been all weekend.

"For a second, because we have to go eat with everyone."

"How about we go get our food and eat up here? Alone, together and talk," Skylar suggested, kicking a pair of jeans to make the floor more inviting.

"That would be amazing," she said, taking out her phone with a frown, and then added, "Let me check my messages in case something important came through."

"Okay, did you want me to get you a plate?" Skylar asked when she didn't look up from her phone.

"No, I need to pick out my own meal. Spicy food has been getting to me lately." She didn't look up from her phone as she typed. "I remember my mom saying she couldn't handle spice, now it's me. I hate getting old."

"You're staying?" she asked before leaving the room.

"Yeah, I'm staying for now," she said, more to her phone than to Skylar. But it was enough. There was still another day, and Skylar planned to spend it completely with Iris.

Chapter 28

Leila kept looking out the window all day on Sunday, waiting for Skylar to show up again, to know she was thinking about her and magically show up. Even Russell was on edge, wondering exactly when the company she was watching for would come.

There was an icy wind, which caused Leila to spend the entire day cleaning her house, a deep cleaning that it didn't need. She even went through her junk drawer and organized it. Which meant she was going far too deep. But she couldn't keep her mind from returning time and time again to that kiss. To Skylar pressed into her so deliciously that she could barely tell where she ended and Skylar began.

Except Skylar was with her girlfriend again, leaving Leila to wonder about the kiss. Had she taken advantage of her friend? Was Skylar upset it had happened?

By midafternoon, she gave up on Skylar coming back. Iris was probably still there and most likely still her girlfriend because they were young and in love with so much in common. Not opposites like she and Leila were.

Tossing a handful of pens from her desk drawer, she jumped when her phone rang. Trying to control herself from diving at it, she almost didn't answer when it came up unknown. Except she didn't have anything better to do than talk to a telemarketer, so she picked up, needing a little human connection today.

But instead of a telemarketer, it was Nissa on the phone. Lauren's Nissa. "So, we were in the area and were wondering if we could stop and look at your puppies. I mean, if this is a bad time, tell me no."

"No, it's a good time." She assured her company. It was exactly what she needed.

"Does it feel weird that your ex-girlfriend wants one of your puppies? Or that I'm wanting your one?" Nissa rambled.

"No, but it's nice that we can admit that this might end up awkward," she said and gave them the directions to her house.

Since they were in town, it only took minutes for them to drive out and park their van in front of her garage, like Skylar always did. Not that Leila was comparing them, but it was the spot she had been watching all day.

Ignoring Russell's barking, Leila went out on the porch. Pulling a sweater around her tightly to ward against the cold, she watched Nissa unbuckle an infant from a car seat and lift him into her arms. Then she helped two school-age girls out of the van before closing the door. Only to have Lauren join her with an infant in her arms also and grab her hand as they walked toward the house.

Seeing her ex as someone else's wife didn't hurt as bad as Leila had assumed it would. In fact, it didn't hurt at all. She was happy for her friend and was only jealous she hadn't found it for herself in the years they were apart.

"This place is so serene," Lauren said as they walked up the porch steps together.

"It doesn't have a brewery, but it's home." Leila held open the door for them to come into the house. Russell barked the entire time.

"Not everyone needs a brewery, but we think it adds a touch of charm." Nissa slipped into the house.

Shutting the door behind them, Lauren was helping the girls remove coats as they tried to get to the dogs on the other side of the fence. They both looked a lot like Nissa, but if they were hers, she had been young when they were born. Not that she wasn't young now, because she had to be close to Skylar's age. Leila hadn't noticed that during their night at the brewery, but the woman hadn't been her focus that night, not when Skylar was close to her.

"This is Mariah and Aleah." She pointed to the bigger girls and then at the babies. "Odin and Aria."

"Nice to meet you girls, and gentleman, did you want to see puppies?" she asked the girls.

The two girls nodded and followed Leila to the mudroom. Russell had stopped barking, but had her nose sticking through the bars of the fence as if she could get closer to the action. The pups were around her and were making all kinds of puppy noises. Leaning over the fence, Leila picked up two and brought them to the little girls, since opening the gate would result in a disaster with puppies everywhere.

The girls, in delight, sank to their knees with the puppies jumping all over them. Leila was happy that they were giggling because the rambunctious little dogs could be a lot to take in. Even when it was only a couple of them.

"They're adorable. Even cuter than the pictures you sent," the older girl said in awe.

"Thank you. I didn't have much to do with it. It was all

Russell." She gave the dog a pet on the other side of the fence.

The littler girl giggled. "Isn't Russell a boy's name? How can their mamma be Russell?"

"Who said names were only boy or girl? I like to think a name is what you make it," Leila argued, like she always did when telling someone her female dog had a male name. "And I wanted to name her Russell, so I did. And if you get a puppy, you can name it anything you want."

"Is Skylar here? I guess I don't even know if you live together or anything," Lauren asked, looking around the house in case Skylar was nearby.

Lauren's question brought up too many images. From fake dating to the kiss, all of which she needed to stop thinking about. One last pet to Russell's head, and she left the girls with the puppies and went back to the couple who were taking off the babies' jackets.

"We don't." Which was the truth. Then she indicated for the couple to move to the living room, since the fire was going in there. Once they were settled, she decided to tell them everything. "In fact, we sort of lied to you. We aren't dating. Just friends."

Nissa made a noise as she curled her feet underneath her and gave Lauren a pointed look. One that even Leila understood, that she had been fully aware of that when they had last met. Apparently, she had told her wife about her theory and wasn't believed.

"Why did you say you were?" Lauren asked, ignoring Nissa.

"Because it seemed desperate to show up single after years after breaking up in order to apologize for ending our relationship. It would have come across as if I wanted you back."

"And you didn't?" Nissa asked, her hand protective on Lauren's leg.

Turning her attention to Nissa and ignoring that Lauren was there, she said, "I don't know anymore. For a long time, I knew I had lost something special when Lauren moved away. But now, seeing her again, I think it was more that I lost my best friend than a lover."

"You didn't want what you had with her again?"

"We didn't have what it took for the long-term. We both know that if we had, there was nothing that would have kept us apart. Instead, when she left, I decided to explore what I thought I was missing and, in the end, I got caught." She bit her lip. She still felt awful about that night. Not about dating, but the getting caught. That was why she didn't chase after Lauren. It was already over.

Nissa shifted in her seat. "What did you learn while you were exploring?"

Leila looked at the kids playing with the puppies and leaned forward. Nissa needed to know, or she could never be friends with Lauren without the suspicion of her wife. And that was what she wanted—her friend back.

"That we were comfortable, not in love. I wanted sex more than a few times a month and needed more. Just … more. I loved Lauren, but I wasn't in love with her. Though I didn't want to hurt her."

"And now?" Nissa asked.

"I'm glad she found the happiness she deserves. The family she always wanted." She smiled at the two babies crawled all over her ex-girlfriend.

Nodding once at the response, Nissa asked, "And you haven't."

"Some people find happiness, and others are happy just to be content," she said, far more philosophically than she felt.

"If you like her, tell her," Lauren said. It was the first thing she had said since Leila and Nissa had started their conversation.

"She's already taken. In fact, she spent this weekend with her girlfriend."

"At least she's not straight," Nissa commented and nudged Lauren.

"She's not," Leila admitted. "But she might as well be. But anyway, she's taken, too young, and my friend's daughter. Which means she's off limits, no matter how I feel about her."

"Oh, you old people with your issues with young people. I heard it all from Lore back when we met. Every time I pushed for more from her, suddenly she was old, or I was young, or anything else. But all her excuses couldn't stop us from falling in love." Nissa gave her wife a pointed look.

"I was making logical arguments, Nissa, which still hold water to this day," she said to her wife before turning back to Leila. "She's still young and doesn't understand everything she thinks she does."

Nissa pushed her away and turned to Leila, asking with interest, "Please, so what was Lauren like in college? All crazy and out of control?"

"No, never. The parties got out of control sometimes, but never Lauren. Laid back is how I would always describe her. Just like she is now. Hilary was the one who was out of control, and not just a little. Still can't see her married," Leila said, happy the conversation was off Skylar. She needed her mind off her for a while.

"And I can't see her like that at all," Nissa insisted. "She is so family-orientated."

Lauren didn't argue it, because she had seen the woman in both cases. Instead, she said, "I like that she found her happiness. I just hope that, in the end, we all will."

Chapter 29

Staring at the ceiling in her mom's room made her miss her even more. She needed someone to talk to and longed for that person to be her mom. She was nothing but a confused ball of a woman lying on the floor under a pile of blankets.

What she should be doing and what she wanted to do were complete opposites. She should have been sneaking into her old bedroom with her girlfriend the moment she thought the kids were all asleep. Instead, she was sure they were all sleeping, but Skylar was still lying on the floor, remembering her kiss with Leila. A kiss that should never have happened. After all, she was still in love with Iris. Still wanting to be with Iris.

Except the more distance and time between them, the harder it was to connect with her. When they lived together, being immersed in each other's lives was easy. Skylar worked and talked about her coworkers and students, and Iris was always talking about her job and how hard it was. That was every day. Now they weren't connecting on even that level anymore. They simply were barely talking anymore.

Iris hated when she talked about all the people she didn't know, and Iris constantly complained about work. It was probably how it always had been, but Skylar had never noticed it before. Instead, she now focused on it; dwelled on it.

She wondered what her mom would say, but knew her mom hadn't liked Iris much. Not even in the beginning, when Iris had tried to win over the woman with complements. But Karla hadn't bought it, which meant Iris had stopped trying, and her mom hadn't been impressed. It was the first time her mom hadn't liked the woman she was dating. The first time she hadn't had that instant approval for what she was doing.

In the first months, she had nearly stopped seeing her because of her mom's feelings. Except she really liked Iris. In fact, she had fallen in love with Iris, or thought she had. So, despite her mom's feelings, she had kept dating Iris and had moved in with her a year before. Another thing her mom was against.

What would her mom say about her kissing Leila, a woman who was closer to her mom's age than Skylar's and a woman she had crushed on years before? Not that her mom knew about that, but Skylar did. Many of her teenage nights had been spent thinking about kissing that woman, not that she ever would have back then. But she had spent quite a lot of time imagining it.

Sadly, her imagination had fallen short of the real thing because Leila Hensley was a grade-A kisser. Something Skylar wished she didn't know, but was glad she did.

As her body warmed at the memory, the door by her head started to open. Turning, she watched Iris slip into the room in her silk nightgown that hid nothing. Though it was dark in the room, Skylar knew it was merlot red because she had purchased it herself. Iris always wore it on special occasions, which meant this was one of those.

Except Skylar wasn't thinking about this woman. Her mind was still on another as Iris slipped under the covers and snuggled into her. Her body was slightly cold from the trek down the hallway.

"Are you sleeping, babe?" she asked in a purr.

"I was," she lied, because what was she going to tell her?

"The kids are asleep, so we can play." Her hand skimmed up Skylar's leg.

"I'm tired tonight. Can we just cuddle?" She turned toward the woman but didn't move in close to her. Couldn't make herself do it.

Iris pouted. "Can we move to the bed?"

"Mom's bed?" she asked in surprise. She hadn't even thought to sleep in the bed herself, much less cuddle with her girlfriend in that same bed.

"Yeah, the floor is hard. I want to cuddle in comfort with my girl." She ran her fingers over her cheek.

"I can't, Iris. It's Mom's bed." Skylar resisted the need to push her away.

"She isn't in it." Iris sat up a little to look at the empty bed across the room.

"I'm just not ready. Sometimes I still think she's here. That this was all a dream, and I can go back to my life again. Our life again. But then I remember it's not a dream, and I'm stuck here."

"You're not stuck here, Skylar. You are choosing to be here. We could get a bigger place, and the kids could move to the city. Or maybe they have friends who they want to live with for a while. We can make that work."

Leaving the kids with strangers didn't seem like a good plan.

"But this town is all they have ever known. I don't want to disrupt them more," she argued, the same argument she always had.

"You need to pull the bandage completely off right now so that you all can heal. The way you are treating this, there will be more and more pain a little at a time."

Groaning, she flopped onto her back. "I don't understand why everyone is trying to tell me how I'm supposed to be grieving. Who gave you all the right?"

"Who else has told you?" Iris asked, sitting up completely. "That lesbian friend of yours?"

Rolling her eyes, she replied, "Her name is Leila, and we are friends. Nothing more. You should be happy I have a friend I can talk to about this instead of being jealous of her."

"Why shouldn't I be jealous? She gets to go on dates with my girlfriend all the time, the same girlfriend I never get to see."

"Because when I go visit you, you're never around. I try, but I don't see you trying." Skylar sat up, not wanting to having this conversation laying down.

"I came here, didn't I?" Iris pulled the blankets around her as she stayed sitting up. "I had an important client meeting that I had to put off just so I could come to this town and spend time with all your siblings."

"If I move them to the city, it will be like this all the time. The kids would be living with us every day, needing my attention all the time."

Iris shifted herself in the blankets until they encircled them both, letting the warmth encircle them both. "But so would you, Skylar. And maybe we could get back to the life we used to live. I want a future with you, but I don't want that from a distance. We aren't doing well with distance."

"You're right; we aren't. We're growing apart." Snaking her arms around Iris, she felt the contentment of just being with her. A feeling she hadn't felt in a long while with Iris.

"I don't want to lose you, Skylar." She snuggled into Skylar's arms. "I love you."

Skylar kissed her hair but couldn't get the words to leave her mouth. Not after what had happened at Leila's. Could she love one woman and kiss another? That wasn't who she had been, and she didn't think she had changed. But right now, she didn't know who she was cheating on anymore.

Because it felt wrong to be in her mom's room in the middle of the night with Iris, and not because of the location, but the person.

Chapter 30

Leila was at work bright and early Thursday morning, and she couldn't convince herself it wasn't so she could see Skylar again. Not that she was thinking about the kiss on Saturday all that much. It had been four days, and in the few times she had seen Skylar, she had said nothing about it. So it was nothing.

All Monday during lunch, Skylar had talked about Iris and maybe moving the kids to the city. Something that Leila had been saying for weeks, but Iris's idea was so much better, it seemed. Not that she had said anything negative about it. This was Skylar's life.

Nissa and Lauren had left on Sunday evening, promising to be back in a few weeks to pick up their puppy. Lauren couldn't say no to her daughters. Those girls had their mom wrapped around their little fingers.

It was something Leila was happy to see, and having the girls at the house made Leila think about doing something about her own life. Maybe bring kids into it. She even decided that kids that were around Lauren's daughters' age would be perfect.

Which meant she had spent the evening during the early part of the week looking into adoption and what the requirements were. There were a lot, but nothing that turned her away from the process completely. From what she could see, they were even accepting of single people and gay people. Both would be a hard stop if they hadn't been.

Four days later, she was still excited about the idea. Though she wondered if she was crazy to even think about doing it on her own. After all, how good of a parent would she be? Because she hadn't had the greatest parents herself. Maybe being a teacher didn't train you to be a parent.

Which was why she hadn't made any moves beyond research, with a few books on order. After all, she was sure she wouldn't do anything until summer. Then she had the summer to devote to a child or even researching raising children more. Whichever she was moving toward.

"I can't believe I listened to you," Skylar demanded from the doorway, her arms crossed over her puffy black jacket, her leather bag still over her shoulder. Which meant she needed to say that more than get ready for the day.

"Excuse me?" Leila asked in confusion, not understanding what she had said that had been so wrong. There had been so many opinions she had given that could have gone awry.

Skylar looked at the ceiling and sighed loudly before saying, "You wanted me to treat Sierra like an adult? Well, what's more adult than her getting pregnant?"

"She got pregnant over the weekend?" Leila asked in surprise and shook her head at her own question. "She didn't, because she wouldn't know yet if she had. Even I know that. Can you just tell me what is going on?"

"This morning Keeley found a pregnancy test in the garbage. It's from this weekend." She didn't move from the door. It seemed they were going to have this discussion from across the room.

"Keeley?" Leila's heart sank at the thought. She was sixteen.

Skylar shook her head. "Swears it isn't hers, and if it was, why would she bring it to me? So that leaves Sierra. What am I going to do with a baby?"

Controlling her smile at her friend being overly dramatic, she said, "Let its parents raise it. You are not responsible for Sierra's offspring."

"She'll have to drop out of college. I can't let her drop out of college." Skylar rubbed her face with her hands.

"Maybe she already has a plan? It's been a few days. Maybe she and her boyfriend have everything figured out already."

"Dane. His name is Dane, and I don't know if I want him in my life forever."

"That's not your choice. It's hers."

"What kind of name is Dane?" She seemed completely focused on the wrong thing.

"Have you talked to her?" Leila asked, because Sierra had a good head on her shoulders. She was probably three steps ahead of her sister on this, since she had a few days to think about it already.

"No, what am I supposed to say? 'Are you knocked up?' She'd probably lie to me." She threw up her arms and turned away from her, going to her own classroom.

Following her, Leila insisted, "Probably not. Why don't you go down there Friday and talk to her? Figure out what's going on. Maybe you'll be surprised how much she has a handle on this."

Getting the door unlocked, she groaned, "I can't wait until tomorrow. No, I'll take the day off and go after work. Except the kids. What do I do with the kids?"

"I can take them, if you want me to. I can watch them," Leila said, trying not to sound overeager about it, but what a great test for her single-parent idea. Actual kids for a few days. She could see if she was really ready.

"Are you sure? They can stay alone," Skylar said, though they both knew that Kayden couldn't. He had been good for weeks now, but that much freedom was going to be too much of a temptation for him.

Leila touched her arm, stopping her from going into her room. Skylar turned to her in surprise, looking at her hand touching her sleeve. Retracting quickly, she insisted, "I'm sure, yeah. You do what you have to, and I'll watch the kids. All weekend if you need the time."

"I'll get everything sorted." She smiled a thank you and headed out the door toward the office.

"You do that," Leila said to nobody because Skylar was on a mission and too far away to hear what she was saying.

Not that it mattered. She had more important things on her mind than a kiss. Her family was going to change completely in the next few months. Whether they were ready for it or not.

And after this weekend, Leila's life just might also be changing. This was a test she had no idea if she was prepared for but was taking. She wanted more from life than a dog and a garden. She wanted a family of her own. And she would di it alone.

Chapter 31

This year Sierra was living off campus for the first time, and Skylar hadn't even been to see her apartment. Karla had gotten her settled in during the summer since Sierra had taken summer classes. Now Skylar felt awkward walking into this place she had never been before, unannounced.

If she had told her sister she was coming, Sierra would question her about it, so she had just jumped in her car after school and came. She'd left Kayden and Keeley to Leila, who was going to take them to her house for the night. Something Kayden hadn't been all that excited about. But Skylar didn't really care right now.

After she had calmed her enough to make it through the day by assuring her that Sierra might be planning what she was doing already. That this might not be another something Skylar had to figure out.

"Skylar?" Sierra's questioning voice came from behind her as she went up the three flights of stairs.

Turning, she saw her sister half a flight below her with her backpack over her shoulder and a frown on her face. A concerned frown crossed her face. "Is something wrong? Are the kids okay?"

"They're fine. I wanted to talk to you," she assured her quickly, not wanting her to think she came with bad news. Or bad news she didn't already know.

"Me?" Sierra asked as she pulled out her keys. "Did something happen this weekend?"

"You could say that." Skylar leaned against the wall and waited, not wanting to get into this in the hallway. "Is there something that you want to talk to me about?"

"Um, no?" she said in confusion as she opened her apartment door and let Skylar inside before dropping her bag on the carpet by the door.

Slipping off her jacket and shoes without being asked, Skylar kept her tone friendly. "Did something happen this weekend that you don't want me to know about? Because I already know, and I think we should talk about it."

"Is that why you came down here?" Sierra was blushing, even if she was trying to hide it as she removed her jacket.

"Yes, we need to talk." Her heart sank. Somehow she had hoped that the test wasn't her sister's.

"Mom already had the sex talk with me, Skylar. Long ago. Unless there is something else you think you need to add. I'm almost twenty. I have had sex and will have it again. So maybe we shouldn't have had sex this weekend, but you know how it gets away from you sometimes. I'm sure you and Iris had sex even if you slept in separate rooms."

"We did not," she insisted, then demanded, "You had sex in the house? I thought I was keeping that from happening."

"You took the kids to Miss Hensley's, and Iris was

locked in her room on the phone." Sierra just shrugged. "Isn't that why you came?"

"We found the test, Sierra," she whispered, giving her sister the chance to come clean about it.

"It's one D, Skylar. Sorry if my head isn't completely in school this year. Mom's dying affected me a lot. Since then, I have worked harder, tried harder, for her." Sierra wiped a tear from her eye, but stood tall in her defense of herself.

"What class did you get a D in?"

"Chemistry, and I have gotten my grade up to a low B, and I plan to keep it there. It's no big deal; it's one test. How did you even find out about it?"

"The pregnancy test, not chemistry," she said, wishing it was with her, except she hadn't kept it because gross.

"What pregnancy test?" Sierra asked in confusion.

"The one you took this weekend and then threw in the bathroom garbage. Keeley found it this morning," she said, needing to keep this on track. One D in a class was nothing compared to a baby. "What are we going to do about the baby?"

"Nothing, Skylar, because it isn't mine," Sierra insisted. "The baby or the test. I've never taken a pregnancy test before. I swear." She crossed her chest like when they were kids.

"If it isn't yours, then whose is it?" Skylar sat heavy on the couch, her mind racing back to Keeley.

As had her sister's. "Keeley?"

"She isn't dating anyone. Not officially, anyway." For weeks Cody had been around her during school, but they hadn't actually gone on an actual date.

Sierra sat down next to her. "She doesn't have to, but why would she show you?"

"And she said it was yours," Skylar said, wondering why she had bought the lie so easily. Probably because

Keeley was sixteen and single, and Sierra was twenty and dating a man.

"Not hers then, that's for sure. If it were, she would have panicked and come to one of us. Plus, how would she have gotten a hold of a pregnancy test?" Sierra leaned back in the chair and looked at Skylar.

"I don't know. Maybe Kayden stole it from someone."

"Let's just forget that you said a fourteen-year-old boy would steal and use a pregnancy test. Was it positive?"

"It was digital and blank. I don't know."

"You came here just because of a test?"

"You don't take pregnancy tests unless you think you're pregnant," Skylar insisted, though she had never taken one or even thought about it. Unplanned pregnancies were straight people's problems.

"Think, Skylar, because you take them when you aren't sure." Sierra tapped her on the forehead because she had assumed it was positive. "It has to be Iris. Nobody else makes sense."

"She'd never cheat on me." Skylar sat up at the accusation. She trusted Iris completely. "I know her enough to say that she would never cheat on me. And not with a guy."

"But she's been with a guy before. And you've been gone a lot," Sierra pointed out.

"You don't know her."

Sierra didn't say anything, just left her with her thoughts. Iris worked and played hard, always had, and had never been ashamed of her past. That included men and women. When they had started dating, she had assured Skylar that past was over, that she was all-in with her.

Skylar believed it was all still true. They were still a couple and still in love. The test had to be someone else's.

BY MORNING, Skylar was still wondering if Sierra was lying to her about the test because there was no way Iris would cheat on her, much less with a man. A woman, sure, maybe. But not a man. They had known each other for years, and Iris had never shown an interest in men.

After having breakfast with Sierra and sending her off to classes, Skylar got into her car and made the trip to the city. That meant driving through Warrington as she went in the complete opposite direction. She didn't even stop as she made her way past the high school where she was supposed to be teaching that day, but teaching was the last thing on her mind. She had to get answers.

It was late afternoon when she pulled up in front of her condo building, the same one she had lived in since she had gotten her first job out of college and had thought she was an adult. Instead, she had struggled with bills and roommates for the years before Iris had moved in with her.

Only then had she found someone she enjoyed living with. In fact, she loved living with her. Even if Iris put in long hours, it was nice when she finally came home to Skylar. When they were together, it was great.

They had met at a club and had hit it off instantly. Within hours, they were back at Iris's apartment, getting to know each other better. It was the first and only time Skylar had ever gone home with someone she had just met and, at the time, had been sure it would last only one night. But by morning, they had both agreed they didn't want the night to end.

When they had started dating exclusively Skylar's last horrid roommate moved in with her own girlfriend, and Iris had moved her stuff in with Skylar. Not that she hadn't been spending nearly every night at Skylar's anyway, since her own roommates were even worse.

Getting out of the car, she knew she had to talk to Iris to get to the bottom of the pregnancy test. To get the answers she deserved.

In the apartment, she saw that her old comfortable couch was gone, a couch that had been there a few weeks before when she had been there but now was replaced by a deep red velvet couch. Something she couldn't imagine sitting on, much less watching a movie on. The only good thing about it was how nice it looked in the place.

After a long day of mostly driving, Skylar fell asleep on the bed she hadn't slept on since Iris bought it. Had only seen pictures of. Not just the bed, but all the furniture in the apartment was Iris's taste and style. Nothing of Skylar's was even still there. She was glad she hadn't taken anything from her mom's house yet. Iris would have sold it before even asking her about it.

When she woke, it was already dark, and it had been the sound of the front door closing that had roused her from her sleep. Checking the clock, she saw it was after seven.

Getting out of bed, she was rubbing her face when Iris rushed into the bedroom with a giggle, a giggle Skylar had heard many times over the course of their relationship. A giggle that meant she was horny. Except she had no idea Skylar was even there, causing her heart to sink. Turns out, she hadn't known Iris after all.

With only the light of the living room, Iris backed into the bedroom. Skylar saw a man's hands around her waist as it was happening. Their bodies pressed close together, no way of seeing it as anything other than intimate.

Flipping the light switch on, Iris screamed, and the man jumped away from her instantly. Guiltily. "I assume this is the baby's daddy?" she asked sarcastically, because she didn't know and really didn't care anymore.

"Skylar, what are you doing here? How fast did you make getting here?" She acted like she had been expecting her.

"Is this your roommate, Iris?" he asked with a smirk, sticking out his hand for a friendly shake. "Kyle Douglass."

"Nice to meet you, Kyle. Skylar Nash. I guess you could say I'm her roommate. Or was." She shook his hand because she was sure he wasn't doing anything wrong.

"Kyle, you should leave." Iris started pulling him out of the bedroom.

He looked confused. "Already? It would be nice to meet one of the close friends. So we can compare notes on you."

"Shall we compare notes, Iris? On you?" The woman was looking from one of her lovers to the other in a panic. The jig was up, and she knew it. Turning to Kyle, Skylar asked, "How long have you been seeing her?"

"Four months officially. Before that, it had been more casual for more than a year as I wormed my way into her heart. As you know, Iris wasn't looking for anything serious, but I was able to convince her we were perfect together. Both lawyers from prominent families in the city. We have the potential to be a power couple before too long. And I was right, wasn't I, darling?" He hadn't noticed how Iris had been completely silent.

"Have you met her parents?" Skylar asked curiously, because she had. "What part of the city are they from again?"

"Not yet, but soon." He was catching on that something wasn't right. "How long have you known Iris?"

"Years. Wasted years, it seems. Since our so-called friendship is over." She didn't turn to the woman but knew she had heard. "Have you two talked about moving in together yet?"

Kyle snaked an arm around the woman, and pulled her to him. "She isn't ready to give up this place yet. It's an amazing apartment."

"Sadly, she has to move out. Perfect timing for her to move in with you." Skylar pushed, knowing that there was another reason she didn't want to move in with the guy.

"Seriously, Skylar." Iris pulled away from him.

Turning to her former girlfriend, she took a deep, calming breath. "Have you told him about the baby?"

"What baby? What is she talking about?" Kyle demanded.

"There is no baby, Kyle. Don't worry about it."

"I would worry about it, Kyle. After all, she took a pregnancy test in my bathroom. So she thought there was a baby," she informed the man, ignoring her now ex-girlfriend completely.

"It was negative. Thank god, the last thing I needed right now was a kid. Or ever." Iris admitted her true feelings about it coming out.

"What was all the talk two weeks ago about having kids? Settling in with a family. Getting a bigger place for one?" she asked, seeing why Iris had suddenly brought all that up. She had thought she was pregnant. As if Skylar wouldn't notice the kid wasn't hers. "Weren't you ready to make long-distance work?"

Iris adjusted her dress. "That was when I thought I might be pregnant. And, after all, who would I want to raise my kid but you? You are so nurturing, always have been. You're a teacher, after all."

"You think I would just want to raise a child with you? One you conceived when you were having an affair?" she demanded, forgetting they weren't alone.

"We're dating, so it's not an affair," Kyle insisted.

"This isn't about you, Kyle," Iris dismissed him as she focused on Skylar.

"It's my kid, so it's about me." He grabbed Iris's arm and turned her attention right to him.

"The test was negative," she reminded him. "So who was going to raise it doesn't matter."

"Iris grew up in a trailer park on the edge of town, and this is my condo," she informed him about her lie, just another in a long string he had been told.

Dismissing it, he told them, "I don't really care where she came from. What matters is who we are together. We are in love."

"I'm glad you feel that way. She'll need someone to live with, because she isn't welcome here anymore." Skylar waved her arm around.

"All my stuff is here." Iris sounded panicked, so maybe Kyle *was* just an affair, and it wasn't love, but that wasn't something Skylar was going to put up with. "I just got the place perfect for us. I bought everything with you in mind since you can't afford nice things as a teacher. We needed nicer things."

Skylar scoffed at the idea. "You bought it for you, and like everything else around here, it was for just you. Did you ever think about me?"

"Why would you buy furniture with her?" Kyle asked curiously.

Turning to him, Skylar broke the news. "Because, Kyle, your girlfriend and I have been dating for years. This was our condo, our bedroom, our bed. So it's you she's having an affair with."

"I can't do this tonight," Iris stated as Kyle glared at her before leaving the apartment with a slam of the door.

With the new silence in the room, Skylar said, "You

have a week to get everything out of this apartment, or I'm calling your boss and hiring the best lawyer they have. I'm sure everyone in your office would love to hear about your lesbian drama. Especially on the heels of your breakup with your boyfriend."

Before she could say anything more, she headed for the door. The drive home was going to be long, but she was most definitely awake now.

"You will regret this, Skylar Nash," Iris insisted as she followed her.

Turning at the door, she faced the woman she once planned to spend her life with. "I only regret that I ever trusted you. You were probably cheating the entire time."

Iris said nothing, which meant Skylar was right and an idiot at the same time.

Slamming the door herself, she stomped down the hallway, wishing once again for her mom. She needed a shoulder to cry on and a calm voice to say she was doing the right thing. Only one person popped into her mind.

Chapter 32

It was almost ten, and Leila had just brought the kids back to Skylar's house. They had decided that they wanted to spend the night in their own beds. When she had agreed to take the kids, she hadn't thought about them sleeping over, something that had never happened since she bought the house. Guests weren't something she ever had, which was why the extra bedrooms were virtually empty, even after all these years.

Thursday night Kayden had slept on the couch, and Keeley had slept on the floor in the living room. Neither of which was all that comfortable, and she would choose to sleep in an empty house herself over doing it again.

Leaving them alone meant she would have to take responsibility for Kayden if he snuck out. But the two were so tired she was sure that wouldn't happen. The days had been long for the teens since their sister had left. Leila had made sure they kept busy.

Her introduction to having kids in her life had gone better than she had expected. Both had been laid back and agreeable. They too, it seemed, were nervous about their sister and knew that Skylar would need to be gone to figure it out. Even Kayden hadn't been too argumentative, just a little.

So far, she hadn't heard from Skylar, so she didn't know if that was what was happening. That meant she had no idea when she was coming home. If she wasn't back tomorrow, she was probably going to go get the kids again. No need for them to be alone when they could be at her house. Though what she would do with them for another day, she didn't know—all her projects were now complete.

After the short drive, she pulled into her driveway. A spike of fear ran through her when she saw a car sitting in front of her garage. Living in the country hadn't bothered her, but a stranger at her house would. Until she got a better look at it, because it was very familiar.

Skylar.

Stopping her car, Leila got out quickly, though she couldn't see the woman in the car or around the car. In the light she had left on in the kitchen, she saw someone on the porch when they got up from her swing and came toward her. It was the familiar walk of Skylar in the pale light. Leila could tell she was exhausted, even from this distance.

Unable to stop herself, she rushed to her, needing to comfort her. Whatever she had learned hadn't been good. The woman looked defeated and tired.

Stopping short of her, Leila asked, "Are you okay? How is Sierra?" Leila resisted the urge to hug her, to try to comfort her. Because even in the darkness, she could see that she was upset.

"Good, she isn't pregnant," she said dismissively, as if that alone wasn't a reason to celebrate.

"Thank god. Not that she wouldn't make a great mom.

But later would be better," Leila said, not knowing what to say in that moment. Maybe Sierra had wanted a baby and now wasn't having one.

"It wasn't her test after all. It was Iris's." Skylar leaned against the porch railing, seemingly unaffected by the chilly air.

"Your Iris?" Leila asked in surprise. She hadn't seen that one coming.

"Not anymore, and not for a while. Today I found out she's been dating some guy from the office for almost a year. More seriously now since I came home, and she had more time with him. She'd been lying to him as well. Why couldn't I see what was happening?"

"I'm sorry, Skylar. You don't deserve that." Leila pulled her jacket tighter around her, wanting to comfort her but knowing that it was just an excuse to touch her, so she kept her distance, even if it was less than a foot. "Do you want to come in?"

"No, I should go home." She said the words but didn't move. "I don't know why I came here."

"I took them home, to Karla's, that is. They didn't want to spend another night with me. I don't have beds, and the couch isn't all that great. They need sleep." She hoped Skylar wouldn't be too upset that she took the kids home after Leila had promised to watch them until she got back. But she would have to understand the sleeping situation, wouldn't she? Then she added, "So they're not here."

"I should've gone home. Keeley texted me that they were at the house. I knew they weren't here, but I still came here. Still waited for you to come back. Wanted to see you. I need to know why you kissed me last weekend. You knew I was dating Iris, but you still kissed me." Skylar's eyes searched her for an answer.

"I, I … you kissed me." She stuttered the correction, not knowing how to answer that. Because Skylar was right, she knew better.

"That's not an answer, Miss Hensley." Skylar reached up and grabbed the edges of Leila's jacket in each hand, then drew her even closer.

"Skylar, you've had a lot happen today. We should talk about this another day. Tomorrow, Monday, when you aren't feeling so emotional." Letting herself get pulled into her warmth, Leila didn't want to add to the strain and didn't want to be a rebound anything. Her heart was too fragile to be broken again.

"Catching Iris red-handed with a man should have been devastating, except it was nothing but a relief. I couldn't stay with her when all I could think about was you. Kissing you again." Straightening, her lips barely brushed Leila's. "So, can you tell me why you kissed me?"

"You kissed me, but I can tell you all the reasons it shouldn't have happened," Leila muttered, not moving, their warm breaths mingling.

"Any of them good?" Her fingers skittered under the jacket and gripped Leila's shirt.

"No," she admitted as she closed the small gap between them and kissed Skylar. Their mouths met and held as Skylar cupped her cheek and took control. The kiss was more desperate than the one in the basement, desperate to get closer, touch more. Be one.

Skylar's tongue delved into her mouth, making Leila moan before it danced out. Shifting, her knees went weak as Skylar captured her mouth again. How long had it been since someone had kissed her like this? Ever? All she knew was that she didn't think she had been kissed right at all before today.

Pulling back to breathe, Skylar rained kisses across to her ear, only to stop and suckle it and whisper things that Leila couldn't make out. Leila could only hold on to her as Skylar's lips skimmed across her neck, pausing now and then to nip or lick her.

"I've wanted this so much, for so long," Skylar whispered as she slipped her hands under the jacket and shirt, touching Leila's bare skin where her jeans ended.

The cold air hit her, and she couldn't stop the shiver that ran up her spine. Or was it because Skylar was touching her? Running icy fingers over her bare skin?

"You're cold?" Skylar asked directly into her ear, causing her body to shiver again, but not from the cold this time.

"No, yes, no. I can't think when you're this close."

"Do you need space?"

"No, I need you," she admitted and regretted it. So much for keeping her feelings close to her heart. Then realized Skylar had been in a relationship with another woman just this morning. She would need time. Pushing her away gently, Leila said what needed to be said, "But we should stop."

"Why?" Skylar didn't let go, but she brushed another kiss across her lips. "Your nose is cold."

"I'm fine," she assured her. "But we need to stop because you need time to process your breakup."

"My girlfriend cheated. No processing needed."

"Skylar, this morning you were in love with her. What if you hadn't found that pregnancy test? You'd still be dating her." Was she reminding Skylar or herself about this? Because Skylar knew, but so did Leila. It was all happening too fast.

"I woke up this morning thinking about kissing you and feeling absolute guilt over it. Now I'm going to." She kissed her, their cold noses brushing as they savored the last of each other. Pulling back a fraction of an inch, Skylar went on, "In truth, Leila, we were never going to make it. Our lives weren't jelling anymore. We haven't even slept together since mom's accident."

Leila was in complete surprise. "But it's been months."

"We never saw each other, and when we did, well, it just didn't happen. We were on different pages and couldn't figure it out. And then I kissed you. After that, when I should have been having sex with her, I was pushing her away and thinking about you. I think, deep in my heart, I was cheating." Her hands, now warm, splayed across Leila's back, keeping her close.

"It was one kiss," she argued, shaking her head, even if it wouldn't matter. Cheating was cheating.

Pressing their bodies together, Skylar kissed her nose. "On you, Leila, with her. I felt like I was cheating on you."

"Oh," she said, liking that Skylar thought of them as a pair, just like she did.

"Yeah." Skylar lifted the shirt she was wearing slightly, and the cold hit Leila's bare stomach, causing her to gasp.

"Can we go inside?" Leila asked, needing warmth, no matter how hot Skylar made her.

Skylar pulled Leila's shirt down and her jacket tight around her before pulling her close again. "Can I come inside?"

The question seemed odd until Leila realized what she was asking. If Skylar went inside, they would do more than kissing. More than touching. She was asking if Leila was ready for that. A sweet gesture.

Backing away from her, she took her hand and kept backing toward the door. "Yes, Skylar, come inside."

Grinning, Skylar stayed silent on the short walk to the door. Only letting go of her hands to help open the door, then close it when they were inside. The moment the cold was shut out, Skylar took control, backing her into the door and pressing their bodies together as she kissed her breathless. Leila let it happen because it was exactly what she wanted.

Chapter 33

"I'd have bought this house just for this bedroom," Skylar said, looking at the vaulted ceiling of Leila's bedroom in the morning light. It made the large room feel massive. Not that the light walls and sparse furniture didn't help, but the entire space was airy.

Last night after Skylar had made Leila come twice against the door, they had slipped to the floor to continue. But coldness chilled them, forcing them to move three floors to Leila's comfortable bed. Once under the warm covers, they had made love again, only this time slower and far more thoroughly. Each spent hours memorizing each other's touch and feel.

Even now, her hands were still around Leila's naked body, still unable to stop touching her. Needing to make up for time lost, because she had wanted to do this for weeks now.

"I almost didn't put my bedroom up here. After all, almost an entire floor of this house is mostly empty. But if I couldn't enjoy the bedroom, who would?" Leila said of the third floor room that was the size of the other floors, with only a bathroom and closet taking away from that space.

"I am. And I would love to spend the entire weekend with you in it, but I have to go home today. The kids are probably getting worried. Or edgy, since Kayden has had freedom that he isn't used to."

"I was going to invite them out to spend the day with me if you weren't back yet." Leila ran her fingers through Skylar's hair, something she had done many times in as many hours. Each time, Skylar loved the tingles that shot up her spine.

"You are so sweet." She shifted them and groaned at how perfectly they fit together.

"I love those kids, even Kayden. Though I still can't stand him sometimes." Leila's lopsided grin warmed Skylar's heart. Kayden was hard to love right now. Then she changed the topic of conversation completely. "What are your plans now with Iris?"

"We are over," Skylar assured her. Leila had to know Skylar wouldn't cheat, or worse, go back to her ex who had used her.

Tracing a line on Skylar's tattoo, Leila asked, "But you live together, right? What is going to happen to that?"

"It's my condo. She's moving out this week. Or at least that's what I told her to do. I have a feeling she will be stalling as much as possible. But she knows what we had is over."

It was more than a little annoying that Iris was there and Skylar was far away. There would be no way to make sure she was really moving out without driving there. Which would take so much time.

Her entire focus was on the tattoo. "Do you really think she would try to stay?"

Shifting so that their eyes met, Skylar assured her, "With me here, she has more power. And maybe she will try to get back together."

"Will it work?" She sounded nervous as she asked, not meeting Skylar's eyes.

"Would I be in your bed if it was going to?" Lifting her chin so their eyes met, Skylar added, "That means no, Leila."

"You have a long past together."

"Which is over, completely. With her gone, I don't even feel the resistance I always felt about moving the kids. It's like a blanket has been lifted," she admitted with a contented sigh. So many barriers had been lifted with the breakup, which was why she was in Leila's bed this morning instead of her own, another barrier that had vanished.

"So you're moving?" Shifting, Leila sat up.

Running a hand down her back, Skylar knew she had to explain. Them being together was all so new, and they probably moved too fast last night. They hadn't talked about them at all, just the past. Now the real talk began. "No, maybe. I don't know. I love living in the city. Since high school, I always wanted to live in the city. And it's exactly like I thought it would be."

"Oh." Leila pulled away and went to her dresser and pulled on panties, not looking at Skylar at all.

"Do you know I had a huge crush on you in high school? You used to wear this faux leather skirt that was a baby lesbian's wet dream." Maybe she should have kept that to herself forever, but she wanted Leila to know she had been attracted to her for a long time.

Turning, she clinched a shirt to her chest. "I, um, didn't see you like that. Back then."

Grinning, she sat up and loved how Leila's eyes zeroed

in on her bare breasts, even as she was hiding her own. "Really, no lusting after your students?"

"Never. Students are just that kids," she denied as she finally tore her gaze away and slipped into an oversized red T-shirt that hid her to mid-thigh before going into the en suite bathroom, leaving Skylar alone.

Fluffing the pillows behind her, Skylar waited for the woman to come back. Running away wouldn't stop the conversation. From her mom, she knew that teachers talked about students and, more importantly, kept track of them after they graduated. Her mom had been able to list where at least half of her students were today. So, had Leila known about her? Asked about her?

When Leila emerged, she had brushed her hair but was still in the T-shirt, which made Skylar want to drag the woman back to bed. One night had not been close to enough for her to learn every inch of her body.

"When did you start seeing me as more than a student? When I started teaching?" She wanted to know and wondered if Leila would tell her.

For a minute, she didn't answer as she dug into her drawer. "I don't know."

Jumping from the bed still naked, Skylar stalked her, though her prey didn't move, except to turn to her in confusion, which made it easy to pin her to the dresser. "Tell me, Miss Hensley, when did you start getting the hots for me?"

Leila dipped her head, but didn't look at her directly. "When you came home from college and didn't have blue hair anymore. You were kind of cute without the garish hair. Not that it mattered. You are Karla's daughter, and I'm basically done with romance."

"Still?" She nipped at her neck, now knowing the exact spot that turned her on.

Leila pushed her away, scowling. "Nothing has changed. Romance isn't something I excel at."

"You seemed pretty good at it last night." Skylar grabbed a shirt from the drawer behind Leila, needing to put on something, but her clothes were all still down by the front door.

Leila took a step from her and folded her arms. "That was sex, not romance. And besides, I don't want to keep you here if you don't want to be here. But I'm here. Not leaving."

Confused, Skylar slipped the shirt on even if she wasn't ready to be done with Leila, since she had no idea when she would be able to spend another full night with her. Not with the kids around. After all, she was a role model now. "You wanted to be a big city reporter once. What changed?"

"Me. I realized somewhere along the way that I like what I do, where I am, and who I am. Being here." Grabbing a pair of pants, Leila pulled them on.

"Doesn't the small-town attitude choke you?" Skylar sat down hard on the bed.

"No, because I have always been who I am here. There isn't a person in this town who doesn't know I'm a lesbian. I'm just me. They either accept me or don't."

"What happens when people say things?" Skylar wanted to know, because she couldn't stand the small-town talk; the judginess of everyone.

"I simply ignore it." Shrugging off the idea, Leila came over to the bed. "They say things in the city as well. Anyway, it's been a long time since I heard anything."

"I still want to go back to the city, eventually," Skylar told her, because nothing had changed about that. "To be able to just walk out my door and go to restaurants, clubs … I like my friends being so close."

"So many people in one place. I'm over that. Maybe when I was your age. But even by then, I was here and really liked it. I guess I just outgrew city life." Leila cupped her chin and kissed her.

Her words stung, because it sounded like Leila assumed Skylar wasn't mature enough to know what she wanted in life. Or that what she wanted was somehow wrong.

"Breakfast before you go?" Leila asked.

"Can we skip it? Have sex instead?" Skylar finally wrapped her arms around the woman and pulled her closer. Food wasn't what was on her mind. Not with Leila so close.

"Who am I to argue with that?" Leila went willingly, with a giggle.

Skylar was happy that whatever had set her off seemed to have passed. Skylar hoped it wouldn't come back anytime soon.

⊏⊐

"CAN I go out with Cody tonight?" Keeley asked in excitement. Skylar was barely in the door before the teenager intercepted her, her bag still slung over her arm.

"When?" She barely understood what she had asked; it had been said so quickly as she slipped the bag to the floor. Skylar was happy the kids had been okay after her night with Leila. That the house hadn't fallen down around them.

It wasn't even noon yet, and she was already planning a nap for that afternoon because she hadn't gotten nearly enough sleep. She wasn't complaining about her late night, but a nap could make her feel better.

"Tonight. Please, Skylar? It's just a movie and pizza

after. Why won't you let me do anything?" Keeley was nearly in tears.

Dropping her bag, she took her sister by the shoulders, needing her to understand that this wasn't worth her tears. "First off, I haven't said no, and second, you can do anything you want within reason. Can you do it another night? I just got home. Are you even going to ask about your sister?"

"She texted me that she wasn't pregnant, so I don't have to." Her lip was quivering. "But what if it's tonight or never?"

"Then you're better off not going out tonight. You know he will wait if you ask, or he isn't worth the trouble." She let her go and turned to see if Kayden was there, since he hadn't greeted her at the door. Was he even there?

Keeley grabbed her arm. "But Skylar, nobody has ever asked me out before, ever."

"This is your first date?" Skylar asked, but knew it was true. Their mom would have shared if Keeley had gone on any date. Karla had been nervous about her third daughter. She had always been in the shadows of her siblings. Maybe that was going to change soon.

Keeley groaned, "Not everyone is as popular as you are, Skylar. You're always dating someone."

"Not now. Iris and I broke up. So I'm not dating anyone." Which was technically true, just not what she wanted, because she wanted to be with Leila for more than one night. She wanted to see if they could make it about more than sex. "And when I was your age, I didn't date, not until college."

It seemed her sister's concerns weren't going beyond herself tonight, because she asked again, "Can I go or not? I think I deserve to go because I spent the entire weekend babysitting Kayden."

"You were at Leila's most of the time."

"But the rest of it was me," she said, as if it hadn't been a few hours, and mostly they were sleeping. "He isn't that easy to manage."

"I guess if you want to, but we were going to Leila's this afternoon because she has a couple coming to look at the puppies," she said, hoping the kids weren't sick of those dogs yet because they were her only legitimate reason to be at Leila's. And she needed to see her again today.

"I saw them yesterday," Keeley complained as her brother came down the stairs, looking like he had been sleeping. Which was perfect. When asleep, he couldn't get into any trouble.

"How about you come with Kayden and me, and Cody can just pick you up there since he lives nearby, anyway?"

"Where?" Kayden asked, annoyed.

"So I can go?" Keeley squealed, making her brother wince.

"Leila's," Skylar told her brother, then turned to her sister. "You can, but there will be rules that you still have to follow."

"Mom and I had the sex talk already, Skylar," Keeley teased her, far more relaxed than before.

Her words took a weight off Skylar's shoulders. She didn't want to tell her about that, but would if she had to. She now just hoped her mom had talked to Kayden. That one would be even harder since she had never even thought about it from a man's point of view.

"You are not having sex with this guy, Keeley. Now you have put that image in my head. Why do you do that?" Grabbing her bag, she headed for her bedroom, needing to unpack. It seemed the kids had done just fine without her. Though she knew that wouldn't have been possible without

Leila. Which meant she had another reason to thank Leila. She just hoped she could do it properly.

Chapter 34

"There is only so much sauce we can pretend we need?" Leila whispered hoarsely as Skylar's hand slipped into her underwear, making her forget why they were in the basement in the first place.

Pressed against the door, they were reliving the kiss of a week before, only this time, neither was stopping. They were not using the shelves, so nothing was broken, and nobody would interrupt them. And they were enjoying it more because there wasn't a girlfriend hanging over them.

"Kayden is playing with the dogs, and Keeley is busy texting her new boyfriend, so we can be down here for hours without them noticing. Not that I need hours." Her fingers skimmed the spot they both knew set Leila off. It had been explored over and over again already. But what harm would one more time be?

"Oh, Sky," Leila moaned just as footsteps on the floor above stopped them both instantly.

"I hate those kids." Skylar slipped her fingers from their position, leaving Leila feeling abandoned. Having sex with teenagers around wasn't something she had ever planned for and didn't really like. Sneaking wasn't in her nature.

"You love them, and have I told you how great you are doing with them? Because you are." Leila kissed her softly one more time and took her hand. "Let's get back upstairs."

"What did we tell them we were coming down for?" Skylar didn't acknowledge what she said as she frowned at the hundreds of jars in the room.

"I can't remember and am sure they won't either." Leila grabbed a jar of jelly and headed toward the door.

It had been four days since they had woken up together after Skylar's breakup with Iris. And though they had seen each other every day at school, tonight was the first time they had spent together. Not that they hadn't spent every evening talking on the phone after Skylar put the kids to bed for hours.

So far, Skylar didn't want to tell everyone about them, though Leila had heard through school gossip that she'd broken up with her longtime girlfriend. Her argument that she didn't want them to seem like a rebound romance sounded logical, but she wanted to be able to be her girlfriend to everyone. Especially in front of the Nash kids.

So they were inventing ways to be together, like tonight's thank you dinner. The kids weren't even suspicious about it. Though Kayden seemed to want to see the puppies more and more often now that four had found new homes. He was still begging for one, but Skylar was still against it. Leila didn't want to let herself believe Skylar would change her mind and stay, but giving in to a puppy would give her hope.

"I don't know what I would have done if you hadn't

taken the kids on Friday. They were lucky that they hadn't had to drive all day Friday from Sierra's to the city," Skylar said, not for the first time, but for the first time in front of the kids.

"Did you make Iris cry when you broke up with her?" Kayden asked with a grin.

"It was a bit more mutual than crying. We both agreed that it was time. That the distance was too much to overcome, and we weren't going in the same direction for the future anymore. We want different things," Skylar explained, making it sound less intense than Leila was sure it was and completely leaving out the fact that Iris had been with a man when it had happened. Which was probably for the best. The kids didn't need to hear that.

"Did you cry?" Keeley asked with concern.

Skylar gave her a hug. "No."

"But you were happy the weekend she came up, even if she was on the phone all the time. Sierra said when we were here, she was yelling at someone almost the entire time," Keeley told them, and Leila looked at Skylar, an emotion she couldn't read on her face.

It hadn't been all that long, and they had been together for a long time. Was Skylar regretting her decision? Did she wish she had given her ex a chance instead of jumping into bed with Leila?

"Good thing she isn't coming back then," Kayden said for them all as the doorbell rang. Cody was there.

Keeley rushed to the door, and Kayden followed because the puppies and Russell were barking and whining. Recently Kayden had been taking more and more responsible for the dogs when he was here.

With everyone distracted, Skylar wrapped her arms around Leila. "Miss being with you."

"Me too," she agreed, but wondered if she was thinking about Iris still. Wanting Iris still.

———

IT WAS FRIDAY, and all Leila had to do was get through the next few hours until she could be exactly where she wanted to be. But until then, she had four teenage girls in after-school detention. Since they were from her own class, she told the office she would do it in her classroom. The four had been late for the third time this week, something that annoyed her. The school wasn't big enough to have issues making it around in four minutes.

Out of the corner of her eye, she caught a glimpse of Skylar leaving for the night with Keeley and Kayden. Since it was Friday, the other woman was in tight jeans and a flannel shirt in green hues. When Leila had seen her this morning, she had loved the new look and looked forward to seeing her lose it layer by layer.

Tonight Skylar was leaving the kids at home, and they were going out. Sure, they were only going to Leila's house, but they were going to be alone. It'd been a week since they had been really alone and not just catching snatches of time together when they thought nobody was looking, worried they would get caught.

"Why do I have to be here, Miss Hensley?" Kelsea asked in a definite whine, as if she didn't already know.

"Me too," her friend Sara added from the back corner, because she never admitted she was wrong about anything.

"Can we talk to Tony?" Kelsea asked. At this point, every student knew their automatic "get out of anything" card came from Mr. Tony Gerard.

"No, you can sit here for another forty-five minutes,

then you can go home." She barely looked up, not caring about their demands.

The four fell silent, and she went back to grading the tests the ninth graders had taken that day. It was going as well as she had assumed it would go. But she knew it could have gone better. That she should have been focusing on her classes, not on the teacher across the hallway. Something that had never happened before and never would again if Skylar left.

So far, they hadn't talked about her leaving again, but it hung over them like a dark cloud. It would until the words were said, and they defined what they actually were doing. Was it just sex, or was it something more?

When the hour was up, she let the girls leave. None of them seemed upset with being detained for an hour, and she was sure that they would do it again without a second thought the next week. Nothing seemed to get through to them this year. It didn't help that the principal refused to actually punish anyone.

Turning back to her tests, she decided she could finish correcting them here as well as at home. After all, Skylar wouldn't be there for another few hours. Since the kids had filled the house with life and action, it seemed quiet and lonely when she was alone—something that had never happened before.

After she had gotten all the tests graded, she was happy she didn't have to bring anything home for the weekend. Though she had stuck around the building for an hour longer than she had planned to, she was happy that she had no homework. And it was an hour closer to when Skylar would get to her place.

Slipping on her jacket, she headed for the door, ready to be done with this week. Ready to be one week closer to when she and Skylar were actually dating.

Walking past the office, she was surprised there were still lights on. The entire school was dark. Had they forgotten the lights on?

Except there were voices, more than one, coming from Gerard's office. One of which was a senior who had a very distinctive voice, especially to someone who had known him for years. Seth Conway. He was obviously angry, based on the elevated tone.

"I'm not doing that," the senior insisted.

"You'll do what I tell you to do, or you will be in juvey. I have kept you out of enough trouble this year to guarantee it."

"Skipping class is one thing, but selling drugs is completely different."

Gerard's voice made her blood run cold when he said, "You're not selling, Seth. You are just the delivery person. Like UPS."

Backing away from the door, she silently rushed out of the building and got into her car. What should she do next? Or, more importantly, what steps was she going to take next? Because she knew she had to call the police, except Seth's dad was a cop, and this would be devastating for the school. Gerard was a drug dealer. And using their school and their students.

So instead, she called the deputy sheriff at home. It wasn't how she should have handled it, but it was how she did it. If she got in trouble, she would be fine with that.

Once she hung up, she called the head of the school board. She wasn't happy about what Leila said or what it would mean for the school. She said to stay put, and she was heading down since the cops were currently en route to the school. So far, neither Seth nor Gerard had exited the building either. Who else had Gerard made do his dirty work? She was sure there were more since Seth hadn't been sent to the principal's office as often as others.

As the first cop car pulled into the parking lot, she sent a text to Skylar that she had to cancel their plans but didn't give a reason, because she didn't know how much she was supposed to say. Didn't know what to say, just that the moment she could, she was going to talk to Skylar. She needed to talk to someone about this development.

Chapter 35

For a woman who prided herself on having no social life, Leila was suddenly busy—so busy that she couldn't even call Skylar back after canceling on her at the last minute. Not even a text.

Not that Skylar was upset, just annoyed. She had spent the entire week working on her surprise for Leila. A surprise that she hadn't even told the other woman about. They had only planned for Friday night, but Skylar had taken it upon herself to expand that. Sierra had come for the weekend without a complaint or even an explanation beyond. Skylar needed time to herself.

When no call came in by midmorning Saturday, Skylar had driven to the city alone. After all, she couldn't stay home with Sierra there already asking questions. So she had made the drive, trying not to think about how much more fun it would be if Leila had gone with her. Instead, she was stuck thinking about the fact that she had just found out Iris had been cheating on her for years, and now Leila was already canceling dates and disappearing.

Was it possible she had met someone? Or had seeing

Leila ruined Lauren and Nissa's marriage, and now Leila was getting a shot at her old love? Would she take a shot with her old love again?

And if not, what was she doing all weekend?

The trip to the city had led her to discover that she had no furniture but, happily, that her ex-girlfriend was gone. Where she had gone, Skylar didn't know or care. Since she was alone with actually nothing to do with Iris gone, she had called her friend and co-worker, Kevin, to have lunch. At which time she had gushed about her almost girlfriend and listened to Kevin's issues with the cuts to the art program. Something she had been aware of since the previous fall but hadn't heard what was happening since the school year had started.

Not that Kevin was interested in talking about school, he was too wrapped up in the drama at home. His roommate was in love, but neither was in love with him.

"What's Beth doing?" The few times they had gone out together, Skylar had felt the other woman was too self-centered for her friend. A trait so different from her friend.

He groaned and leaned back in the booth. "She's engaged, met a guy on vacation in August, and is now engaged. So I guess I don't have a chance with her. In fact, Rick has just moved in with us. Nice guy, but I hate him so much."

"Are you going to live with them?" She wanted to know. She had known that this would happen one day, since Kevin had never been brave enough to take a chance with her.

Seeing the man so upset was hard. Kevin had always been upbeat and optimistic. It was one of the things that drew her to him when they met as first-year teachers. Beth wasn't a bad person, but she wasn't his person. Now maybe he would put some time into finding the one.

"Yeah, I have no place else to go. It's been years, and I don't want to find a new roommate again. We get along, so I don't think I'll be going anywhere, but watching them be all touchy-feely isn't fun."

Skylar snapped her fingers and grinned. "You can move in with me. Well, not *with* me, because I'm not even there. But into my place. Iris took all the furniture, but it's a two-bedroom."

"I can't," he refused quickly, putting up his hands in defense.

Leaning toward him, she saw a solution to her own problem of an empty apartment. "Kevin, I have an empty apartment, and you need a place to stay. It's perfect. I can't see myself staying in Warrington forever, and when I come back, I don't want to look for a new place."

"What about when you move here with the kids?"

"I'll give you fair warning before that happens. Besides, I don't think it'll be happening. I'm going to apply for my mom's job full-time. The kids are there, and it's better not to move them. In a few years, when they both graduate, I think we can move here. "

"We? Is there a we? Iris is barely out the door, Skylar!"

"It wasn't planned, I swear. Leila, that's her name. She works at the school with me. There's just something about her that drew me in like nobody before her. I can't even explain it. I like her so much." She covered her face with her hands, embarrassed by what she had admitted.

"Are you in love? You never gushed before about a woman."

"I'm not in love. We barely started seeing each other, and we're not even in the open."

"She's in the closet? I don't understand why you would put up with that?"

"No, no, not that. She just doesn't want everyone to

know about us. Since we work together, and I just broke up with Iris, and the kids. She has a point."

"Or are you just accepting what she is willing to give? Again?"

"I'm not," she argued, but in the back of her mind, she was thinking about the fact that Leila had canceled their first actual date. She had accepted it without a single explanation. Just like when Iris had over the years.

Kevin took her hand and squeezed it, bringing her back to here and now. "I will take you up on your offer of a place to live, but not just for me. You need to decide if you want to change every plan you ever had for a woman who doesn't want to be seen in public with you."

That was two days ago, and she was still thinking about his words. Was she moving from one bad relationship to another without a break? Destined to get her heart broken again?

By Monday morning, she was determined to talk to Leila about them before school. Except there was a surprise staff meeting. Surprise meetings for the entire staff were not something that happened often, but when they did, it wasn't usually good news.

In the back of her mind, she wondered if it was about her and Leila—not that she had seen the woman all weekend, but that would explain why. But if the school had found out about them and were not happy about it, wouldn't Leila tell her that? And why would every member of the school need to be at the meeting?

Walking into the teachers' lounge, she looked first for Leila. There was no way she would miss a meeting, which made Skylar a little worried. Now she wished she had tried harder to get a hold of the woman this morning or yesterday. What was happening, and why was she worried that it was all about her?

"What's going on?" she asked Kris, the science teacher.

"No idea," Kris whispered in concern as Skylar sat down next to her. "You?"

"Nope." She looked for Leila again, but still nothing.

Before she could ask the two teachers on the other side of the table, Carol Donnely, the head of the school board walked into the room, making all conversations stop. But Skylar wasn't looking at the older woman, but Leila, who was walking behind her. Neither looked happy.

Skylar waited for Leila to turn in her direction to get her attention, but she didn't look her way once. Her entire focus was on the woman despondent beside her or the clock in the back of the room.

"Thank you, everyone, for coming in on such short notice. I don't know how else to say this but to just tell you. Mr. Gerard has stepped down as principal of our school as of Friday evening. It was sudden and unexpected, which made for a busy weekend for our school board. As of yesterday, Leila Hensley has agreed to be our acting principal as we assess what we will need in the future. There will be a long-term substitute needed to fill her position in English, an opening that we would like to fill as soon as possible. So as of right now, bring your concerns to Miss Hensley."

"I have a question?" Kris asked instantly. She always did.

The older woman waved off the question. "I'm not able to answer any questions at this time. And since the school day is about to start, there will be no questions."

The woman then walked out of the room, and Leila followed without saying a word. Nor had she made eye contact with Skylar. It didn't even seem like she had noticed she was there.

At least now she knew why Leila was so busy. But why

hadn't she called? Why keep it a secret? What was really going on? What had happened?

———

BY THIRD PERIOD, Skylar couldn't take the unknowns anymore. Since it was her open period, she made a beeline for the principal's office because she needed answers. Now.

Ignoring Jan's protests, she walked into the office that Gerard had been in Friday and was surprised that there was nothing left of the sports trophies and his pictures around the room. Instead, it was mostly empty except for nails in the wall and Leila at a surprisingly clean desk.

"What happened this weekend?" she jumped in with, not knowing how long they had.

Looking up, Leila seemed surprised that she was there, though Skylar knew she should have known she would come at some point. And she would also know this was the period she would choose. So there shouldn't have been any surprise.

Getting up, Leila came around the desk, saying quietly, "I can't talk about it, Skylar. Let's just say it was sudden, and there was so much going on for most of the weekend. I didn't know what I could or couldn't say."

"You could have called Leila and said that." Hadn't she deserved more than a text when breaking off their date?

"Skylar, we need to talk." Leila shut the door and leaned against it.

"We're talking now. Sierra came up for the weekend so I could get away." Stepping closer to her, she knew Leila would know exactly what that meant. What had been missed out on?

"I'm sorry, you didn't say that was the plan." She shook her head nearly unperceptively. "We can't see each other, not when I'm acting principal, and you are a teacher."

Skylar took a step back and bumped into the desk. "What? There are no rules about that."

"You and I both know that there are rules, and then there are expectations. This is only an interim position. And as interim, I'm being judged on everything I do and say. This is a trial to see if I can handle the job. I want to be offered the job at the end of the interim."

Gripping the desk behind her, she demanded, "Is this why you wanted to keep us a secret? Because we're gay?"

Stepping away from the door, Leila was silent for a few moments while she walked to her desk and sat down in her chair. Skylar watched her go and wondered what she was thinking, how she could not deny it instantly, completely and adamantly.

Folding her arms on her desk, she finally spoke. "That's part of it. Anything untoward could jeopardize my job. It's probably the reason I was passed up before. I don't want to give them any reason to do it again. I have wanted this for too long."

Skylar was mad. This wasn't what she expected from Leila. She had been her gay rights hero for so long that seeing her deny who she was for a job was a surprise. Mostly because there wasn't anyone in this town who didn't know she was gay. She had lived with a woman for nearly a decade and hadn't hidden it. Until it was Skylar.

"You just said a week ago that you didn't care what others thought about your sexuality, yet now suddenly you want to hide it. I don't understand this at all."

"Not hide anything, Skylar. We need to stop seeing each other completely," Leila said with so little emotion, Skylar didn't know if she knew her at all.

This wasn't how you broke up with someone. But then

again, had Skylar put more into the relationship than Leila had? They had never discussed it. Right now, Skylar knew the answer to what they were to each other. It had just been sex.

"I guess I can't change your mind." She turned back, heading for the door, needing out. Before she did, she added, "Good luck finding a math long-term sub, because you're going to need it."

Chapter 36

Skylar hadn't slammed the door when she left. Worse, she had left it open, so Leila couldn't even break down without Jan telling the entire town about it. She had to push down her emotions until later, when she was alone.

Knowing she had to end her relationship with Skylar and doing it had been two different things. When she had agreed to be the interim principal, she knew they would have to break up. It was simply a this or that decision. Skylar had been in her life for weeks, but Leila had wanted to be a in this office for years.

And even before she had to make the decision, she knew Skylar could head back to the city at a moment's notice. Then what did she have? The same things she had before. So she had said yes to the job and no to Skylar, which shouldn't have been that hard. After all, she had been without a girlfriend for years, she could do it again. But breaking up with Noreen had been very different than breaking up with Skylar, no matter how long they had been together.

Sitting at her desk, she pulled out the file she had found

yesterday evening as she had organized the desk. Gerard hadn't taken anything, so she had boxed up all his personal stuff and left it in a storage closet, so she didn't have to look at it. Didn't have to think about all the crimes that had taken place in this office.

By midnight Friday, Seth had turned on Gerard completely and was willing to tell the cops everything. And everything was a lot. From the drugs that Gerard was handing out and forcing his favorite students to sell to the fact that most of his inventory was hidden throughout the school. From the Library to individual classrooms. It had been part of his stash that Leila herself had taken the day she burned herself. Which was something she didn't know and hadn't told the cops about.

After the drug dogs had been through the school from top to bottom on Saturday, they had searched the office she was now sitting in. Though there were no drugs found, there had been files on students and teachers for various reasons. From those who would sell his stash to those that he admired. Even with detailed notes of where the women lived and some of their habits. Information he wouldn't have unless he had been following them. The files with the most information had been Skylar's and a kindergarten teacher who was also a first-year teacher. Both were young and pretty, and neither had shown him any interest despite his best efforts.

What the cops had found out after questioning him about that she didn't know and probably didn't want to. The more troubling files were about student girls in the school. There were notes in those also, but the notes were far more cryptic. What she saw of them she couldn't make out, but she was sure it wasn't anything good. It never would be.

Since the cops had taken all those files, the desk was

mostly empty, except for a drawer that contained over a dozen applications for Skylar's job. Some had come in before Skylar had even walked into the building. Gerard, it seemed, was keeping the position open for his own sick reasons.

But that meant finding a full-time teacher for the position wasn't going to be an issue, nor was filling her position based on the applicants. Flipping through them again, she didn't want to call any of them because that would mean she was letting Skylar leave, which she didn't want to do. She wanted her forever. But Skylar herself had said she didn't want to stay here and never had wanted to be here. That she was only here until she could decide what to do with the kids. She had only taken the job because they were desperate.

But now weeks later, she wasn't desperate anymore. She was doing great with the kids, and they were settling in with her as their parent. And now that she wasn't going to be working at the school anymore, she would leave. Like she should have right away. They would be settled in the city by now if she had.

In the last week, she had become close with the two kids. She had really enjoyed spending Thursday night and Friday evening with them. The feel of others in the house had been a different feeling that she liked, but that was over, just like her relationship with Skylar. Even if it had been a week, she knew she would miss having someone to talk to. Someone to snuggle up with. Someone who cared for her. It had been a long time since that had happened.

Maybe her life as a principal wouldn't leave her enough time to want kids. Would she be so tired of the kids in school that she wouldn't want them at home? Did she really want to raise kids alone?

Chapter 37

Skylar had been pissed since Monday, since the meeting with Leila. It wasn't how she felt when Iris had said the same thing, that a job was more important than she was. Something that had been there from the beginning. But this time, underneath, the anger was hurt. A lot of hurt. Because she didn't believe Leila would be that way.

Why she hadn't felt this hurt when Iris had betrayed her, she didn't know. Had she already lost interest in Iris when they were apart? Lost the feelings she had for her over their weeks of separation? Had it been that easy to get over her? Would she just as easily get over Leila?

It was only Thursday, and Leila had been all professional this morning when she had told her that they had already hired a new math teacher, someone who, luckily for them, had a wife that was an English teacher. They would fill both positions the school had openings for. Though the math would be full-time, and the English would be a temporary position. Because Leila wasn't the principal, just the acting one for as long as they needed her. After that, she would have her job back.

So far, there had been very little information floating around the school as to what had happened with Gerard. Most assumed he had gotten bored with the job and left on his own. Even his neighbors claimed they hadn't seen him since the week before. The only reaction from staff was a sigh of relief because he had stepped on far too many toes as he tried to be friends with all the students and actively worked against the staff with discipline.

So as of today, she was jobless, which felt a little more troubling than when she had resigned from her job to move back here to take care of the kids. No, it felt more like a choice than it had been before, when it wasn't her choice as much as it had been her responsibility. Even if this time it wasn't a choice at all and that time it had.

Skylar wasn't sure why she hadn't told the kids she wasn't staying on at the school, because she should have been spending the week planning. Instead, she had put off planning. But who knew it would only take four days to hire someone?

With her breakup, or whatever it was, with Leila, she was now determined to live her life again. She was tired of putting it off completely. Her mom wouldn't have wanted that. The kids were her charges. They would be until they went to college or became adults. She no longer wanted to put her life on hold for years, so they could have the life they wanted when they didn't know anything else.

Which was why she was going to tell them tonight. Over pizza with Sierra there, because she was going to sell the house. It would just sit empty otherwise. Selling it made the most sense, no matter how much she hated doing it. It wouldn't bring her mom back.

"Pizza? I thought we were going out to Miss Hensley's tonight. She has that couple coming to look at the puppies," Keeley said as she walked in on Skylar pushing a frozen pizza into the oven.

"Nope, just a family night." Grinning, she tried to make it sound fun.

"But she doesn't like to sell the puppies and wanted us there." Kayden followed her in. It had been exactly what they had told the kids last week when a different couple came to get a dog. But it wasn't true then or now. It had been their excuse to spend time together. Now it was biting her in the ass.

"Miss Hensley said she would be fine by herself." She gritted her teeth at Leila's name. "Sierra's coming home."

"With her boyfriend?" Keeley groaned as she slipped into a kitchen chair.

"No, alone this time. She should be here any moment now." Looking at the clock, she hoped so, at least. This week hadn't been an easy one, and she tried to be upbeat as much as possible, but mostly failed. "Go get washed up so we can eat as soon as she gets here."

She pushed them from the room, only to be distracted when Sierra herself walked in the front door. At least she was happy to have what was being served, even if it was only frozen pizza. Something she probably had more often than not while living on her own.

As Keeley and Kayden went upstairs to wash their hands, Sierra followed her into the kitchen. "How are you doing since the breakup?"

Skylar looked at her in shock. How did she even know about the breakup? Then realized it wasn't her break up with Leila but with Iris she was asking about. To her, it had been so long, she had forgotten it was just two weeks before.

"Good, then bad. But I'm going to be okay." She hoped so, at least. She was tired of being sad this week.

Tired of seeing Leila, who seemed unaffected by the entire thing.

"She was a bitch," Sierra started, setting the table without being asked.

Flinching at the words, Skylar reminded herself it was for Iris and not Leila. Sierra liked Leila, after all. And she hoped all the kids would think back on her with fond memories like Skylar once had. And maybe one day Skylar would again.

"Yeah, but I don't want to talk about that now. We have some stuff to go over tonight. As a family." Skylar pulled on an oven mitt, ready to take out the pizza when the buzzer rang.

"Like what?" Turning to her, Sierra stopped what she was doing.

"Like me moving back to the city with the kids and selling the house. It will only sit empty otherwise. You are going to school for art. There is no way you are coming back here when you graduate."

Sierra sat down heavily on a chair. "What about Keeley and Kayden? What if they want the house one day? It's their home, too."

"It's just a house in a small town. We need to move on with our lives. I can't stay here anymore." Sitting down next to her, Skylar took her hand.

"You have a job here," Sierra said quietly as she looked around the kitchen that had always been a part of her life. She probably always thought it would be.

Shaking her head, she admitted, "As of Monday, I don't. They hired someone for Mom's job full-time. I can sub in the city until jobs start opening up for next year. It will be easier to move now than during the summer. Meanwhile, I'll get them settled."

"Is that what you want?" Sierra asked, her blue eyes sparkling with unshed tears.

Biting her lip, Skylar wondered if it really was what she wanted. A month ago, she knew she wanted out, but now she had fallen in love with the town and the people. With more, but she wasn't going to think about that.

"The kids will be fine in the city," she lied. She knew the kids would have a hard time in the beginning. They had never moved schools before and had always known every teacher they ever had before entering the classroom.

"What city? What are you talking about?" Keeley asked behind her, surprising her because Keeley wasn't usually so quiet that she could sneak up on her.

The timer went off, but nobody moved. "Us moving. I don't have a job anymore. It's time to get back to my life. Or what's left of it."

"I thought after you broke up with Iris, you would stay here." Keeley folded her arms and pouted, the same as she did when she didn't get her way.

Getting up, Skylar stopped the timer and pulled out the pizza. "It has nothing to do with that. I want to get back to where I was. I'm bored here."

"You have never said you were bored. Why now? Did you and Miss Hensley have a fight?" Keeley demanded.

"Miss Hensley?" Sierra looked at her and grinned as if she knew more than she had been told, which was nothing. "A fight?"

"She was made principal on Monday, and Skylar has been moody ever since. I think her trip to the city made it all sink in." Keeley shared her gossip with her sister.

"Nope, she was moody before she went to the city." Kayden decidedly came into the room, grabbing a piece of hot pizza before she could even plate it. "And I'm not moving, not ever."

"Me either. I just got a boyfriend, and now you want to move. Do you hate me so much?" Keeley stormed out of the room, pizza ignored.

"Is there a boyfriend?" Sierra came to the stove to grab herself a piece.

Skylar handed her the plate that was supposed to be the teenager's. "There is, Cody Sather. Nice kid, and not the reason I'm moving."

"Miss Hensley is," Kayden said, around a bite of food.

Glaring at her little brother, she told them, "Leila is nothing to me. I just feel it's time. Can we just drop it now and eat?"

"Okay." Sierra took a bite of the pizza and chewed slowly. "I'm okay with selling the house. I want some things to remember Mom by, but the house isn't one of them."

"We won't sell anything, but life can't stop because she died," Skylar told them and watched as Kayden grabbed another piece of pizza on the way out of the room, away from this conversation.

Sierra watched him also. "I know. You just have to convince the kids of that."

It was then that Skylar realized how old her sister had become since their mom had died. That she had to stop treating her like a kid because she wasn't that anymore. But sadly, none of them were. Not even Kayden and Keeley had come away from Karla's death the same. They were wiser than they needed to be for being so young.

But she was still in charge of them and couldn't stay here anymore. No matter what they needed, she needed to be far away from here.

Chapter 38

Leila had only been at her job a week, and she was exhausted. The students had been acting up more than usual with the shift. Though word hadn't gotten out of what had happened, they knew something was up, and it was enough to knock everyone off balance. All week she had been dealing with kids who she rarely had issues with.

Keeley had been in her office this week more than once, simply crying. It was from her that Leila learned Skylar was moving, then they were all moving. They were leaving soon, and Keeley hated leaving her boyfriend and everything she knew. She knew how the girl felt, because she felt it with Skylar leaving her behind. Though it wasn't unexpected, it still hurt.

Which was why she was spending Saturday alone and in the quiet of her living room, trying to read. Usually her favorite pastime, but now it was something she couldn't get into. Not with the knowledge that Skylar was leaving.

When exactly she didn't know, because Skylar wasn't talking to her at all. But then again, there was no actual need for it, and now they wouldn't see each other every day. The two new teachers were starting on Monday, and Leila was sure they would be a good fit at the school. She had talked to them Friday morning when they had stopped by the school with their two kids who were not quite in school yet.

The family had been nice, and Leila wanted to hate them, even if she was the reason they were there. She just wanted to turn back the clock a few weeks and teach across the hallway from Skylar. Really, she wanted to have another conversation with Skylar.

The teachers that she had gotten along with for years were now treating her a little differently, a little more reserved, and those who did talk to her were talking about students or classes or anything but personal stuff.

Which meant she had lost most, if not all, of her friends. So far, she hadn't been able to talk to anyone freely. Not a soul wanted to eat lunch with her. What she wouldn't give to have Karla back in her life. The woman befriended anyone and everyone in the school, and she had been Leila's first and best friend for years.

A loud knock on her door snapped her out of her thoughts, which was for the best. She just hoped it was someone she wanted to see, someone she missed seeing already, and she hadn't even left yet.

"Are you home, Leila?" Lauren called from the front door, making Leila realize how stupid it had been to think it was Skylar.

"Yeah, come in." She got up from the couch and went to the door. She had completely spaced that Lauren and Nissa were coming for the puppy today.

It had been Nissa who had emailed her midweek and said that Lauren had agreed to a puppy. And it had been with Nissa she made arrangements for them to come and get the dog. Leila wondered if it was because Nissa didn't want her and Lauren to be speaking yet. Not that Leila saw Lauren that way. They were only friends now.

"Are you okay?" Lauren asked as she set the little boy in her arms down on the floor as her wife followed her inside, carrying another toddler.

Leave it to Lauren to pick up on her mood instantly. To know something was up. That she wasn't happy.

"Yeah, just fine," she lied, because her moods were not Lauren's issue now. Hadn't been for years. "Have you looked at the pictures I sent?"

"Over and over again, they were so cute, and we couldn't decide." Handing the baby girl to Lauren, Nissa went to look at the four remaining dogs and Russell, who seemed to miss her pups for a day and then get on with her life with those who remained.

"Take them all then," she joked, but actually wanted to be done with the puppy-selling business. It was too hard on her.

"Not a chance. One is enough," Lauren argued. "Can I sit? Aria is still tired and heavy."

Leila pointed toward the living room and was glad she had started the fire today. "Sit down, then."

"Babe, you and the girls pick out a cute one," she called to her wife as she carried the girl with her to the living room. Sitting down, Lauren adjusted the baby on her lap. The girl in tiny bibs instantly snuggled into her mom and closed her eyes again. "She had just fallen asleep."

"She's adorable," Leila said, for once wondering if she could ever have her own kids in her life. But realized instantly that there was no way it was happening with her putting her career in front of everything, and that meant there would be no homey scenes like this in her future. She was destined to be alone.

"Looks like her mom, beautiful." Lauren looked over at the woman in question and smiled at her from across the room, who was holding the boy as she took out a puppy for the older girls to hold. The love between them was so thick, Leila could almost see it. "How is your love life?"

"There isn't one," she admitted. It was over.

"Skylar?" Nissa asked in question, walking away from the puppies and the two girls.

"Moving back to the city, taking her brother and sister, and moving away," she explained as much as she wanted to. "It's for the best, really. There is nothing for her here and, well … there's nothing for her here."

"But you," Lauren said as her wife sat down beside her.

Shaking her head, she told them, "Not anymore. I'm the new interim principal. I can't date teachers."

"That's not a rule. I know that for a fact." Nissa ran a gentle hand over her sleeping daughter's hair. "I went to school to become a principal. In fact, most principals are married to teachers or staff members because it's statistically easier to meet someone at work."

"You went to school to be a principal?" she asked in surprise. She was a bartender now, wasn't she?

Lauren leaned over and kissed Nissa's cheek. "My wife has a double major in business and education administration. I told you she was the brains, and I'm merely the brawn in the relationship and the business. I've accepted it."

"It's more than that. There was something happening at the school that I can't talk about," Leila argued, because there was no way around that.

Nissa wasn't letting it go. "Which she probably understands. She had been in education long enough for that."

"She is moving back to the city. Soon. She doesn't want to stay here, and I don't want to go with her. Not that she asked. And anyway, I have my job and my house, and my life is here." Leila watched the little girls each hugging on a puppy and what seemed like a fight, which they wanted.

"Doesn't she have a girlfriend?" Nissa asked and nudged Lauren's shoulder with a grin.

"They broke up," she admitted simply, now feeling embarrassed that they had started anything the day she broke up with Iris. No wonder it lasted a week. "Her girlfriend was cheating."

"Does she have kids? You said she has a brother and a sister?"

"Yeah, and they are upset. Keeley cries every day, and Kayden is unusually quiet—which would be great if I wasn't so worried about the outburst that's coming."

"Can't they stay here with friends? At least for a while?" Nissa asked, concern etched over her features.

Leila shook her head. "No, there isn't anyone I would trust them with."

"You wouldn't trust?" Lauren asked with a look at her wife.

Nissa nodded her head and asked, "How about you? You seem to love the kids, why not take them in? You have the house for it."

"Skylar would never let me take the kids." Leila looked around the room.

Even if Skylar agreed, there was still the matter of the empty rooms. The kids barely made it through a night on the couch and floor. How could she ask them to do it for months? Years?

Lauren broke the silence. "Maybe you should talk to her."

"Maybe you should keep your nose out of my business. I don't tell you how to live your life," she snapped at Lauren.

Lauren just took it with a grin. "So you don't need a girlfriend, and you don't need her kids around either. Maybe you are doing perfectly okay being alone."

"I am happy, too," she insisted, but knew it was a lie. She wasn't happy without Skylar. But she had made her decision, and it couldn't be changed now.

"I can see that," Lauren said as her daughters brought over a puppy, the chosen one.

Within an hour, the couple, kids, and one puppy were gone. Heading back to their happy lives. She knew the puppy was heading for a new home. A family. Something she never would have gotten if she had stayed here. There were no families here, just her. Alone.

Chapter 39

They were on load three with the trailer to get furniture from their mom's house to Skylar's apartment. Saturday, they had taken everything from the living room and kitchen, and boxes upon boxes she knew she would have to go through, or she wouldn't be able to move into her apartment.

Thanks to Kevin, she had extra muscles, even if moving her in had made it impossible for him to move in, and he would have to stay with his crush and her boyfriend for a while longer. Thankfully, he wasn't complaining about it.

Though she had been dreading today for as long as she had lived in town. But the group had done everything in their power to make it fun and not the emotional day it was. Now after a few hours the house was just a house and not the home she remembered it to be.

Today it was the beds and bedroom furniture, and she was starting to think that they would have to make another trip. But this one would be the last this weekend. Tomorrow was Monday, and she had to enroll the kids in school and get everything straightened out about that. And she would have to inform her former school and a few others that she was available for subbing. Which would fill her time quickly.

Also, as of Monday, the house she had been raised in would go on the market. The realtor she had talked to had assured her it wouldn't be for sale for long. It was a cute house in a great neighborhood, and there were so many people looking, which had surprised Skylar, but then again, she was looking to leave and assumed nobody was interested in staying.

When she asked if she should paint it, the realtor had assured her that the new owners would probably want to paint it themselves, something that made her a little sad. Her mom had a flare for color, and she hated to see that be painted over.

Sierra had invited her boyfriend and his buddy to come down and do most of the heavy lifting. Which they seemed happy enough to be doing, which left her to pack up.

Box after box was quickly packed, since they weren't really looking at anything. It made Skylar sad, but she was already mad at herself since she had months to actually do this and hadn't. And she would have to go through the boxes in her small apartment, made smaller by having more people than bedrooms in it.

She was shoving photo frames into a box with card games when Keeley came rushing into the room. "Miss Hensley's here."

Skylar's heart skipped a beat at the words. Leila was there. She almost smiled, but the memories crashed through her mind, and she was pissed at the woman again. Pissed that the moment they started something, Leila was no longer interested.

Pushing the box away from her, she got up to face her

again. Something she had thought she was over doing. That was the reason she was pushing so hard to get out of this town as soon as possible. To avoid running into Leila.

Coming down the stairs, she saw Leila in jeans and a brown jacket, her hands stuffed in the pockets as she looked around the nearly empty room. As usual, her hair was resting on her cheek just before she brushed it behind her ear. A move that Skylar had seen so many times and thought was adorable.

Forcing herself to sound cheery, she asked, "What can I help you with today, Leila? As you can see, we are very busy."

It seemed she wasn't ready for her because the woman jumped at the sound of her voice before turning slowly to meet her eyes. "I can see that. I was hoping to talk to you for a moment."

"Sure, talk away," she said, not knowing what they would talk about now. There was nothing between them.

Leila looked around the room and added, "In private."

"There is nothing you can say that the kids can't hear," Skylar stated, because there wasn't.

Sierra came into the room and looked from Skylar to Leila and back again. "Hi, Miss Hensley."

Leila gave the girl a smile, something she hadn't given Skylar. "Hello, Miss Nash. I mean Sierra. How is college treating you?"

"Good, I'm enjoying everything about it," Sierra assured her, then added, "I was going to take everyone out for lunch. How about you stay here, Skylar?"

"I don't need to." She was sure her sister had picked up on the tension between them. How could she not?

"Yeah, you do," Sierra assured her before getting everyone out of the house so fast Skylar couldn't seem to stop it. Maybe the entire group was as tired of packing as she was.

Once the front door closed, Skylar demanded, "What do you want, Leila? I thought we had discussed everything already. Back when you decided we were nothing to each other."

Leila actually flinched at the words but recovered quickly, and all emotion left her face. "We did. About that. This is something else."

"What?" Skylar demanded, wanting this over.

"I was thinking, wondering, am thinking, about Keeley and Kayden. Are they still not wanting to move?" she asked, her toe tapping, belying her nerves at asking the question.

Rolling her eyes, she knew Keeley had been going to her for support. "Do you even have to ask?"

"Would you be interested in leaving them here?" She kicked into the hardwood floor with her boot. "With me? I can take care of them during the week. Bring them to you on Friday, pick them up on Sunday evening. It's not ideal, but it would allow them to stay here and give you the freedom you deserve."

"I deserve?" Skylar wanted to know what made Leila think she deserved freedom.

"Deserve is a strong word, but Karla wouldn't want you to feel trapped raising her kids. You're still young and don't need this. Nor does Sierra."

"But you're fine with it?"

"I'm already here, already know the kids, already settled."

"Wouldn't it be a conflict of interest to have the kids at your house?" she asked, because Leila was so interested in those lately. "You're the principal. Aren't you supposed to use this time to impress the board, not raise someone else's kids?"

"I'm asking, Skylar. You're not forcing it on me."

"You don't even want kids." It was what Lauren had told her once.

"They'll never be my kids, just like they will never be your kids. They'll always be Karla's kids. I just want to be there for them when they need someone and let you live the life you want at the same time."

"They don't need you. They have me."

"And they will always have you." She scuffed her foot into the hardwood once. "That was all I had to say. It was just a thought. Good luck."

"I don't need luck. It's my life."

"Sorry for getting in the way of that," Leila said so quietly that Skylar barely heard her, but she did.

Before Skylar could say anything, Leila slipped out of the house and walked to her car. Skylar just watched her leave, wishing she could call her back, but what would be the point? Leila had chosen her job over what they had. Skylar couldn't change that.

But what about her offer? Why would she suddenly be interested in taking in the kids when she never had before? Was it really because she wanted to help Skylar?

But they did it feel like she was just proving to everyone that there was only one Nash kid she didn't like?

Chapter 40

Late Sunday night, the temperatures dipped, and it was snowing, which Leila wasn't ready for. There was one puppy left. So at the end of the day, she had gone out with Russell and Puppy, as she was calling her until she could find a new home for her. It shouldn't be hard to sell her, because it was as easy as opening her emails and responding to one of the dozen requests she had gotten, but she kept putting it off. As if having that one puppy would fill the gap in her life. The one the Nashes used to fill.

As she waited for the puppy to stop sniffing the dead leaves in the yard, she wondered when her life had gotten so lonely, because she had never noticed it before. And having a friend like Karla hadn't filled the gap before Skylar came to town. Unfortunately, the gap had appeared when Skylar had, but it didn't seem to vanish when she had.

And Skylar was gone. She may have left already or was leaving in the morning, but she was gone from Leila's world. And there was no getting her back. She had her chance at happiness, if even for a little while, and had blown it.

Beside her, Russell let out one of her deep, menacing barks, drawing her attention to the road as a lone car went by. It was Sunday night, but it not everyone was home tucked away from the cold and snow.

To her surprise and the puppy's great fear, the car turned into her driveway. An even bigger surprise was that it was Skylar's car, something she had been sure she would never see in her yard again.

As she watched, the puppy pulled on the leash and was free before she could grasp it tighter. The puppy was gone and running straight to the car, just like her mom. Except Russell knew to stay away from the front and tires, something her daughter didn't.

In horror, she watched as the car kept moving. Skylar hadn't noticed the little dog running in the dark. Not until she was right in front of her in the headlights. Then she slammed on the brakes.

Running toward the car, she was more concerned that if Keeley or Kayden were in the car, they would have witnessed the accident. They would be traumatized by it. And it would be their last memory of her house. Death.

Skylar jumped out of the car and raced to the front, getting there just as Leila had made it there. Neither wanting to look, but both needed to.

Skylar was already in tears. "Oh my god, I hit it, didn't I? She came from nowhere."

"It's not your fault. I should have kept hold of her better. Way better. I don't know what I was even thinking. Why didn't I just sell her this week? Why was I so fucking selfish to keep her?" She kicked at the ground, hating herself. Nothing she did was right anymore.

Skylar touched her shoulder. "Leila, you weren't being

selfish. She would have been so happy here. So happy here. You are an amazing pet parent. Look at how great of a dog Russell is."

"No, I'm not. I'm not good at anything." Leila turned to walk to her house, away from this woman who kept showing up and breaking another little piece of her heart. Showing her what she was missing in life. That she would never get.

Before she made it three steps, Skylar grabbed her arm and spun her back to her. "Leila, stop. Is that her?"

Leila looked to where Skylar was pointing and watched the puppy run around the stopped car in the dark, barely keeping up with Russell, safe and happy. Her little legs going as fast as she could.

"She's okay." Leila sank to her knees, and the puppy and Russell both went running to her to lick her face and get pets. "You gave Mama a scare there, girl. Why did you do that?"

Skylar squatted down also and added more pets before turning to her. "I want you to take the kids. I mean, we had a family discussion, and the kids want to stay here during the week like you said. With you."

"I don't want to take your kids from you." Wiping away tears, she didn't know if they were from the puppies or from the offer. She wanted the kids to stay in her life so badly.

The snow was still falling in big flakes, covering Skylar's dark hair in white, something she didn't even seem to notice. But then again, neither did Leila. Her entire focus now that the puppy was safe was being with Skylar, if only for a few minutes on a Sunday night, in the snow.

"You're not, honestly. You're solving a problem we had no way of solving. I don't have room in my apartment, and I don't have a job right now. On top of that, they don't even want to leave. They want to stay with you. If it gets too much, we can work it out then. This might not be the perfect solution, but it might be something close to it." Skylar got to her feet and brushed the snow from her jacket.

"And the house?" Leila followed, looking over at her own. The one that would soon be filled with teenagers. At least for a while.

"We are still selling it. It's too much for any of us right now, and though Mom loved it, she loved other things, too. Those are the things we will keep. The smaller things."

Leila shoved her hands in her pockets, suddenly planning for something that she hadn't even dreamed possible an hour before. "I don't have beds or anything."

"They already have those. We can move them in tonight if you want. Or wait if it's too late already. Or you need time. It's a big change, after all. I know, I lived it." Skylar brushed dampness from her cheeks, either from the snow or tears, or possibly both.

"Tonight works. As long as you're sure," she asked again, not wanting her to change her mind but letting her if she needed to. After all, it was her family.

"Yeah, I'm not ready to be a mom yet. Time hasn't changed that, and time never will." Skylar pulled her phone from her pocket and sent a quick text.

"Thank you," Leila said quietly, hoping Skylar didn't hear but needing her to just the same.

"For what?" Skylar asked, picking up the puppy to hug since it had run back to her.

"For sharing your family with me. I know I don't deserve it." She knew this took a lot from Skylar. Her family was her everything.

"No, you don't." She handed the puppy to her and went back to her car. "But you're the only person I would allow my siblings to live with. They deserve the best, and that's you."

Before she could answer, Skylar got into her car and reversed out of her driveway. Leila didn't have much time to get the house ready for two teenagers and all their things, but she was going to be ready if it was the last thing she did.

Because if she had the kids, Skylar was free to be a single woman in the city again. Leila knew for a fact that she wouldn't be single long. Leila knew how easy it was to love her. Now, even before it happened, she regretted taking the kids in. She didn't want to see Skylar in love with someone else and being in a front row seat as it happens.

Chapter 41

"You're sure you're okay with the kids being here?" Skylar asked again, because she didn't want to ruin a perfectly good relationship, even if it was just a roommate relationship.

"Of course. It's just for the weekend, and now that your mom's house sold, you can't keep going to Warrington every weekend," Kevin assured her again as he flipped through the channels on the TV.

It had been three months since Leila had taken the kids, and every weekend, she had made a point of going to Warrington to spend the weekend with them. Even Sierra had made it half the time. And once, when she had been sick with a cold, Sierra had gone alone.

The kids seemed to be thriving with Leila. Their grades were improving, and Keeley was still dating Cody. As far as Skylar knew, Kayden hadn't been in trouble.

This would be the first weekend she would have them come to stay with her. Without the house, there was no place for her to stay other than at Leila's, and she wasn't ready for that yet.

Despite their relationship being short, it had lasting effects on Skylar's life. She missed her. Even after all this time. Iris, on the other hand, was a memory she didn't like to revisit, but not because she still had feelings for her. It was just a reminder of how much she had accepted and shouldn't have.

Leila was driving the teens to the city, and Skylar would drive them home on Sunday. Home. It was odd how she still considered Warrington home, even if there was no place for her there anymore. The apartment had lost any of the appeal it had, even if it was full of the furniture her mom had so lovingly picked out over the years. It still wasn't home.

Kevin was a great roommate, which had been a slight surprise because they didn't seem compatible in the living-together way. But he was neat and tidy and made meals that melted in Skylar's mouth—something she was sure his old roommate was missing.

On the job front, she was still subbing but managed to work almost every day and could turn down any day she wanted, like Friday or Monday, depending on which end of the weekend she wanted to make last longer. Jobs for the next school year would be opening up soon, and she had her resume ready, but would miss the short weeks. This time she was going to be picky and not take the first job that opened up. She had a great job once, and she could find another one.

Kevin didn't take his eyes off the TV. "I was going to go out tonight, anyway. Clubbing. Maybe I won't even come home."

"As if you would find a woman who would take you home," she teased him as she cleaned the dishes from the night before.

"It could happen. I am, after all, a catch," he assured her with a confidence he didn't actually possess.

She chuckled at him. "No argument here. If I was the least bit interested in guys, I would date you."

"See? I just have to find another, just like you. But straight, and possibly blonde or a redhead." He winked at her. "When are they getting here?"

"Soon. Leila had to work until four, and then they were heading out." She glanced at the clock and knew it would be any minute unless Leila got stuck in traffic, which she could. But maybe she would have left early.

She wished she could tell herself she was excited to see Keeley and Kayden, but she knew it was Leila she wanted to see. If only for those few minutes before she drove away. It was never enough time, but neither seemed willing to invite the other inside during the drop-offs. So it was just a few moments they shared.

"We should go out for supper. I know this great burger place the kids would love," Kevin said, seemingly wanting to spend time with them.

"Jonesing for a burger?" she asked, wondering if he would really go out clubbing tonight or just stay in. Either was fine with her. Kevin got along with the kids when he helped them move.

"I'm not going to say no to a burger," he said happily.

He had been so much help during the move she wouldn't tell him no. He had even stayed at Leila's to set up the beds and put away some of the kids' clothes before they headed out. It was after midnight before they got back to the condo and then had to deal with the mess that it was. That had all been done with no complaints.

Ten minutes later, Leila was ushering the kids into the apartment. They were right on time, and Skylar hadn't had to worry too much or call once. Which she was grateful for.

Each kid had a backpack for the weekend trip, but space was still going to be limited. Both also had an air mattress and would be sleeping in the living room. This would either be the first of many weekends spent like this, or the last. Skylar would just have to rent a hotel room in Warrington every weekend if this didn't work out.

"Hi guys, how were the roads?" she asked because they had gotten snow this week, and she had worried about this weekend actually happening.

"They were fine, no issues," Leila said, pulling off her mittens.

"Good. How was school and everything?" She grabbed an air mattress from her.

"School's fine. Leila says I have to join a team sport this spring," Kayden argued, as if Skylar had been involved in this discussion. Which she wasn't, but she would back whatever Leila decided.

Tucking her mittens in her jacket pocket, Leila argued right back at him, "You are running all the time Kayden, you could just as well join track."

"I don't do team sports," he grumbled and sat down next to Kevin.

Shaking her head at her brother, she said, "It would be good for you, Kayden. Keeley, how are you doing?"

"Awful, Cody's a jerk." She headed for the bathroom, slamming the door behind her.

"They broke up," Leila mouthed at her.

"Too bad," she said, but didn't mean it. Keeley was too young for a serious boyfriend, but she couldn't be told that.

Leila gave a silent agreement as Keeley came out, still upset but not crying. Skylar hoped the weekend would take her mind off her misery. And if she knew anything about teenage love, they would probably be back together in a week.

"Hey Leila, how are you?" Kevin asked, getting off the couch.

"I'm good, Kevin. Busy, but good." She pulled her mittens out again.

"Who's in the mood for burgers?" Kevin asked the room.

The kids instantly jumped on the idea of eating, but Skylar's stomach was twisted as she grabbed for her jacket before turning to Leila. "You can join us."

"Ahh, no thanks. I should get going." She put the mittens on.

"Are you doing something while you are in town?" Kevin asked, because he knew Skylar wanted to know but just wouldn't ask.

"Just going to head back. It's been a long week," she said, stifling a yawn.

Skylar straightened and asked with concern, "Why didn't you say that? I could have come and gotten the kids."

"No, it's fine." She waved her off.

"Why don't you two talk, and we'll get burgers," Kevin stated and pushed Skylar back into the apartment gently. Before closing the door, he leaned toward her and whispered, "Talk to her."

Skylar couldn't even argue before Kevin and the kids were gone, and she was alone with Leila. Completely alone. They barely even talked since the kids had moved in with her, and when they did, it was completely about the kids.

"I should get going," Leila said, but she stayed where she was.

"Can we talk? Without the kids?" She waited for agreement before going on. "Are they really doing okay?"

"Yes, I think they are. Still miss their mom and you, but they're focusing more on school and friends than they did before. Neither is getting into trouble, at school or at home." Nothing had changed. Kayden still got into trouble, but far less than he did at the beginning of the year. It seemed he needed a steady hand, and Leila had it—something his mom and sister didn't.

"Good."

"And how is big city life?"

Skylar just shrugged as she took her jacket off again. It wasn't all that great. She didn't feel the pull to go out. To meet up with old friends or even to meet new friends. Instead, she stayed in and was mostly bored. Missing the kids. Missing Leila.

"We need to figure out how to do this exchange stuff. Maybe I just should come and get them and bring them back. Less pressure on you." She could take the day off now. Next year would be different, but they would deal with that then.

"I'm not busy. I can bring them," Leila argued.

"It's Friday night. You can find something to do," Skylar suggested, but shouldn't have. The last thing she needed to think about was Leila out in a bar, alone. Or not alone.

"Yeah, I guess you're right. I should be able to find something to do." She backed slowly toward the door of the condo. Except Leila didn't walk out the door at that moment. She stopped, lingered.

"Do you need any suggestions?" Shoving her hands in her pockets, Skylar took a step toward her.

"No, probably not." Licking her lips, Leila looked at hers. "I should probably just head for home."

"Probably." Taking another step, she was close enough to touch her but didn't.

"I can't leave Russell alone for long," she said breathlessly.

"And that puppy you had to keep?" she added, because Leila still had the last puppy, which the kids loved. They had named her Alice. A name Leila had been against, but the kids had won out, as they always did.

"Kayden wanted to keep her." Her eyes were on Skylar's lips.

"I wish more people knew you were such a softy," she teased her, breathlessly. "I'm going to kiss you."

"Kiss me." She pulled Skylar close, their lips meeting.

Wrapping her arms around her jacket and all, Skylar kissed her with everything she had. All the pent-up frustration and need came out, and based on Leila's response, she was feeling it, too.

Pulling off the woman's mittens, Skylar tossed them over her shoulder, paying no attention to where they landed. Only then did Leila's hands start roaming her body, sending shivers through her as she did.

Leila said into her skin, "We shouldn't do this."

"I know, but I need you again." She was too busy ridding her of the jacket, needing to feel the woman against her again.

Leila's warm hands were quickly buried under Skylar's sweatshirt and cupping her breasts. "Once, just once. To get you out of my system."

"Once." Skylar pressed her into the door and captured her lips in a searing kiss. It was exactly what she needed, except she wasn't sure she could stop at once. In fact, she was sure she couldn't. She needed Leila more than she needed to breathe.

Chapter 42

Spring was finally making an appearance in Warrington, and Leila was ready. She had actually been ready for weeks since the snow had melted, but she had wanted to share the experience with Skylar. The kids also, but she had wanted to do it during the weekend with everyone. But the seasonal window to plant her garden was almost closed, so they needed to get it done today.

"Skylar, it's time to go downstairs." She kissed the bare shoulder on the tattoo she loved to trace and smiled when Skylar groaned and stretched.

It had been weeks since her first trip to the city, and Leila hadn't brought the kids there since. Instead, Skylar came to Warrington and stayed with her and slept on the couch. Which was where she started, but when the lights went out, she would find her way into Leila's bed. Not by accident.

Which meant that Leila was looking forward to the weekends and was happy the weekdays were flying by with her job and kids. There was so much to do that she hadn't even over-planned her garden. Something she was prone to do, buying far more seeds than she would ever use in a season.

Today she was happy she had those extra seeds, because she hadn't been able to get away to buy new seeds. Even when Skylar was there, she hadn't felt the need to leave. How could she waste a moment of time with her?

But today she needed to get it done. This was the latest she had ever planted since buying the farm. And this was going to be the first time she had help with that task. A lot of help with the teens and Skylar.

"One more minute," she said into her pillow.

"That's what you said last weekend, and Kayden almost caught you coming down the stairs." She kissed the center of her back. "We could just tell them."

She shook her head into the pillow. "No, they will think I'm only coming every weekend to see you and not them. I don't want them to get the wrong idea."

Leila pulled away from the woman and sat up. Maybe she herself was getting the wrong idea. Was she letting herself feel too much? Maybe this was nothing but a fling for Skylar. They hadn't talked about it; just let it happen. And continue to happen.

So what if it was just a fling? Why couldn't Leila be happy about that? What is the harm in this going nowhere?

Except Leila was tired of not going anywhere. She wanted more. But what more would entail, she didn't know.

"You should get going," she said, maybe more gruffly than she should have because Skylar sat up behind her.

"Are you okay?" Skylar looked at her.

"Yeah, just fine."

"Good. What was your plan for the day? We are

heading out to see Sierra. Have lunch with her and Dane. Still hate the name, but the guy is growing on me."

"Just going to work outside." Getting up from the bed, she had lost her excitement for the day. They were leaving, all of them. Now it was going to be just another year where she planted alone. As if nothing in her life had changed since last year.

"You can come with us," she said from the bed, though Leila had left it, wondering if Skylar being with her was just a convenience. That she never planned to tell anyone that Leila wasn't who she wanted people to see her with. Hiding her away from her real life until she had no use for her when the kids were gone.

Grabbing her robe from the chair beside the bed, she slipped it on, feeling she had missed something in their relationship, like the fact that there wasn't a relationship at all, just a bed for the weekend. A convenience.

"I wouldn't want to send the wrong idea to the kids." She headed into the bathroom, not looking back at her, tired of the conversation.

When she emerged ten minutes later, Skylar was gone, and she had even made the bed so Leila couldn't even imagine her there. But that was the point of hiding their relationship, after all. Leaving no traces.

Taking her time, she got dressed. After all, it was Skylar who made sure the kids were up and fed today and, since they were leaving, dressed. When she was in the clothes her garden clothes, she decided to just ask them during break-fast to change their plans or modify them. Not that she wanted to come between the family or force herself on them. That was the last thing she wanted to do.

Going down the stairs with her plan in place, she realized that the house was unusually quiet, unusual for a morning. Kayden like to talk and talk loudly. Which meant one thing. They were already gone. They had left without even saying goodbye to her.

Fighting back tears, she headed for the door. No coffee needed today. She just wanted to get the project done as soon as possible. All the earlier excitement and joy were lost now.

Once in the morning sunshine, she reminded herself that the Nash family wasn't hers, and they would never be hers. One day, they would leave and wouldn't have a reason to return. Just like everyone else in her life.

Today was as good as any to distance herself from them, so her heart wouldn't be broken when that day came. It would take everything inside her to do it because she wanted nothing more than to spend the rest of her life with the Nashes. Except they weren't hers and never would be.

—

THE BELL HAD WRUNG at least five minutes ago, and even from a distance, Leila knew exactly who was in the corner of the hallway that she always hated because it gathered young couples in love. Keeley and Cody were late for class, and based on how long the kiss was that she was interrupting, they were back together. Their on-and-off relationship made Leila's head spin most days. It was either love or hate with those two.

Keeley rebelling wasn't what she needed today. Before she even made it to her desk that morning, she had been told that during a science test on Friday, the entire sopho-more class had cheated, same with a math test on Monday. All twenty-eight of them.

From what she had learned in the hours since then, one of the students in that class had gotten a master key to the school from Gerard months before. Since then, he had been breaking into the school regularly to get test information. Lately, he had started bragging about it to his classmates and, for the first time, had proceeded to give everyone in the class a copy of the test that included the answers. How many had used it, she would probably never know.

The repercussions were going to affect the entire school. And her performance as the principal at the time. After today, there was no way she was getting the job full-time. In fact, if she were on the school board, she would fire herself. She wasn't any good at this job.

Even after knowing everything she now did, she hadn't thought the kids capable of cheating en masse. Some of them, sure, but not all of them. So now they had to punish an entire class. She was just happy that neither Keeley nor Kayden were in that class. Though she knew every other student in it.

Now it was up to her to dole out the punishment, and with only a month left of school, she didn't know what would be the right move. Go easy on them because it's the end of the year, or make an example of them. All she knew for sure was that without Gerard's influence, this would never have happened.

Gerard had admitted to so much wrongdoing when confessing his misdeeds, but not giving out keys to the school. So what else was coming their way? Tonight, the entire place was getting new locks.

Her stomach was rolling at the thought of having to deal with yet another Gerard-created problem. In the weeks after he left, she was putting out more of his fires than were actually created by the students. In recent weeks, she had thought that was over, but now she was thinking it was never going to end.

This wasn't what she needed today, not with her already worrying about the distance between her and Skylar since the weekend. They hadn't spoken since Sunday, either on the phone or by text. For days, it was complete silence, and she could feel the wall going up around them. The calls to say goodnight like they had been doing for weeks had stopped cold.

The Nashes had been gone all day Saturday, only returning well after dark. During that time, Leila had planted her garden alone and ignored that she was losing her future with a woman who didn't even want a present with her.

Sunday hadn't been any better. Skylar had left early because it was a friend's birthday. Something she hadn't mentioned until she was already packed up and leaving. They hadn't had a moment alone together because Skyler, for the first time in weeks, hadn't ventured upstairs. Instead, she had slept on the couch. Leaving Leila to wonder what she had done and if she could fix it.

But how could Leila argue? They had no relationship, so they had no connection. If Skylar thought Leila was in the way, why did she come to the farm? Why not ask Leila to bring the kids to the city? Why keep coming?

So she just had to get her emotions under control and not let Skylar breaking her heart bother her. She couldn't let anything bother her, not even Keeley's relationship, that the longer it went on, the less she liked it.

"What's going on here?" Leila asked as the two jumped apart, looking guilty.

"Nothing, just going to class." Keeley adjusted the books in her arms and dared Leila to say anything more.

"Cody, get to class. Keeley, I need to talk to you before you go." She glared back at the girl she'd been raising for months.

Cody didn't say a word to her as he hurried down the hallway to class. He knew better than to get between the two women. In the months since she had moved in, she had relaxed enough to argue with Leila a lot. Sometimes Leila enjoyed it as the teen being just that, a teenager. But not today.

When the boy had gotten to his class, Leila turned to the girl and stopped being her principal and became the woman who was raising her. "Keeley, I thought that you'd broken it off with Cody? That we decided you wanted to focus on your studies?"

Taking the familiar defensive stance, Keeley glared at her. "You decided, not me. I don't want to be alone again."

"That's no reason to date someone."

"What do you know? You never date."

"I, I …" she stammered because Keeley was right. She didn't date, not even with Skylar. Was it considered dating? Which made the accusation completely true, but it made it hurt worse to hear it said out loud. "My personal life isn't part of this conversation."

"Neither is mine. It's my life, so you can just leave me alone."

"We will talk about this tonight. Go to class."

"I need a pass." She held out her hand as if she deserved one.

Leila shook her head. "No, you were late before I stopped you. You're late now. Go to class."

"I need a pass," she said again, insistent now, and a lot louder.

"I said no." Leila wanted to knuckle under and give in, not wanting the girl who lived with her to be upset. But she also knew Keeley was in the wrong.

Keeley stomped her foot and yelled, "You're a poor excuse for a mother, do you know that?"

Leila saw teachers looking out their open classroom doors at them, watching. No one shut their door to let Leila and Keeley do this in private. Instead, everyone was listening to them. Judging her.

Lowering her voice, she insisted, "I'm not trying to be your mother."

"That's not what it looks like to me. You are so desperate for a family that you've glommed onto mine. Well, we don't need you. You will never be the mom my mom was. Your aren't even mom material."

"Keeley Nash." She had nothing else to say. It was true, after all. All of it.

"I wish we never moved in with you. Skylar should never have allowed you to raise us! I'm calling her to tell her what you are doing." She walked down the hallway a few steps before turning back to her and added, "And you are failing as principal. Everyone can see that."

Leila was speechless. There was no comeback. She had wanted too much and had gotten it, but she couldn't control any of it. Her life was spiraling out of her control, and she couldn't stop it. Did she even want to try anymore?

Her stomach rolling, she rushed back to her office, grabbed her car keys and purse, and walked out. If she said anything to Jan, she didn't know. All she knew was that she needed to get away from her mistakes and bad decisions.

With a call to Skylar had to leave a message. Her not answering her phone meant she didn't want to talk to her anymore. Rambling she to tell her to come and get the kids as soon as possible, Leila drove away from Warrington, needing to be as far away as she could possibly get, fast.

Chapter 43

Playing the voice mail back didn't ease Skylar's worries any more than hearing it the first time. Because hearing Leila's voice crack at every word made her foot press even harder on the gas pedal to get to her. That the kids didn't love her was ridiculous; that they were better off without her was even more preposterous. The kids were thriving for the first time since their mom died because they were in her care.

But what Leila had right was that they couldn't go on anymore like they had been. Skylar knew she didn't want to be in the city anymore, not when Leila wasn't there. For weeks she had been living for the weekends, working just to make money, not for the enjoyment. Something she had always had before. But instead, she just missed her days at Warrington more and more.

It had been Leila's sudden coldness that had made Skylar return to the city early by pretending there was a birthday party she needed to get to. After all, she had waited until the entire family was gone before she planted her garden. Skylar had been waiting for her to say she was going to do it and was going to make a point of being there for it. Instead, she had said nothing and done it when nobody was around. Which just told her that Leila was tired of everyone being there all the time.

So was she tired of the kids or just Skylar? That was the question that circled her mind. A question she didn't know if she wanted the answer to because either one would break her heart.

That was why she had walked out of the class she had been subbing in without a word, which meant she wouldn't be subbing there again, and there was no possibility of a job later. She had burned that bridge to the ground, but she was fine with that. She knew where she had to be, and that was with Leila.

The school day wasn't even over yet when she pulled up to the school. As she got out of her car, she saw the school board president, Carol Donnely, walking into the building from her car. Carol owned a real estate firm in town, the only one, and rarely came to school during the day. There was simply no need. Was Leila in the building? Was Leila gone? What had happened here today?

"Carol, wait a moment," she called, needing to know what the other woman knew.

She stopped and turned, greeting her with a smile. "Skylar, good to see you. How is everything going since the move to the city?"

"Good, very good. What are you doing here? You don't usually end up at the school during the daytime."

"Just some odds and ends to work out. I'm sure that Leila informed you of the cheating scandal that was uncovered on Wednesday."

Skylar wished she had been a better girlfriend and just called her instead of letting Leila dictate their relationship. Now she knew there was more going on with Leila than just their personal issues. Something she should have realized. Leila had a stressful job now.

"Why would she do that?"

"I thought that you two were ... Well, never mind. With an entire grade involved, this will be Leila's first big test as a principal. Based on everything I have heard and seen, she's passing with flying colors." Carol started back toward the building.

"That's good to hear. I know she wants to apply when the listing opens. She loves the job. Not that she didn't love teaching, but she truly loves being the principal." Skylar knew she was laying it on a little thick, but she wanted Leila to have everything she wanted.

"She has the job as far as we're concerned. Passing her up the last time was a mistake—in more ways than one. I wanted her, but others didn't feel she was right for the position. Between you and me, it serves them right to have hired a drug-dealing stalker over a gay woman. Right? If you ask me, I think she should have told us to shove it after we passed her up. I would have, but then again, I have a temper. She is a damn good teacher and goes above and beyond for her students. Always has."

"Yes, she has," Skylar agreed, not following the conversation. Gerard had been caught selling drugs? Stalking someone or someones? If any of that was true, there was a good reason to install Leila in his place so quickly and quietly. Was she sworn to secrecy and couldn't tell anyone? Is that why she hadn't?

"I might be old school, but you need a little strictness in these kids' lives. Not every teacher needs to be strict, mind you, but a few. Your mom was the complete opposite, as are you, and kids need that also. A balance."

"I love her balance," Skylar gushed and opened the door to the school for the woman. "Leila is the reason I became a teacher, not my mom like everyone thinks. Looking back on my life, she was a big influence on me. Nothing that she taught, but how she taught, how she treated her students, how she treated life. I came out to her in high school, even before my mom."

"You're not the first student to say that." Carol nodded in agreement.

Surprised at her words, Skylar stopped just outside the school offices wondering how many others had said something. How many more would in the future? "I wasn't the only one who came out to her?"

Carol shook her head. "Not that part. I wouldn't know that part. But she's an amazing teacher who makes her mark on many of her students. We have always been lucky to have her in our district."

"We are dating. I mean, I didn't say all that because we're dating, but we are. Or we're sort of fighting right now. Not that it matters … We will get over it. I know we will."

"You didn't have to tell me." A knowing grin spread over her face.

"I know, but I also don't want to hide anything from you or anyone else." She wanted to pull the words back instantly because beside Carol was Jan, and she had heard everything. Dread washed through her because it was up to Leila to tell her staff, not anyone else who would tell everyone before morning, based on the excited glint in her eye.

Before she could say anything to the pair, she was rushed by Keeley, who it seemed was back with Cody again based on his being near her and her not glaring at him in annoyance. Kayden was slower at coming toward them.

"Where is Leila? Jan said she left early, but she didn't say anything to us about it. Just told us to ride the bus home." Keeley rolled her eyes at the mere suggestion of taking a bus anywhere.

"Leila needed a break," Skylar said, knowing that Carol and Jan were listening to everything that was said.

"From us?" Kayden asked, his voice cracking like it hadn't done in months.

"I don't know. Can we just go out to the farm and see her before I put words out there that she doesn't mean?" She headed for the door again, letting Keeley and Kayden follow. She needing to get away from the older women before she said too much again.

"She isn't answering her phone," Keeley stated, but that was something Skylar already knew.

"I know. She isn't answering my calls, either," she admitted, not telling them how many times she had called since getting in her car and heading back to Warrington. Instead, she insisted, "Let's go talk to her in person."

Half an hour later, they realized in person wasn't going to happen because she wasn't at the farm. Russell and Alice seemed like they hadn't been outside all day, which meant she hadn't stopped. But where would she go? Why wouldn't she come here? This was her happy place.

"Did something happen today?"

"There was a cheating scandal at the school," Kayden said, all-knowing.

"It's huge. The entire sophomore class is involved. Nobody has heard anything about the punishment yet," Keeley interjected from the couch.

Sitting down heavily on the couch, she knew that wasn't enough. Leila could handle that with a hand tied behind her back. There had to be more. "Anything else?"

"Keeley went off on her. Everyone heard it happen." Kayden pointed at his sister.

Keeley shot her brother an annoyed look. "She was butting into my life. I don't need that."

Her brother ignored her. "Keeley yelled at her in front of the school. Everyone heard it. By lunch, that's all anyone was talking about."

"What did you say to her?"

"She was lecturing me about Cody, as if she has any say in my love life. So I just reminded her that she isn't my mom and that I should move in with you." Keeley looked all smug at what she did. "She should be happy I didn't bring you up."

"Why would I come up?" Skylar wanted to know.

"Oh, please, Skylar, you use her as a sex object when you are around and then forget about her the moment you leave. Using her to get over your breakup isn't healthy for anyone. And Leila deserves better."

"I was not using her to get over my breakup. I like her a lot. We were trying to keep you two from feeling like I wasn't interested in you by coming here."

"Why would we think that?" Kayden asked in confusion.

"I don't know. You're kids." All of Skylar's arguments went out the window. She had no idea why she thought these two wouldn't understand.

"We aren't babies; we understand. And for the record, we like Leila a lot more than Iris. God, Iris was such a pill. Leila is ..." Keeley stopped, as if she said too much by admitting she liked Leila in her life—despite what she told the woman today.

"Like a mom," Kayden said and glared at his sister. "More like a mom than you were, Skylar."

"I wasn't trying to be your mom. I was always just your sister. Nobody will ever take the place of Mom in your lives. In our lives."

"Sometimes we just needed a mom-type person. Like Leila." Keeley curled her legs under her.

"For the record, I wasn't using her. I was falling in love with her. Or not. When did I fall for her? But then you guys moved in and, suddenly, she had people around her all the time. I didn't want her to regret taking you guys in and feel that I'm using her."

Keeley asked, "If you're not using her, why do you only come on the weekends? Your job is open again. You can be here all the time if you wanted to. It seems like you like your life in the city and weekend here because we are here, and you get sex."

Blushing at her sister's insinuation, which on the surface looked true, Skylar sat down heavily. "Leila didn't tell me that my job was open."

"Maybe she wanted you to be interested in her and not a job," Kayden tossed a pillow at her.

Grabbing the pillow from midair, she tucked it into her, knowing that wasn't true. It was deeper than that. It was that she wasn't sure Leila would allow herself to be in a loving relationship. Because she admitted months ago that she hadn't allowed herself to love someone. Noreen hadn't been love; Noreen was just a person who was there. It hadn't been enough. Was Skylar?

Chapter 44

Walking into the large car dealership, Leila felt like she was a teenager again. How many times had she walked into this place? It looked completely different from when she had last been there, modern and flashy. But the feel of it was the same. Fast-paced and cutthroat.

Her mom had been the center of that attitude. From the time Leila had been young, Donna Hensley had been a better businesswoman than she had been a mother. She had wanted nothing but perfection from her only daughter. Leila knew she never got it and had been disappointed until the day Leila walked away.

A disappointment she knew still lingered, even after she had been gone for nearly half her life. Her mom had never been easy to forgive or forget, and Leila had committed many sins on the way out the door back. Changing her degree to journalism and being gay had destroyed every plan Donna had for her daughter. Plans that included taking over the dealership and marrying well.

Before she could turn and run away from this place and the memories, a man in a crisp white shirt and khaki pants rushed up to her with a fake smile. He was around her age, but she could tell he was trying to act younger, more in touch with the younger customers since he had an iPad clinched in his hand and a haircut that didn't match his receding hairline.

He made eye contact with her. "Can I help you find your next great ride?"

That was the same line her mom used to use with every customer who walked in. It still sounded weird and put her off buying a car completely. It was why she rarely bought a different vehicle and was only on the third since she last walked into this place. She had gotten rid of the first only because that car had been damaged beyond repair before she even graduated from college. The second had a major engine issue from five years before. One that she was driving, she hoped, would last as long as that one. Though it was already having more issues than she liked to think about.

"Can I talk to Donna Hensley? Is she even still here? I'm sure she's not." Turning to leave, she knew this wasn't going to help her, anyway. In fact, she knew her mom would do nothing but see her as the failure she was.

The man touched her arm lightly, making her stop and turn back to him. His smile was a little more genuine this time. "Of course she's here. She's here every day. Can I say who wants to speak with her?"

"Her daughter. I mean, Leila, just tell her Leila," she said quietly, maybe too quietly, because this man would surely not know Donna Hensley had a daughter. Nobody here would know anymore. It had been too long.

"Sorry, I didn't recognize you, Miss Hensley. I'll go tell her you're here." He looked up toward where she assumed her mom's office was. "Take a look at the cars while you wait. Maybe you will find one you can't live without."

"I'll …" Stopping, she had no idea what to even say, but it didn't matter because he was already gone.

Did he say he didn't recognize her? But would he have? Did she know him? But he called her Miss Hensley like he had. But she knew she didn't know him.

As she waited nervously, she walked to the shiny red cars in the middle of the showroom. Her mom always liked to have matching vehicles in here. It seemed that hadn't changed, and today's color was red. Looking inside an SUV that was far bigger than she needed, she saw the price tag was far closer to the price of her farm than the price of what her actual car had been. It was also twice the size of what she currently drove.

Even from the outside, she could tell the kids would love this SUV a lot more. They would have room to stretch out and even bring along a friend, or three friends. But then she remembered that she didn't need something bigger; she was just her after today. Skylar would never let her see the kids again. Not that they wanted to see her. She wasn't who they wanted in their lives.

"Leila?" A familiar voice from her past said her name from behind her in wonder.

Turning, she saw an older version of the mom she had last seen. The woman before her wasn't as polished or controlled as she had been back then. The career-focused business woman was still there, but she had softened.

But could she soften enough to accept her this time?

"Hi, Mom," she said, fighting back the threatening tears as if she were still a child, one who was in trouble.

The words were barely out before Donna Hensley did something she had never done before by pulling her into her arms for a hug. Arms wrapped around Leila made her feel something she hadn't felt in so long. Unconditional love.

Years ago, this wouldn't have happened. Her mom never let her employees see her emotional. And hugging her daughter was showing a weakness that wouldn't be tolerated. But today it was as if they weren't on the showroom floor where anyone could see them.

Today, for the first time, she could hear the tears in her mom's voice. "Leila, you came back to me. How have you been? Are you alright? Are you happy? Do you need anything?"

"Nothing." Pulling out of her embrace, she only answered the last because she wasn't alright, and she wasn't happy. But her mom couldn't fix that.

Donna had tears in her eyes as she looked into Leila's, as if she could see her life through those eyes. But maybe her mom could. She could see a lot more than anyone else she had ever met before. Her lip quivered. "This car? It's yours if you want it. Anything in here, or outside, or anywhere on the lot. Just ask, and it's yours. You can have it all if you want."

"I don't want it, Mom," she assured the woman. Her mom had tried to buy her love all her life when all she ever wanted was time with the woman, time and attention. Something that couldn't be bought, so it was never given.

Pulling away and with tears running down her face, Donna looked Leila up and down. "Look at you all grown up. You're beautiful, simply stunning, and look so much like your daddy. I know you always did, but now so much more than before. You cut your hair."

Leila reached up and touched it as if it hadn't been years since she cut it off. "I did."

Donna wiped a tear from Leila's eye that she hadn't even known was there. "It looks gorgeous like this, all of you does. I've tried to find you, you know. Over and over again through the years. Never with any luck. Where have you been?"

She looked around to see if anyone was watching, but to her surprise, nobody was. The showroom was empty of anyone. "A little town called Warrington. Since graduating from college. I got a job and stayed."

"Are you married? Do you have kids?" She took both Leila's hands in her own.

"I used to teach English and have been the acting principal at the high school for months," she said and realized how little she had achieved in the years they had been apart. There was nothing there that would allow her mom to brag about her to her friends.

"No, Leila, that's your job. I want to know about you and your life. The important stuff," she said as if she hadn't been a workaholic Leila's entire childhood.

"My job is my life. Just like you. Except I'm failing at it, I can't do anything right anymore." Leaning against the car in depression, she bounced off, remembering how much it cost. She didn't need to damage it and be forced to buy it.

Donna just frowned before opening the door and pushing Leila into the driver's seat of the super expensive SUV. "Get in the car."

Not wanting to argue, she got in and let her mom slam the door shut, before Donna walked around the car and got into the passenger seat before stating, "Hensleys don't fail, sweetheart."

Letting the new car smell surround her, Leila gripped the steering wheel and stared out at the quiet showroom. "This one does. You said I would, and I am. I guess I'm here to be told I told you so. It's what I deserve, after all."

Reaching over, her mom took her hand and gripped it hard as tears slipped from her eyes. "I made so many mistakes with you, Leila. The biggest ones of my life. Sadly, I was too self-centered to even realize it for years. Then one day, it hit me. I had lost everything when I lost you. That you wouldn't coming back groveling and doing what I wanted you to do. That you were going to make it on your own. Without me to even see it happen."

"I'm still gay, Mom," she reminded the woman, as if her mom could forget the reason she had disowned her in the first place. The reason they had been apart for so many years.

Not letting go of her hand, Donna shifted in her seat until she was nearly facing her. "LeLe, I assumed you would be. My therapist tells me that doesn't change over time, no matter who wants it to. She also reminds me that you being gay doesn't change who you are, that you are still my daughter. Will always be my baby. That I can love you no matter what."

Tears sprung to her eyes. This was what she had always wanted to hear from her mom. The fact that her mom, the woman who needed nobody, saw a therapist was a surprise. Almost as big as knowing her mom was following the advice given.

"No, you shouldn't. Nobody can love me. You said it yourself—I'm unlovable." The words had circled her mind since she drove away that day. Words that had proven true over and over again since then. The ones that were still true, even if her mom accepted her sexuality, that would remain the same.

"Oh, Leila, I didn't mean that. I was angry and hurt and took that out on you instead of realizing that you needed a better me than you had known before. For a long time I tried to control you, but I couldn't, and I shouldn't have tried. You were always going to be your own person. It took me a long time to realize that."

"I should have just done what I was told. I have made so many mistakes and have nothing to show for it."

It was something she had been slow to realize. Maybe if she had stayed, she would have built a life that wasn't so loveless and lonely. One where she would never have met the Nashes. Never had her heart shattered.

"LeLe, you can have this entire company if you want it. Just say the word, and it's yours. It's always here waiting for you. But only if you want it. I will never force it on you again."

Leila didn't want to say yes. Even now, she couldn't bring herself to say the one word her mom wanted. So instead, she deflected. "How many dealerships do you have now?"

"Just three. I stopped buying more when I lost you. What was the point, after all? Then five years ago, I went through a cancer scare and sold the others. The first three I bought are the only ones I have. The ones your dad and I bought together. I just can't let them go," Donna admitted, looking out at the dealership. This was the first her parents had purchased, the one that started everything. Which was why she walked into this one. Why had she known this one was where her mom would be?

Touching her mom's arm, she told her the truth. "You would've still been my mom."

"Can we go home?" she asked tentatively before adding quickly, "Or are you going somewhere? Do you have plans?"

She shook her head. She had no plans, not for a long time. "No, nothing. Just driving and the road seemed to lead here. No plans at all."

Her mom jumped in with, "I would love to spend more time with you. Did you want to go home? Stay the night with me? Your room is just how you left it. I couldn't bring myself to change anything."

Her words surprised Leila. She had assumed her mom would redecorate her room the instant she was gone. Not just because she had said she was never coming back, but because Donna had always wanted her to change her room. To make it a grown-up room.

"Sure, I'll just get my car." She reached for the door handle.

Instead of getting out, her mom reached over and grabbed her arm. "No need. We'll just take this one." With her other hand, she reached over and honked the horn. Which caused a garage door behind them to open up slowly.

It seemed her mom wasn't ready for them to spend a moment apart, but since Leila truly had nothing but her phone in her car, she decided to let her mom have her way. As of right now, she didn't need her phone, anyway. Skylar wasn't on the other end anymore. Probably never would be again.

Raising her hands, Leila asked, "Do you want to drive? This is too expensive for me to just drive off with."

"No, you look good there. Do you remember the way?" She buckled her seat belt.

"Yeah," she admitted. She would never forget the two-mile drive to the house she had been raised in.

As she drove out into the sunshine, her mom said, "I'm glad you came back, Lele."

"Me too." She wished she had come back years ago. That maybe it was she who had held the grudge and not her mom. Was it possible that they both just overreacted and both were too stubborn to admit it?

Chapter 45

It was dark and hours since Skylar took the kids home from school, hoping that Leila was at her house. Leila loved her place, and she had been so sure she would be there. Now she was just hoping she would return to the house again. Soon.

As she paced the living room, she worried. Where was she, and why wasn't she calling her back, or the kids? Would she leave her dogs alone?

"What's for supper?" Kayden asked from the doorway to the kitchen. He acted like he hadn't been eating almost nonstop since they got home. Keeley, on the other hand, had been in her room. Which was for the best since Skylar blamed her for Leila leaving. Probably unjustified, but it had been after the argument that Leila had vanished.

To her credit, she had taken both dogs to her room, something Leila wouldn't allow, but Skylar didn't stop. At least the dogs weren't missing their human as much as the other humans in the house were.

"Make whatever you want." She waved him off. She wasn't hungry and wouldn't be until Leila was back.

"Leila was going to make her famous homemade pizzas tonight. You can make that," Kayden said, but Skylar could order take out like a champ, not cook. And never when she was stressed.

"I have no idea how to make that. Aren't there any frozen ones?" She knew there was. Since the kids had moved in, there were always frozen pizzas in the house.

"Yeah, but I like the ones Leila makes better." Shrugging, he kicked at the rug. "Is she coming back?"

"Yes, this is her house."

"Will she still want us when she does?" He asked the real question.

"She loves you guys. No matter what Keeley did today or you do, that won't change," Skylar said, but it didn't answer his question because she didn't know anymore. "In fact, I am thinking about moving back here. To be with you two more."

"But I like it here. I don't want to leave. I'm tired of being moved around all the time."

Staring at him, she wanted to laugh. He'd moved once in his life, and that was in with Leila. But managed to hold back because he didn't need to be laughed at tonight. "You kids are the most important thing to me. I'm not moving you. In fact, I shouldn't have left you to begin with. If she'll have me, us, I want to move in with Leila and for us to be a family. With Leila."

"What about your apartment?" Kayden asked an oddly adult question for the teenager.

"Kevin will take over the lease like we had decided before I moved back." Though she hadn't talked to him about it, she was sure he would be okay with it. He liked the place and would even keep the furniture since she would have no need for it here.

Not that she and Leila had talked a moment about this,

but it just felt right. Or maybe Skylar was reading this all wrong. Was that why Leila had left? Was she watching the house, waiting for them to leave? Should they just leave? But where would they go?

"You love the city, don't you?" Keeley interrupted her thoughts as she came down the stairs quietly.

Turning to her sister, she said, "I thought I loved the city, but the city is missing everything I do love. You and Kayden, this town."

Keeley sat down on a step. "Leila?"

"And Leila, you're right. I love her," she admitted to the wrong people. She should tell this first to Leila, not everyone else.

"I didn't know that, and I 've ruined your relationship." Keeley started to cry.

"No, you didn't. We did that all by ourselves. Or I did," she said, defeated. She had wanted nothing but to talk to Leila.

"Where is she?" Keeley asked, looking out the big window into the darkness.

"I don't know. She still isn't answering her phone." Skylar touched the phone in her pocket, the one that had left so many unanswered messages with the woman.

"Isn't there anywhere she would go?" Kayden wondered out loud, not for the first time that night.

Skyler pulled out the phone and looked at it, at a website that could be the only place Leila would go. But if she was there, what then?

Reluctantly, she admitted, "There's only one place I can think of, but I don't think she would go there."

"Can we go look?" Keeley got to her feet in excitement.

"No, I will call. You two go make something to eat. No need to go hungry, not at Leila's house." She gave them a wan smile before turning her back and pulling out her phone.

She dialed the number, even if the last person she wanted to talk to was Lauren. What would the other woman say about Leila leaving? Would she tell her that was the first sign Leila wasn't interested? Or maybe not even the first sign, but a big sign. Would Lauren know before Skylar they were over? If there was anyone, it would be her.

"Hello, Lauren. It's Skylar Nash."

"Leila's friend Skylar. How are you?" Lauren said cheerfully.

"Not great, Leila's missing. There was an incident at school today, and she left. I was wondering if she called you? Or if she's there?" Skylar didn't want to get into small talk, not when there were more pressing things to talk about.

"No, not for a few days now. Maybe a week or so." Lauren sounded concerned.

"She left me this weird message and then vanished. She didn't come home. I don't know where she is." Pacing again, she needed to keep moving, or the worry would be too much.

"What did the message say?" Lauren asked.

"Something about failing and the kids didn't want her in their lives and that we couldn't go on anymore." Something she hadn't told the kids.

"She doesn't take failure well, or didn't when I knew her, because of her mom."

"Still doesn't. I just want to find her. Talk to her." Skylar sat down on the couch and fought back her tears.

"She hasn't been here. Nissa even says no. I wish I had something to tell you."

"When you were together and fought, where did she go?"

"We didn't fight," Lauren said with a chuckle.

"No, seriously." She didn't need their perfect relationship thrown in her face tonight.

"I am. We were not fighters. Hilary used to be so annoyed that we didn't fight, telling us it wasn't healthy to always be agreeable to each other. Even when we broke up, we didn't fight. I just walked away, and she let it happen."

Rubbing her forehead with her free hand, Skylar admitted, "I guess you were the perfect girlfriend. Who can compete with that?"

Nissa came on the phone. "You can. It wasn't a healthy relationship. Arguing, fighting, making up makes a good relationship. What they had was friendship with the benefit of sex. And not often enough is what I got out of Lauren. They weren't going to last forever."

"But I'm not like Lauren," she said, knowing she couldn't compete.

Nissa blew out a breath into the phone. "And I'm not like Leila, but we are what the other needs. Leila loves you. I saw it in her eyes when she spoke about you. She loves you, not Lauren."

"I just wish I knew where she was." Skylar felt the tears threatening.

"She will come back. Her home is there." Lauren had the phone again, it seemed.

"What do I do until then?" she asked, even if she knew they didn't know the answer to that.

"Wait for her. It's all you can do," Lauren whispered.

It wasn't what she wanted to hear, but knew Lauren was right. Leila was coming home, and when she did, Skylar was going to be there. No matter when it happened.

Chapter 46

"Do you still eat eggs and toast for breakfast?" Donna asked, the spread already on the counter, which included more than a continental breakfast with its choices. Far more than the three types of eggs on offer.

"Not really. Usually just toast and coffee these days." Stomach growling, Leila sat down at the island, still amazed the kitchen hadn't changed, not one bit. Though it had been recently remodeled when she was last here, she had assumed it would be completely different now.

It was the same with the entire house. Nothing had changed. The night before, as she walked in, it was like stepping back in time. From the flooring to the paint on the walls, it was all the same. True to her mom's words, her room hadn't been touched except for dusting because there wasn't a speck in there. Even the comforter was the same pale purple she had loved in high school.

The night before her mom had been down in the kitchen cooking while she had explored. Finding her college freshman yearbook, she had sat down and paged through it. That had been her last memory of the night before.

At some point, her mom must have found her sleeping and covered her with a maroon blanket from somewhere else in the house and set the yearbook on the nightside table because she didn't wake until the sun was coming up. Which was a relief. She'd assumed her mind wouldn't rest to let her sleep, not until she had faced everything she was running from. Now she could face them fresh.

"Did you find your phone? I had Galen bring it over last night. You were already asleep, but I left it on your nightstand. I hope that's all right. You said you didn't need it, but I think everyone needs their phone," her mom rambled as she put two pieces of toast in the toaster, despite the fact that Leila was already filling her plate with the food available.

That explained that mystery. When she woke up, she'd seen the phone and wondered how it got there after leaving it in the car, but was thankful because she had been able to send a message to Jan that she wouldn't be at work today. There was no way. She was hours away, and the school day was starting in two. Yes, she could have just called in late, but she wanted to spend time with her mom, enjoy the woman she had become since they were last together.

The second thing she did was search her old bedroom for clothing. Hers were wrinkled and smelly from the day before. To her surprise and delight, all her clothes were still in the drawers and closet. Except nothing actually fit anymore. Sadly, she had gained weight since she had last slept in the bed, and her out-of-date jeans told her that stark truth.

She had almost been reduced to wearing her clothes for another day when she found a pair of joggers and an oversized sweatshirt with her college logo on it. They had been Lauren's from way back. Why they were in her room at home, she didn't know, but she slipped them on and was happy they actually fit.

Her mom brought over the newly made toast and set the slices on her plate. "You look better today, Lele."

If this was looking good, Leila wondered how badly she had looked the night before. Seeing herself in the mirror this morning as she washed her face and brushed her teeth, she barely recognized herself. A brush and a good night's sleep were no longer enough grooming. She needed a shower and makeup for that feat.

But instead of arguing, she took the compliment. "Thanks, Mom. Sorry, I fell asleep last night. I know you were making something for us to eat. You should have woken me up."

"You needed sleep more than food, and in reality, I deserved being stood up by you after how many times I used to do it to you. I know I messed up a lot while you were growing up, and I could easily explain it away as my parenting style or misguided judgement but, in reality, I was an awful parent and, sadly, the only one you had for most of your life." Donna sat down next to her but didn't put anything on her empty plate.

Choking down a dry bite of pancake, Leila turned to her mom. "You did the best you could."

Shaking her head, Donna went on, "Of course, I didn't. I was so busy trying to prove myself at the dealership that I barely noticed you for to long, and when I did, I was trying to make you more like me. Which wasn't you."

Pushing her plate away, she admitted, "You're wrong. I actually am so much like you. I've spent my life working, with nothing outside of work that I enjoy. Not letting emotions control me. The only thing I do for myself is garden and canning. But maybe I do that more to relive the past than for the food it provides. I don't share it with many people, so it's a waste of time in the end."

"I remember you and Gin canning all the time. It was something I never enjoyed, but you two spent so many hours at it every year. Now I'm so glad she was there for you when I couldn't be. She was such a big part of your life."

"You never liked her. Why not?" Leila asked, curiously. She had never known the reason for their animosity, but it had been there her entire life.

"I liked her well enough. But when marriage with your dad hit the rocks, she took his side. I never forgave her for that. But in truth, she should have been on his side, and I was in the wrong about it." Her mom placed a spoonful of eggs on her plate.

"You were still married when he died," Leila said in confusion. Their relationship had always seemed strong to her. They were a team at work and at home. But she had been eight when he died, so maybe she hadn't gotten the entire picture.

"Yes, we were still married, and I still loved him, but he had changed by then. Back when he was in high school, he was the quarterback, you know that. Do you remember the pictures at Gin's house? He loved the game, but senior year of high school, he took a bad hit. Really bad. It ended any chance he had of college ball. We were already dating by then, in love. But that hit changed him instantly." She had a far off look in her eyes as she told the story.

"It's called traumatic brain injury." Leila told her something she worried about with her student-athletes.

"Now it is. Back then, it was just Dale not being man enough to take a hit. Dale being a wuss for not going back out there to take another. Without the football scholarships, he went to work with his dad at the shop. It took hard work to get that shop turned around and me selling cars to make it something. By the time you were four, we were planning a bigger family, a bigger business. Then Dale's dad died, and we were the sole owners of the biggest used car lot in the city. We were big. But Dale was getting worse." Her mom stopped talking and focused on the backyard, lost in the past.

"How?" Leila wanted to know because she had never heard there was anything wrong with her dad.

"He started to forget things. Little things at first, then bigger. Then he would forget your name, my name, his mom's. By then he wasn't working because he couldn't remember how to. I was suddenly supporting us all and all our workers as he sat in the office watching TV. And at home, he was angry more and more often."

"I don't remember that."

"You were eight, and I tried to shield you from most of it by sending you to Gin's house as often as I could. By the time of the accident, I knew he shouldn't be driving, but I also couldn't stop him. His memory was shot, but his strength was still there." Picking up her fork, she set it back down.

"He forgot how to drive?" Leila asked, pushing her on since she seemed lost in the past.

"The real facts of how he ended up with his car wrapped around that tree, I'll never know. And the truth is, I don't want to. I loved that man, but he wasn't the man I loved anymore." Donna looked at the ring still on her finger. No matter how much money she had, she still wore the small diamond ring.

"You never remarried?"

"Sometimes you only get one true love."

"You never even looked again?"

"Oh, I looked. But you would be surprised how few

men want to date a woman who works all the time and doesn't need the money he's offering." Donna seemed to snap back from the past and took a drink of orange juice.

"Not all men are like that," Leila said. Though she had little experience with men, she was sure there had to be at least one out there for her mom.

"The ones I dated were. So I stopped looking."

"I stopped too. Looking, wanting, for a long time. I thought that my college girlfriend was the love of my life, and I ended up messing it up." She watched her mom for any reaction to the word girlfriend, still unsure that her mom had changed. "But still I was devastated and haven't been able to love anyone since. Not that I tried much. Why try when you're just going to get hurt in the end?"

Donna tucked a lock of hair behind her ear before kissing her cheek. "I wish I had met her if she was such a big part of your life. I regret not accepting you back then. It's the one thing from my past I would change. That day."

"Not the day of dad's football game?"

"No, because despite that, my years with him were the happiest of my life. We had you and were starting something together. But after you were gone, I was left with nothing."

"You had the dealership."

"The dealership wasn't going to want to have lunch with me or argue with me over politics. The dealership was never more important than you. I let you go over a career choice I didn't understand and because of who you loved that I couldn't control."

"I shouldn't have dropped it all on you in one day. But I was stupid enough to think if I came out to you, she would do the same, and we would be together again. Except instead, I lost her and you and everything all at about the same time." She had never told anyone that was why she came out. It sounded stupid now, and it was stupid then. One action would never cause the other reaction.

"Do you still think she's the one that got away?" her mom asked softly.

"No, she's just the ideal because my life was perfect for that moment in time. I recently ran into her again. She's married with kids, and I felt nothing but envy. Not for her wife and wanting that life, but for her for finding that life for herself. I wanted that. A family of my own."

"With someone special?" her mom pushed.

"Skylar, but she's over me. I don't even know how or why or even when. Just last weekend, everything changed. I fell in love with her, but …" She stopped, not able to go on.

"That's why you came? Because your love life is on the rocks?" her mom asked skeptically.

"No, it's not just that. It's so much more. My entire life's out of control. I've lost Skylar, and I'm losing my job." She was losing everything at one time, just like in the past. Back then, she had managed to create a life from the ashes, but she wasn't going to be strong enough this time. This time, she was losing so much more.

Donna touched her chin, and their eyes met. "Thinking it doesn't mean it's true. And until it happens, you can fight for it. It's what we Hensleys do best."

"It might be too late for everything."

"Then you will do something else. Losing a job isn't the end of the world," Donna reminded her.

Which was true. Maybe she would never be the principal again, but she would always go back to teaching. The cheating scandal wouldn't affect that. And if she had to change schools, she would. Even towns. She would find another place to call home.

But finding another Skylar wasn't going to happen. Not

in this lifetime. If Lauren's loss had effected her for so many years, how long would she long for Skylar Nash?

Her mom seemed to see her thoughts because she added, "And maybe you just need to talk to this woman. She might not know how you feel. She might even feel the same. You wouldn't know until you say the words."

Chapter 47

Skylar was trying to fill all her time waiting for Leila to return with chores. The laundry was near done, and the house was completely free of dust. Now she was tackling dishes that could be washed in the machine, but that wouldn't take enough time. Wouldn't be distracting enough.

That morning, Skylar sent the kids to school. They had left reluctantly and, so far, she had gotten three texts from Keeley. Right away, she got one that said Leila wasn't in school. Then one came in before lunch asking if Leila had returned, and the last was to ask the same thing a few minutes ago.

Noticeably, Skylar was alone on the farm today. Late last night, when she couldn't sleep, she had found Leila's daily planner on her desk in the bedroom. Until that moment, she hadn't even known Leila kept something like that. In it, she had tracked everything in her life, even their relationship, right up until the end. Because her daily updates on her life stopped Sunday.

Alone in the quiet house, she had read it, and in Leila's

careful, familiar hand writing last weekend she had written, *plant garden with the Nashes*. Which hadn't happened and, instead, Leila had crossed out the words *with the Nashes*.

If she had wanted them to help her, why hadn't she said anything? Why had Leila done it herself and alone? Skylar knew she would have immediately changed her plans if Leila had asked. Just by her asking, she would have known she and the kids weren't in the way. That Leila had wanted them there.

Seeing those words, Skylar knew she'd been over-thinking their relationship. Why hadn't she continued to go along with the flow? Instead, she analyzed Leila's every move, every word, but missed all of the little cues. Because those said she wanted her there, them there.

Now Leila was out there believing she wasn't anything special to Skylar. Just a bed to sleep in when it was convenient. Except Skylar saw her as home. Coming here had turned into home since she'd sold her mom's house. Not that her mom's house had been home in years, but neither was her apartment. It was just a place to sleep. Home was with Leila, wherever Leila was.

Behind her, a door opened softly, and her heart leaped in her chest. A gust of chilly air and two dogs that were supposed to be doing their business while she cleaned up the kitchen came in with the new arrival.

Turning from her sink full of dishes, Skylar grabbed a towel to dry her hands, knowing that school wasn't over yet, so it wouldn't be the kids. Which left one person. A person in joggers and a sweatshirt, something Skylar had never seen Leila in before. No matter how dressed down the woman got, it was never to the point of joggers. Not that it mattered. She looked great in them, but she looked great in anything to Skylar. Or nothing.

Not daring to move away from the kitchen sink, she tried to hide her relief. "You're back?"

Leila seemed just as taken aback that Skylar was there as the dogs circled her and wagged their tales in excitement. "You're still here? I thought that you would have packed up the kids and been gone by now."

Ignoring her question, Skylar did what she had wanted to do since she realized Leila was missing. She rushed across the room, avoiding the equally happy dogs, and threw herself in the woman's arms.

Hugging her close, Leila's body was tense in her arms, but Skylar held on until she felt the woman relax. if only slightly. Skylar regretted the tension between them. Not letting her go, she whispered, "Where have you been? I called, texted, messaged, and you never got back to me."

"Are the kids still packing?"

Pulling back, Skylar didn't let her go despite her flat tone. "No, they're at school. I barely got them out the door this morning. They're worried about you, same as me."

"I'm fine."

When she tried to twist away, Skylar let her go. She was in the house now, and she hoped she wouldn't run away again. "I'm not. Babe, I haven't slept since Sunday when you wouldn't talk to me. Then you vanished. I was worried I'd never see you again. I thought that I would never get to tell you how much I love you, Leila Hensley. How much I want a life with you."

Leila gasped, putting distance between them. "Don't love me, Skylar, I'm a dead end. You need to get on with your life. Find someone better than I will ever be. You're all better off without me."

Standing her ground, she argued, "You're wrong about all that. My life is here. I want to be with you here. The city has lost its charm for me. The things I used to enjoy I don't anymore. Now I want quiet mornings and rainy afternoons, you in the garden. Us together."

"You'll only be bored here. Give it time, and you'll miss all of that. We have no theater or take out or night life." Leila started pacing the room, the dogs following her as she did.

Watching the group, Skylar said, "We can go into the city now and then to do those things. Together. Since we turned into a we, I have spent my weeks waiting for the weekends, missing teaching here and spending time with Keeley and Kayden every day. But most importantly, I've missed being with you. Missed you."

Stopping her pacing, Russell flopped down to lay at her feet with an audible sigh. "When did we turn into we? I thought we were just having fun until you got bored. A distraction."

"I know I never said that, because I never saw us as that, Leila Hensley. And we became a we the night I broke up with Iris. Maybe before, because I couldn't stop thinking about you when I was with her. To the point that I couldn't even sleep with her in the end. All I wanted was you."

"You never said, I assumed you just wanted …" Blushing, Leila stopped talking, but started to pace again.

"Sex?" Skylar said the word that her lover couldn't.

"Yeah, sex. That you came here because of the sex. You didn't want to tell the kids because there was nothing to tell beyond the physical." She turned and nearly tripped over Alice, who yelped and ran to her mom for comfort.

"I was so worried about hurting the kids' feelings that I ended up hurting yours. I have been afraid you would regret taking in the kids or start resenting us being here all the time. Losing your alone time. But I came, Leila, every weekend because I wanted to be here. You were taking on a lot by taking in the kids. I didn't want you to ever regret that or resent us in the end." Skylar wished she had said all this weeks ago. Her not wanting to hear Leila confirm her suspicions had made her chicken out time and again.

"I have loved them here. It made my house a home for the first time. I didn't even realize it until they were here. Until then, my life had been empty, now I can't see it without them. I just wish they didn't want to leave. I'm going to miss them."

"They don't want to leave. Keeley was just lashing out. They both told me they liked living with you better than living with me."

"I can't keep them with me for long. Once I don't work at the school anymore, it's going to become impossible."

"Why won't you be at the school?" Skylar needed to know. Leila loved her job in Warrington.

Leila started pacing again, this time without a dog following. "The school board is going to fire me. There was this huge cheating scandal that happened on my watch. I thought I was doing alright and then suddenly, I had missed so much of what was happening at the school. Too much to excuse. I wouldn't excuse it."

"Because you're too strict," Skylar said and realized Leila took it the wrong way when she stopped and hung her head. Rushing to her, she took her hands in hers. "In a good way. Strict in a good way. Your standards are so much higher than anyone else's. We both know kid's cheat."

"But it was me who let it happen."

"Nobody lets something like that happen, Leila. Kids cheated. That's not on you. Nobody expects you to have known it was going to happen. Nobody but you."

"I left school without telling anyone. I walked off the job."

"You took time off. You are allowed to take time off,

even unplanned. If they fire you for that, there are more schools out there than in Warrington. I wouldn't worry too much if I were you, you'll get another somewhere else, in teaching or as a principal, anything you want. It's not the end of the world." Skylar brushed a lock of hair off Leila's cheek before adding, "I'm the unemployed one here. And I can't work at the one place I want to because my girlfriend is the principal, and I feel there is a conflict of interest there."

"How so?" Leila leaned into the touch.

"I am interested in her in an unprincipled way."

Laila raised an eyebrow. "Was that a joke?"

"Not a good one. But seriously, if your job was in jeopardy, the kids would have said something. Heck, Carol Donnely would have said something to me when I talked to her," Skylar admitted.

"You talked to Carol Donnely?" Leila squeaked.

"Yesterday at the school when I was looking for you after you left that message. I was so worried I drove straight here. After I walked out on my subbing job." She smiled shyly, and it was so similar to what Leila did. But Skylar told nobody she was doing it. "I might have let it slip we were dating, even if we weren't. Or sort of weren't, but now hopefully are."

Leila rolled her eyes at the addition, but didn't seem upset. "What else did you and Carol talk about?"

"She told me about the drugs and Gerard. Why didn't you say anything about that to me?" Skylar asked, needing to know.

"At first, I couldn't. Then I didn't want you to worry about Kayden. I made sure he wasn't involved."

"Thank you, but you should have been able to talk to me. Lean on me. You had to take over after dealing with that, but are worried you will get fired for taking time off?

I'm so proud of you and how much you have done in such a short amount of time. I'm lucky to be dating you." They wouldn't keep it a secret, not from anyone. Not again.

"Dating?" Leila asked.

"Living with, loving." Skylar wrapped her arms around her as she slipped her hands into Leila's joggers and grabbed her butt. "I hope I get to see these again one day. Where did you get them?"

"Actually, they're Lauren's."

Instantly, Skylar pulled her hands out and stepped away. "I called her, and she said you weren't at her place. That liar, I should have known she wouldn't be truthful with me."

"You called her? Why?"

"Because she was your first love. Maybe you wanted her back," Skylar admitted. It was her biggest worry. Lauren was so much a part of Leila's past the threat had been there.

Leila took her and pulled her into her body, pressing them together. "No, Skylar, not in a long time. And I never loved her like I love you. I have never felt anything like this before. But she was right. I wasn't at the brewery. They just happened to be at my mom's house still. And sadly, I don't fit into anything I wore when I was twenty. These I fit in. And they were clean."

"I love you, too." Loving to hear that, Leila felt the same. Nuzzling her neck, Skylar couldn't get enough of the smell of her. "You went to your mom's?"

"Yeah, I just needed to see her again. Ask her something." Leila pulled back, putting distance between them.

"Did she regret what she did to you? Rejecting you? Or did she do it again? Are you okay?" She shoved her hands into her pockets, suddenly nervous about what Leila had been through in the last twenty-four hours.

Turning to the clean dishes, Leila started to put them away. "Yeah, I'm fine. Going back was nothing like I thought it would be. She's been in therapy about our past and tried to find me a few times. She loves me still, probably more than when I was a kid. It seems it took my leaving to get her to figure all that out. We talked a lot."

"Is she planning on being a part of your life now?" All she wanted to do was take Leila in her arms, but her every move told her to give her space.

"I think so. She wants me to come another weekend, for longer than a day. Next time I need to bring luggage. There isn't anything else in my closet that fits me." Picking up a glass, she looked at it in confusion for a moment before putting it back down in the sink drain.

Leaning against the counter, Skylar asked, "What's she like?"

Shrugging but not moving, Leila said more to the sink than to Skylar, "A lot like me. We have the same personalities and our ability to keep everyone at arm's length."

"Everyone else, because I won't let you push me away again." Skylar grabbed a sleeve of her shirt and pulled her close, wrapping her arms around her.

"I don't want to push you away again," she admitted and leaned in for a kiss.

Whether it had meant to be a light kiss, Skylar didn't care as she turned them until Leila's body was pressed between the cupboards and her, their mouths not separating as hands searched for skin.

They were deep in the kiss when the door burst open, and a blast of cold air washed over them before they jumped away from each other guiltily. Turning, the kids looked at them in surprise.

"Whose car's outside?" Kayden asked as he turned dramatically away from his sister and teacher kissing.

"Mine, I guess." Leila sounded uncertain as Skylar took her hand, because the kids had better get used to them together. Not that they hadn't been aware before, but now it was going to be in the open. No more hiding, no more secrets.

"You mean I get to ride to school in that?" Keeley demanded.

"What's wrong with it?" Skylar asked curiously.

"It's a monster," Kayden said approvingly.

Leila just shrugged. "I thought we would need more room than my old car provided."

"Old car?" Skylar let go of her hand and walked over to the window, and looked out. "It is a monster. A red one. I never thought you would buy a red car."

"It's a bit big, but when your mom tries to buy your love, you go big."

"Can she buy my love?" Kayden asked as he gave her a hug. Something that neither seemed completely comfortable with, but that didn't stop it from happening.

"If you play your cards right," she said as she patted his back before they pulled apart.

"No, seriously, did you let your mom buy you a car?" Skylar asked. That was completely out of character for her girlfriend to have accepted.

"It's not a big deal," Leila assured her.

"Those things cost a lot," Kayden assured them, like he had been buying vehicles for years.

"It's not a big deal," she said again, even if nobody was buying it.

"Is your mom rich?" Keeley asked.

"I'm sure she is. She owns Hensley Automotive Group."

Kayden turned to her and demanded, "Your family owns a car dealership?"

"No. I mean yes, she does. When I was in college, she owned seven. Now she just owns three." Leila smiled and held up the appropriate number of fingers.

"I'm getting a car for graduation!" Kayden announced, and hugged her again, only this time with far more enthusiasm.

"Only if you get straight As," Leila said with a big smile.

He let go of her and announced to everyone, "I can work with that. I better get to studying."

"He isn't getting a car when he graduates," Skylar said, a little unsure as Keeley followed her brother upstairs.

"He's not getting all As either. So we are pretty safe." Leila grinned because they all knew Kayden's grades weren't that good.

Skylar pulled her into her arms. "Your mom gave you a car? Does that mean she excepted you for being you?"

Shrugging, Leila pulled her into her as she leaned into the counter. "She says she does. All these years, I thought she was done with me. That there was no need to talk about it. You were lucky your mom accepted you. I'd accepted that mine didn't long ago. The day I told her, she said she never wanted to see me again. I accepted that and never looked back."

"Until yesterday," Skylar reminded her.

"I wasn't thinking straight when I went there. If I had been, I wouldn't have walked into her dealership. Mom wasn't one to change her mind. But I think I just needed to be reminded how much I had failed her as well. Since I had failed so much in one day." Leila rested her head on Skylar's shoulder, leaning heavily into her. Finally, letting her support her.

"You failed nothing, Leila," Skylar reminded her.

Their conversation was interrupted, but neither moved

as Keeley raced down the stairs, Kayden on her heels. The teen was jiggling Skylar's car keys in her hand. "How about I take Kayden and go spend the night with Sierra? Let you two be alone."

Leila frowned and looked at them. "I don't know. You haven't had your license very long. And it's a long drive, especially in the morning, because you two aren't missing school."

Keeley waved off her concern. "You two have stuff to work out, and we shouldn't be underfoot. You need some alone time."

"I like you two underfoot," Leila admitted and gave Keeley a hug.

Hugging her back, Keeley's voice cracked. "Consider this an apology for what I said yesterday. I didn't mean any of it. I love living with you; we both do. We'll be back in time for school tomorrow. I promise."

Leila turned to Skylar with concern as they left the dogs whining their own disapproval as the door closed. "Are you sure you don't want to drive them?"

"No, I need to be here." Skylar took her hand and was already heading for the stairs. "Keeley's right, we have stuff to work out, but first, I need to show you how much I missed you. Every inch of you. The moment I get you alone, I am going to make you promise to never do that again."

Chapter 48

Leila parked her new SUV in her old spot—not that there was assigned parking, but most people seemed to park in the same place. Even her. But her new SUV was so much larger than her old one, and she was nervous as she pulled in. Nervous because she had walked out two days before.

With the car parked, she pocketed the keys, grabbed her bag, and headed for the building with more confidence that she felt. It was better to get this morning over with. She knew she still had to deal with all the students caught cheating and contact their parents. Something she was dreading almost as much as the repercussions of skipping yesterday.

"Morning, Miss Hensley," Jan's cheerful voice welcomed her into the office.

"Morning, Jan. Sorry I didn't make it in yesterday."

"Don't worry about it. I had that same thing over the weekend, and I wouldn't want to be stuck here in the middle of it, either. Best to deal with that in privacy," Jan assured her and handed her a file. "Carol Donnely and Lloyd Bennett are already waiting in your office. They were here bright and early yesterday as well, but you left so quickly."

Leila's stomach dropped. If they were both there, it wouldn't be good news. They were the chair and vice chair of the school board. One word from either of them had the rest falling in line. And they were in her office, so it was about her. But she knew it was about her. She had left work the day the scandal broke out. She wasn't doing her job.

"Do you know why?" she asked, because Jan knew everything. Or so she prided herself. Leila just hoped that the gossip hadn't found out about her getting fired before it even happened.

"Their only request was a list of parents and students who were cheating. They are taking this one very seriously. Probably because neither has a kid in that class." She looked down the hallway to make sure nobody could over-hear her.

With a weak smile, Leila headed down the hallway, knowing it was probably for the last time. She was even sure they wouldn't want her to stick around to teach English anymore. She was done here. How many years had she dedicated her life to this school, and she was booted for one day's infraction? What if she'd actually been sick?

"Hensley, come in. We were hoping you wouldn't be sick again today," Lloyd said, waving her in. He was already at the head of the table, using her desk chair as his own.

"Nasty flu going around this year. So far my family has been spared, but we don't usually get sick," Carol announced with a smirk. Neither Leila nor Lloyd commented on it, so she went on asking, "Do you think Skylar Nash will be available again now that she's in the area?"

Leila wasn't expecting to talk to these two about Skylar right away. In fact, she had hoped to not actually talk to them about her at all. Since she wasn't planning on working in Warrington. "She's at the farm for the rest of the week. She's starting to look at what's available nearby, probably more for next year since there isn't a lot of time left in this one."

Now that they weren't hiding their relationship from the kids or anyone else, she was freer to be at the farm without explanation. Not that they were announcing it to everyone, just hoping word would get out on its own. Small-town rumors were good for that sort of thing.

"Can't she apply for her mom's job? It's open with Mrs. Powell wanting to be home with her kids. You know that." Lloyd leaned back in the chair, and it creaked under his extensive weight.

"I know the job's open, but I didn't think it was a good idea for her to work here when we are ..." She stopped, not wanting to open that can of beans with the school board today. So instead added lamely, "Friends."

Lloyd took interest in her reason and leaned forward, making the chair squeak. "I don't see how that as an issue. You worked together before. You're friends with everyone on the teaching staff. What makes her any different?"

Sitting up straighter, she proclaimed confidently, "We're dating."

Carol was quick to jump in. "So? Rick Hardy was married to Deena the entire time he worked here, and she worked down in the office for years. There was never an issue with them."

"You're okay with her working here, with me? And us dating?" Turning to the woman, she needed to verify, because a few months before they didn't want to hire her because of her sexuality after being single for years. Now she was dating someone who was going to be working for the school. Did they really want that?

"We've had so many headaches this year. Let's just get the math position finally filled and move on," Carol said, giving Lloyd a look that brooked no argument about it. When he merely nodded, she went on, "Like to this cheating issue, we decided that we would call all the parents and students in for a little discussion about retaking the test. This time under their parents watchful eye. With your permission, of course. This way everyone will be treated the same, and nobody can complain that some of the students got special treatment."

"You already have it planned?" she asked in surprise. All this time, she had thought it would be all on her.

"Of course we do. You've only been on the job for a few weeks. Rick Hardy worked here for years and never had something this big happen. Not even close," Lloyd said as the chair creaked again. "We had Jan gather all the phone numbers of the parents. I feel setting this meeting up for just after school would be the perfect time. The kids will have the most memorable pop quiz of their lives."

"You can say that again." She liked the idea more and more. It gave them all a chance to retake the test and their parents to understand what had happened. It was like a weight was lifted off her shoulders, and all at once, she let out a pent-up breath she didn't even know she was holding.

"What's the matter, Leila?" Carol asked from beside her.

"I assumed you would be firing me today," Leila admitted to the two.

"What the heavens for?" the woman asked in surprise.

"Missing yesterday, leaving early the day before. This cheating happened under my leadership. I assumed I was going to be let go." She adjusted herself in her seat as she explained.

"You were sick, and this all started under Gerard. This year has been one disaster after another. We are just hoping next year will be better." Lloyd shifted, and something on the chair snapped, but he stayed seated as if he hadn't heard.

Carol smirked at Lloyd and added, "I wanted Hensley the entire time. You wanted change. Look what change brought us. Not that Leila won't bring change, but at least she won't cause us embarrassment or criminal charges. We need the stability she will bring to the school."

Lloyd slid the file folder toward her as he got up from the chair. "Now, I need to get going. I expect to be back a little before the end of the day."

Carol got up also, taking her folder with her. "I'll have Jan contact Skylar Nash about the job. The sooner we get her in here, the better."

Leila almost told her that Skylar hadn't applied for any jobs yet, but held her tongue. She wanted Skylar back at Warrington, and a job here would be perfect. More than perfect.

She just hoped Skylar saw it that way.

Chapter 49

Unpacking her bags in Leila's bedroom, Skylar felt very alone in the big house. Though Russell and Alice were there, they were both sleeping in the corner after the ruckus of the kids and Leila leaving that morning.

Yesterday had been so stressful trying not to think about the awful things that could have happened to Leila that she hadn't bothered to unpack. That and she was nervous. Leila would kick her out and thus make her start packing again, so she had left it. But today was a different story.

She decided that the next weekend she would go back to the city and get more of her things. She wasn't planning on moving back there, so she wouldn't need anything. Kevin would be ecstatic to get the place to himself again. Not that he complained when she was there, but he had grown used to her being gone and living alone.

In her jeans pocket, her phone rang, startling not only her but the two dogs, who lifted their heads in unison. Neither were happy with their nap being interrupted.

Glancing at the screen, she saw it was the school, and

not one in the city, but Warrington High School. Confused, she didn't know why they would be calling unless the kids had acted up. Which was probably what had happened.

Kayden hadn't been in trouble since moving in with Leila, and she hoped he hadn't started up again. What he had needed was a steady hand, and Leila was that. It had been nice to not have to worry about him.

But in the last few months, Keeley had also changed. Since dating Cody, she had gained a confidence that Skylar hadn't been aware she was lacking. That confidence sometimes got her into trouble, and Leila was usually who she took her frustration out on.

"Skylar Nash," she answered as formally as possible, hoping it was Leila again. It had been months since that fateful phone call that lead her to working at the school with her. She couldn't believe how amazing that had turned out.

"Morning Skylar, this is Jan at the school. Are you busy?" Jan asked, as if she didn't have the most recognizable voice in town.

Looking around the bedroom, she admitted, "No. What can I help you with?"

Jan barely let her finish before saying, "We were hoping you could start today, unless you need more time than that. Do you?"

"Start what?" she asked in confusion as she shut the dresser drawer.

"Math, teaching Math again," Jan said, as if it were the most obvious thing in the world. "Didn't you apply for the job? With Powell wanting to leave, this would be a perfect way to get back here. Get your foot in the door for next year."

The words almost made Skylar laugh. The woman was scheming for no reason. Though she had wanted to go back to work at Warrington, she didn't think she would get the opportunity, not with Leila working there. But if Leila wasn't there, would she want to work there?

"I didn't apply, though," Skylar admitted, not knowing if she should say yes before talking to Leila.

"I'm confused. Carol Donnely and Lloyd Bennet were in here this morning and approved your being hired full-time. Leila was in the meeting, so I would assume they talked about you two dating. Not that it should be an issue at all. It never has been before." Jan suddenly was whispering, "We're in a pickle here, Skylar. Powell wants out now. I am afraid she's going to just stop coming in one day. Her kids are sick constantly, according to her. We just need someone who wants to be here every day. And the kids really miss you."

"Leila and I didn't think my working at the school would be a good idea," Skylar admitted to her, even if she knew she would tell anyone and everyone she said it.

"So, will you be coming in today or tomorrow?" Jan completely ignored what she had said.

"To-today." She looked at the clock and then at what she was wearing and smiled. "I can be there by the end of first hour."

"We look forward to seeing you." The woman didn't hide her smugness before she hung up on her.

An hour later, she walked into the school with a smile she couldn't contain on her lips. Feeling like she belonged for the first time in years. Even before her mom died, she hadn't felt that everything was as perfect as it was today. Not her professional life and not her personal life. Somehow she knew something was off, or everything, as the case may be.

Once she was walking down the empty hall, she realized she maybe should have taken the time to change from her blue jeans and college sweatshirt into something more professional. Something like what Leila usually wore. Except that really wasn't her, and she wanted to be herself here now.

"Morning, Miss Nash." A student came up to her in excitement. "Are you going to be teaching math again?"

"I am," she assured the kid with a grin she couldn't stop.

"For how long?" he asked, because she had always been temporary before.

"As long as I can, and that hopefully includes next year." She waved at Jan sitting at her desk, just watching her head for her classroom. Not her mom's anymore, hers. "You have to get to class, and so do I."

The student kept going down the hallway, but she walked into the room just as her brother threw a paper airplane at his friend. Grabbing it in midair, she crumbled it up and carried it to the front of the room before tossing it into the garbage.

"Good morning, class. I hope you remember me. I'm Miss Nash and I will be your teachers until the end of the year."

"Boo," Kayden said, but with a smile.

The rest of the room was far happier about the situation.

"Can anyone tell me where we're at in the textbook?" she asked, and couldn't stop the feeling that this was her place.

Within minutes, she had them working on problems on the board when she caught Leila lingering in her open doorway. Her smile was as big as Skylar's because this was what they both wanted but couldn't hope to get. Now here they were, working together again. Though Skylar would miss her across the hall, she knew she would see her more often throughout the day now. Tomorrow would be different because they would come to work and go home together as a family.

Instead of coming into the room, Leila gave her a thumbs-up and walked away. It was all the approval she needed. But if Leila had been against her working here, she wouldn't here.

Today was so different from the beginning of the year, when Leila's words of disapproval had stung so much. They were in different places in life and neither thought the other not capable of anything.

They were back working together, though very different than the last time. And more importantly, at the end of the day, they would go back to the same house together. Their home.

Epilogue

"Did you wake up the kids?" Leila asked as Skylar came down the stairs. She was running late and wondered how long it would take to get her internal clock back to work mode after the long summer.

"I did, but neither were ready to get up." She wasn't exactly ready to leave herself, since she was still in her pajamas from the night before. Or actually, they were put on this morning as she left their bedroom, since she didn't actually sleep in pajamas.

"We're supposed to be leaving in fifteen minutes, Skylar." Leila's tone didn't hide that she was annoyed.

It was the first day of the new year, Leila's first full one as principal, and she was desperate to get started. And to be the first one at the school today. Which was fine for her. The rest of them, not so much.

"Except only you need to leave in fifteen minutes, not the rest of us. How about I drive in today also? This way, we all don't have to be there over an hour early." It was too early for anyone except Leila, who Skylar knew had been up for two hours already only because she had looked at the clock before rolling into the other woman's warm spot and fallen back to sleep when she left their bed.

Leila let the dogs into the house and tried to avoid getting any of their hair on her black slacks. "But you said you want us to ride together to save gas. What happened to that argument?"

Skylar regretted saying anything about that because Leila brought it up constantly, but the summer had been long, and they had taken more vacations than they should have. Wanting the kids to get out in the world had been important to Skylar, so she pushed for it. Leila had been happy to tag along and never complained.

Grabbing Leila's abandoned coffee cup from the counter, she filled it for herself. "Tomorrow we save money, love. Today we save my sanity and let the kids sleep a little longer. This way you can finish that podcast I can't stand listening to."

"It's about Jane Austen and all the adaptions of her work. How can you call that boring?"

"Quite easily, actually." Skylar took a sip of coffee. There were a few things that Skylar had yet to learn to love. Leila's taste in podcasts was a big one. Not that Leila liked any of the cool ones she did. So, in the end, they listened separately and let the other enjoy what they wanted to. There were a few that they both enjoyed, but only a few. And none that all four of them agreed on.

Leila grabbed her keys from the peg on the wall and stopped. "You want to take the SUV, don't you?"

Smiling over her coffee cup, she admitted, "I'll have the kids with me, so it only seems logical."

Putting them back, Leila grabbed the other set that was there, the one that wasn't used nearly as much over the summer. Since when they went anywhere, they seemed to all go together. "We should talk to Mom about getting you something new, bigger. Keeley can use this one since hers is on its last leg."

"Last week, you said you were thinking about trading the monster for something smaller. Something more suited to our little family."

"I did, and I do. This one is too big, except I have learned to like bigger. We couldn't have done the camping trip without it. And Kayden's knees poke the back of the seats in the car, and I don't think he's done growing."

"I'll tell your mom since I know you won't." She winked at the woman, who just nodded in agreement. The mother-daughter relationship was so much better before, but there were still some things Leila didn't like to talk to her mom about. Money was one of those.

Since the weekend Leila had spent with her, Donna had been a part of their lives. There had been two long weekend trips to see her over the summer. She had taken to the kids as if she was their grandma, even if she and Sky never pretended to be the kids' parents. They never wanted to take the place of Karla in anyone's life.

Her acceptance of Skylar had been the most amazing thing. Not once had she said anything about Skylar's age or gender. Not to Skylar, at least. Maybe she had said something to Leila, but she was sure that hadn't happened. Leila had spent most of both trips testing her mom's change of heart toward her lifestyle. Looking for any excuse to leave.

"We can buy our own cars," Leila argued half-heartedly.

"Or, now, hear me out. We can save money by having your mom give us one. She wants to do it. We can just let her."

Groaning, Leila dropped a kiss on her lips. "Her love language is gifts."

"Let her love us, Leila," she whined.

"Okay, but let me talk to her." Leila grabbed her briefcase heading for the door. "Love you, see you later."

Skylar talked to Leila's mom more often than Leila did. She knew and would let it slip, then she would have to beg Leila for forgiveness, which would be far easier than actually waiting for the other woman to ask her mom for anything. Leila had forgiven her mom for nearly everything, but there were still little things that she couldn't get over, and her mom's neglect during her childhood was one of those things.

"Love you too, babe," Skylar called after her as she leaned against the counter. "See you at school, Miss Hensley."

She would never get over the fact that Miss Hensley of her teenage dreams was her girlfriend. That they were building a life together. They were here, and she never wanted to leave.

She loved their lives and couldn't see them happy anywhere else but in Warrington. All the things Skylar had once hated, she now loved. But maybe that had more to do with Leila loving her than the town itself, because she knew she'd be happy anywhere Leila was. That she had almost missed out on all this because of her stubbornness wasn't ever far from her mind. Now she was her amazing girlfriend.

Now that school was starting, they wouldn't get to spend every hour of the day together anymore. Though they would be in the same building, they wouldn't be across the hallway. At least at the end of the day, they would all come back to the farm together.

A loud thump from above her reminded her that she had to get ready for school. That she still had a lot to do before she could leave the house and knew that tomorrow she would happily ride into town with Leila. In fact, she was a little upset with herself for letting her go alone today. For losing those few minutes with her.

———

WITH THE FIRST day of school over, Leila sank into her chair and just let herself relax for a moment. This was the first time she had been in her office all day. It seemed she spent the entire day putting out one fire after another.

Not that she hadn't enjoyed every moment of it. She had. She was still strict and demanded respect, but now she also tried to be an ear when wanted and a friend when needed. Someone the students liked without being a pushover.

"Are you regretting your decision to be principal?" Skylar asked as she stepped into the office. This morning, she had been in her pajamas when Leila had left the house, so she hadn't seen the outfit her girlfriend had picked out for the first day of school. She was not disappointed. In fact, the slim charcoal pants showed her amazing ass, and the red short-sleeved blouse let her tattoo peek out on her arm.

"No regrets, loving it, but it does take a lot out of you." She sat up. "Where are the kids?"

"I sent them home in my car. Figured you could use a few child-free minutes."

"They don't really count anymore. They are too much a part of my life." The few times they had been without the kids in the last few months, something had felt off until they were all back together.

"How about I say I needed a child-free few minutes because the first day is always the hardest?" She let out a sigh.

"I always felt the kids were the most well-behaved the first day," Leila argued.

"They are, but I don't want to be here the first day. What happened to summer?" Skylar whined.

"It is behind us, but I think we savored every minute of it." Then the shadow of Skylar's past crossed over her. Their relationship was strong, and she never doubted her love, but did she want to stay in the small town? Was that still there? "Do you miss your old school?"

Shrugging, Skylar shut the door before coming further into the room. "No, I never felt this deep connection with the students I do here. I mean, I know most of their families, and if not, I will soon enough."

Skylar didn't stop until she was sitting on Leila's desk, right in front of her. Close enough to touch, but she had promised herself no touching at school. She didn't want to break that rule on the first day.

"That's why I never thought to leave, though it took time to get to know everyone."

"I got a call from Paige Green-Andrews today," Skylar said of the social worker they had been working with for months now. When she had moved in with her, they had started the process almost immediately.

Whoever said fostering kids was easy, she was sure had never done it. Every time the woman showed up, there was a list of things that had to be fixed at the farm, and that was before a child had even been placed with them. Leila was sure they would never actually get a kid after all this time.

"What new hoop has she come up with now?" She felt a headache coming on that she hadn't had before the woman's name was mentioned.

Skylar tucked a strand of hair behind her ear with a

smile. "None, she has a little girl she wants to place with us."

Sitting up suddenly, she nearly knocked Skylar off the desk. "What? Really? Are you sure?"

"Yes, completely sure." Skylar laughed and steadied herself.

"When?" She felt it was all happening so quickly. So suddenly.

"This weekend, if possible. I know it's the worst timing, but I couldn't say no either."

"We will make it work, just like everything else. Together, we will make her life perfect for as long as she stays. How long is she staying?"

"No idea." Skylar grabbed her hand and held it tight.

"It doesn't matter. We are so ready for this," she said, because they were. They had been hoping and planning since they got together. Leila had already been thinking about it, and Skylar had thought it was the perfect idea. Kids needed families, and they were a family now.

"We are, aren't we?" Yanking, she pulled Skylar onto her lap and hugged her close.

Adjusting herself, Skylar looked into her eyes. "I love you, Miss Leila Hensley."

"Thank you, Skylar, for wanting me. For believing in me, for loving me. For changing my life in so many unexpected ways. So many times." She kissed her, forgetting completely about any stupid rules she had made for herself over the summer.

"Let's go home and tell the kids that our lives are about to change again," she said, but didn't move.

Nor did Leila, which was just fine. They rarely got a moment alone, and soon that would be even fewer. But neither would change that for anything. Life was perfect.

Bonus Epilogue

Bonus Epilogue

"Looking sharp, Principal Hensley." Skylar handed her a cup of coffee. Not unlike most mornings, except this one was one they had been looking forward to for years now.

Leila looked down at the black slacks and light blue blouse that she would pair with a blazer by the time she left today. It wasn't much different from what she usually wore to school, but she felt it was a little more fancy for a graduation.

"I would say the same thing about you, but you are wearing Bart Simpson pajamas." She leaned into the woman and kissed her, anyway. She was adorable with her pink-painted toss and sex-messed hair.

Giggling, Skylar snuggled into her. "I believe you gave them to me for Christmas."

"We gave them to Kayden, who outgrew them within a month, and now I can't seem to get you to stop wearing them."

"You know exactly why I like to wear them." Skylar

winked as Keeley came into the kitchen in search of coffee of her own.

Leila liked the design, not the character on them. With a handy opening just where she liked one to access Skylar's panties. Something she had used over and over again over the years since she confiscated them.

Not taking the bait, she smiled at the now twenty-year-old. "Morning, Keeley."

After two years in college, she did seem like an adult, one that had fit into college life far better than she had high school. Happily, the on-and-off with Cody had been off for over a year. And with the gushy way she spoke of a Spencer, there wasn't a chance at Cody coming back.

"Morning Leila, Skylar," she said to them, not ready for conversation yet this morning as she went back the same way she came, coffee clenched in both hands.

"I think she's hungover," Skylar whispered with concern. Keeley had gone out with a few of her high school friends the night before and hadn't returned until late.

"She's still in that age bracket," Leila admitted and didn't feel as overprotective of the college student as she had when she was in high school. Skylar hadn't let up yet.

"Can't you ground her or something?" Skylar demanded.

"Can't you?" she told her back, because she couldn't. The kid was only home for short amount of time; no need to give her a reason to come home less.

"I like to be the nice cop. You play bad cop so well."

"You enjoy bad cop," she said and pinned her to the counter, pressing her body to hers deliciously. It had been four years, and she savored every moment Skylar was in her arms.

Nuzzling her neck, she breathed in the familiar scent as

she kissed along her shoulder, loving how the woman below her shivered at the touch. And the way her hands skimmed up her body, drawing her closer.

"Can't I get a day away from the smoochy-smoochy when I graduate? Wasn't that the only thing I asked for?"

Kissing the neck one more time, she turned to him. "You asked for a car. I don't remember anything about kissing Skylar on that list."

"Not kissing Sky." Correcting her, he looked in the fridge. For years, he had been the tallest in the family and hadn't stopped eating. As he shoved an already made sandwich in his mouth that was intended for the party after graduation, then grabbed another before saying, "And you will never get me a car, so I asked Grandma. She will give me anything."

"I told her no to a car," she said about her mom. Cars were given out like candy from the woman. Keeley had gotten one before she went to college. And all Skylar had to do was hint that hers was getting old, and Donna had one sent to them by the end of the week.

"She said if I got straight As, she would give me a car." He closed the fridge and grabbed a bag of chips.

"You didn't get straight As," Skylar stated, though his grades were great compared to what they were after his mom had died.

"Close enough." He waved off the comment.

"Were you guys talking about me?" Her mom walked into the room, already dressed and ready for the day, dressed up even more than Leila was.

"No car for Kayden," she told the older woman.

"He needs something, Lele," her mom whined, and Kayden gave her a hug.

"Yeah, he needs something, Lele." Kayden's voice mimicked his grandma's.

When Donna Hensley said she had changed, she hadn't been lying. There hadn't been a holiday or big event in anyone in the house's life that Donna wasn't a part of. From holidays to birthdays and even for Sierra's wedding, she made the drive. Not once had she put pressure on anyone to take over the dealerships. Though Leila was sure that she was pinning all her hopes on Kayden. The girls had too much Karla in them to want to sell cars.

"He can keep using Skylar's old one until he learns he has to obey the rules of the road. He got another ticket last week."

"Again, Kayden, you said you were going to work harder at that?" Donna turned on her favorite grandchild.

"I did. I only got one." He held up the sandwich to the woman, and she angrily took a bite.

"I have to get going, get everything ready at the school." Looking at her watch, Leila kissed Skylar despite Kayden's moans of annoyance.

Heading into the living room, she stopped short when she nearly tripped over Ophelia, standing watching the action in the kitchen. At twelve, she was shy, and too many people scared her. But she had been with them for almost four months now, and she was thawing. She wasn't their first foster child and wouldn't be the last, but she might be the one that stayed. Skylar had already said she had gotten attached to her, and Leila was feeling the same way.

"Morning, Ophelia. How did you sleep?" She slowed herself down. No need to rush out of the house when she could give the girl a bit of undivided attention.

"Okay." She looked into the kitchen again.

"You can just go in there. It's just Skylar, Kayden, and Grandma. You know all of them. Skylar will make you something for breakfast."

"I guess." She just shrugged her frail shoulders.

The report on her past had been sketchy, but neither had imagined saying no to taking her in. Back then, she barely left her room when they were home, but just last week, she had yelled at Kayden. Not usually something that Leila would allow, but she couldn't find it in her to punish the girl.

"Do you want to change quick and spend the day with me?" she asked, even if she had no idea what she would do with a little girl when she had so much to do.

"Can I?" she asked, knowing that she would do anything to get out of the house before more people came. And everyone knew that Sierra and her husband were coming soon.

"Yeah, you change. I'll tell Skylar and grab you something to eat." She patted her shoulder before the girl ran off.

Turning, she caught Skylar's eye, and there was a tear in it.

⊏⊐

"Look at your name on the door, Hensley," Lauren said from the doorway, making her jump.

It had been an hour since anyone had been in the school but Ophelia, who was quietly helping her put diplomas in envelopes. There weren't that many, but the girl was dedicated to her task. Her pink tongue stuck out the side of her mouth as she worked.

"Lauren, when did you guys get to town?" She jumped from her chair and hugged her friend, then her two daughters, who were with her. They were getting older.

Happily, they were friends again, though it had taken a few years for their respective significant others to completely trust them alone together. Not that either saw the other as anything but a friend. They didn't really remember their past as a couple. Not like their significant others did.

"We just rolled in, and Skylar told us to drop me at the school, mostly to get you home. You were supposed to be picking up a cake or something."

"It's already in the back of the SUV. But it's nice to know the wife doesn't trust me to actually pick it up."

"I think she's getting nervous," Lauren correctly assessed Skylar's mood. "And who is this?"

Walking over to the girl, she put her hand on her shoulder, but the girl had been staring at them since they came into the room. "This is Ophelia, our foster daughter. Ophelia, this is my friend Lauren and her daughters Mariah and Aleah. Aleah is your age."

"Hi," she said, a word Leila didn't think would come from her. She usually was silent around strangers.

"Do you go to school here?" Mariah asked.

At that, she only nodded. So far she hadn't gotten used to living in a house with a lot of noise. She had only recently stopped flinching when Kayden was simply talking. Leila knew it would take time for her to be completely comfortable with the family. She and Skylar were letting her take that time, because even if Leila and Skylar both knew she was safe with them, Ophelia didn't know that yet.

"Can we look around?" the older of the two kids asked Ophelia.

"If she doesn't want to, she doesn't have to, Riah," Lauren said to the girl, who was always the more outgoing of the two.

"I'll hold your hand if you want me to," Aleah said, a smile playing on her lips.

"Okay." Ophelia slipped off the chair, her task forgotten, as she went to the other girl and instantly took her hand.

Mariah turned and rushed out of the room, but the two others stood looking at each other for a moment before Aria said, "I'm Aleah."

"Ophelia," the girl said, as if Leila hadn't already told them that.

"I just know you're going to be my best friend." Aria started out the door with Ophelia's hand still in hers.

"I know," Ophelia answered in complete agreement.

Once they were gone, both she and Lauren looked at each other in confusion. "What was that about?"

Lauren sat down heavily on the chair Ophelia had just vacated. "I want to say they became friends, but I think Aleah just fell in love."

"They're twelve." Leila looked at the door they had left.

"Fell in like, a lot of like," Lauren amended, and let out a sigh.

"What does that mean?"

"That this school is some sort of romance epicenter, and I should have kept my kids away."

"Epicenter?" Leila questioned as she set the readied diplomas on the edge of the table, ready for her to grab later.

"You and Sky, and now this. Some school." Lauren looked at the picture on the desk of them together earlier in the summer at her mom's house.

"It is." She grinned, loving her life more and more every day.

⸺

"Once again, you pulled off an amazing graduation party." Leila squeezed her hand as they waved goodbye to another friend, leaving the get-together.

"I had to after following that graduation you put on," Skylar complained. It was so much work, and she was glad this was the last one for a long time.

"It's the same every year. You just only pay attention when your siblings graduate." Leila wrapped an arm around her as they started back for the party.

"I pay attention. I know all of them, after all," she argued, but she didn't. Not really. Graduation was just the signal that the year was over. Some kids she was happy to see gone and others she would miss terribly. "What's up with Ophelia and Aleah? I haven't seen her so accepting of another person before. They were inseparable."

"Lauren thinks they're in love," Leila said, as if they weren't twelve-year-old kids.

"Is there something wrong with our child being gay?" Skylar asked in surprise. Leila had always been so accepting of everyone and everything. This wasn't like her.

"Nothing at all. But twelve is too young," she argued, but they both knew that it wasn't. Sure, at twelve, sex wasn't what was on their minds, but attraction was. And being with gay parents should allow them to explore their feelings without fear. Stopping Leila, she turned to her. "You called her ours."

Her eyes swept the lawn before she answered, "She is, isn't she?"

"Yeah, she will be the first we adopt," Leila said with conviction.

Skylar felt a rush of pure joy that they were on the same page on this. They both had fallen for this kid in a completely different way than any of the others they had fostered. "There will be more. But for now, I want her to be our only. Kayden is leaving next week to spend the summer with Sierra and Nick. By fall, we can open our hearts to another. But this summer, just Ophelia."

Leila took her hand in the familiar way that still left her wanting more of her touches. But instead of pulling her close, Leila said, "I think that is a perfect plan. Except one thing."

"What?" she asked, worried.

Leila, still holding her hand, dropped to one knee. "Let's get married."

"What?" She was so surprised she couldn't wrap her head around what was happening.

"You, me, rings, a cake, and all our friends."

"I thought you wanted to wait."

"I changed my mind. I want you to be mine." Leila pulled a ring from her pocket and slipped it on Skylar's hand.

"Hey, this is my graduation party, not some engagement thing," Kayden hollered from the garage, though even from a distance, Skylar knew he was smiling.

"Skylar Nash, will you marry me?" Leila asked again.

She looked at the ring through her tears. "I thought you wanted to wait."

Getting up, Leila pulled her closer. "No more waiting. Let's start the rest of our lives now. All our tomorrows start now. Together."

"Did she say yes?" a voice asked from somewhere, and Skylar didn't care who it was, but she knew that everyone was watching them now that Kayden had turned all the attention to them.

"Of course she did. Nobody says no to a Hensley," Donna said with the same conviction her daughter could.

Leila laughed her nervous laugh, as she may have realized everyone was watching them. "My mom is maybe wrecking this moment."

"Your mom and everyone else are perfect. Just like you and this moment." Tears spilling from her eyes, Skylar leaned in and, with their lips millimeters apart, she answered the question, "I'll marry you anytime, anyplace. Just say the word."

"As soon as we can." Leila promised and kissed her, not caring they had an audience. Not caring about anything but her fiancé.

The End

Thank you for spending time in my world. I hope you enjoyed my story. I hope you loved reading it as much as I loved writing it. If you want to know more about Lauren and Nissa's love story, you can read <u>Not Asking for More</u>.

About the Author

Lindsey Pennington happily lives in Minnesota and writes in her spare time. When she isn't writing she works her day job and traveling as much as possible.

If you want to keep up with my next release on www.lindseypensaromance.com

Also by Lindsey Pennington

Risking her Heart

Finding the One

Still the One

Not Asking for More

Love's Learning Curve

Made in the USA
Monee, IL
27 May 2023